(UN)PLANNED

SAINT STEPHENS LAKE
BOOK 2

K.C. BROOKS

*For the ones who have felt invisible, or that they needed to change
to live up to someone else's standards.
Find your path, make the choice, and remember that you never
need to bend to fit someone else's mold.*

AUTHOR'S NOTE

This book contains on-page, sexually explicit material. It also makes references to parent and grandparent death (off-page and in the past), strained parental relationships, and estrangement between family members.

Although this author has tried to approach all of these subjects with sensitivity, if it is a trigger, please skip this one.

Protect your peace lovelies.

PLAYLIST

1. You're On Your Own, Kid- Taylor Swift
2. Keep It Up- Good Neighbours
3. Nervous Energy- Glades
4. Admit Defeat- Bastille
5. Lose Control- Teddy Swims
6. I Like Me Better- Lauv
7. Like Real People Do- Hozier
8. Terrified- Vincent Lima
9. Losing Me- Gabrielle Alvin & JP Cooper
10. Homeward- Dermot Kennedy

PROLOGUE

Focusing on the quiet waves, I tried to force my tears to dry. They'd been pouring down my cheeks for what felt like hours, and there was no sign of them stopping. I hated that I was crying, hated that *he* was the cause of it.

Before my mother married my stepfather, David, we were happy. Or at least that's how it felt looking back on it. Our family was always together, smiling our way through life. Even though my real dad was starting to become a distant memory, I still could feel the weight of his love for me, like my favorite blanket that I dragged everywhere, despite Laurel telling me it was for babies.

Everything changed so quickly when my dad died, and my mind was still struggling to connect the pieces. After his car accident, there was no more laughter, no more impromptu family adventures or slow dances in the kitchen. Our whole lives became about appearance, about how we *should* act.

Especially me.

It only got worse when my mother and David got married earlier this year. Even though she tried to sell it as a fantastic opportunity for our family, it really only benefited her. As the wife of a prominent businessman in the city, she got the name and the money.

All the while, Laurel, Devyn, and I were pushed off to the sidelines, only brought out when they needed a picture of a happy family to accompany his company's newsletters. At first, it was fine. I was old enough to be left on my own. Being fourteen meant I wasn't a baby anymore; I could handle myself.

At least when David and my mother left me alone, they weren't trying to shape my future to mirror their own. I glanced down at the brochures clenched in my hands, my fallen tears marring the pictures of happy, smiling children.

This weekend was supposed to be a trip away from all the stress of the city—a chance for my newly-minted stepfather to spend time in my mother's childhood home, to see the legacy that her family built and what made this town so special.

Instead, it became an all-out assault. David launched into a list of my shortcomings before dinner could even be served, dragging up everything from my report cards to my taste in friends. And that wasn't even what burned the most. No, it was how my mother sat there, not even bothering to look up as he dove into my failings. I mean, what did he expect me to do? Throw on a power suit and become his shadow? That was never going to be my goal.

I knew better than to think Laurel would stand up for me. She idolized David and already declared that she was going to be just like him when she grew up. It wasn't surprising; Laurel was always quick to follow my mother's lead.

Devyn had no problem causing a scene, screaming loudly across the table at our new stepfather. Even though she was only a year older than me, Devyn was my fiercest protector. Still, even she couldn't stop David once he started scolding me. I loved her for standing up for me, but at the same time, I just wanted to keep my head down and hope that, eventually, he'd move on to another target. But that was before he started mentioning boarding school and all the excellent opportunities it could afford me.

As my nose started to tingle with a fresh wave of tears, someone settled into the seat next to me. I didn't even have to look up to know who it was. The familiar scent of cigars and cedar always reminded me of home.

"I should have known I'd find you here." My grandfather, Poppy, took the seat next to me.

The isolated dock was where we always went when we needed an escape from everyone. Even though my grandfather owned and operated the largest hotel in the region, he carved out this little space for himself and my grandmother when he took over the Isadora. Even fifty years later, it's still one of the few places off-limits to guests. The same beaten Adirondack chairs have sat on the shore my entire life, overlooking the lake the town was named after.

I have vague memories of sitting in this very chair with Grammie, her fingers dancing through my waves as we watched the sunset over the mountains. She died when I was seven, so most of my memories were borrowed from others, but certain feelings always come up when I think of her. I know Poppy misses her every day. It's in his smile; it has dimmed since she died.

I sniffled, wiping my face with the back of my hand. "David wants to send me away." I held up the crumpled pamphlets. "He's going to ship me off to boarding school."

"And what do you want?" Poppy asked.

"I want to stay here, with you." I glanced up at him. Everyone said I looked just like my grandmother—maybe that was why Poppy and I had such a good connection. "This place feels more like home than that stupid apartment."

Penthouse, David corrected me in my mind. We'd moved in

a couple of months before the wedding. My cozy, decorated bedroom had been traded in for something stale and cold. Even a year later, it still had no personality.

No, the Isadora Resort was my favorite place in the world. I counted down the days between each trip, waiting impatiently to walk through the lobby again. Maybe I was weird because I preferred living in a hotel, but it was a part of me.

My grandfather just sat by my side, offering silent support. I had no doubt he'd let me live with him if I asked. I half expected him to offer when he shifted toward me. "Calla bug, you know what we say about running from your problems?"

"It makes them go away?"

He laughed, the sound deep and hearty. "No, my love. It just saves them for another day." He patted the back of my hand. "I'll talk to David about boarding school, but I also don't think hiding up here will solve anything."

"Never know until you try."

He squeezed my hand before turning back in his seat and letting out a content sigh as he looked across the lake. "Remember what happened when we went sailing last summer?"

"The day with the storm?" He nodded. "The sky looked clear, but once we got the boat out, it started to pour. And then, once we were back home, the sun came out all over again." I shook my head. "It was like the weather was trying to mess with us."

"That's life, Calla bug," Poppy said. "Just when you think you've gotten your bearings, something will come and knock you off your feet. Sometimes it's good, sometimes it's terrible, but either way, you need to face it." He knocked my chin with his knuckles. "Life won't stop just because you're afraid. But it's in those moments you'll learn your strength, what you're capable of. And I know, no matter what life throws at you, that you'll find your way, my love."

"How will I know I'm making the right choice?" I asked, brushing my tears on the back of my hand.

He smiled slowly down at me. "Listen to that big, beautiful heart of yours, Calla. It'll lead you where you need to go."

ONE

Calla

The sound of a blaring car horn ripped me out of my dream. My eyes barely had time to open before I slammed into the dashboard of the moving truck, my hands hitting the hard plastic right before the rest of me.

"Oww…" I groaned as I pushed back into my seat, rubbing my probably-bruised skin.

"What the fuck?" Cole screamed from the driver's side, rolling down the window to continue screaming at the passing cabs.

As my eyes adjusted to the brightness, it took me a minute to get my bearings. Just a moment ago, I was on the pier with my Poppy, replaying a forgotten memory. The next, I was in the middle of downtown Manhattan, the cacophony of traffic and congestion filling the world around me. I might have spent most of my childhood in New York, but after years upstate, the abrupt shift was jarring, to say the least.

"Are you okay?" Alex, my best friend, asked from the middle seat, as she checked me over.

I waved her off. "All good. Just trying to wake myself up."

"I bet," she chuckled. "You've been snoring since we hit the Thruway."

That wasn't surprising. Cole insisted we leave Saint Stephen's Lake at a ridiculously early hour to get on the road before rush hour began. For the past four hours, the three of us had packed into the cab of a moving truck heading toward my new apartment in the city.

All my belongings were piled into boxes in the back, far fewer than I thought I'd have. Then again, most of my clothes were still hanging in my closet back at the Isadora, my family's hotel in Saint Stephen's Lake—the same hotel my mother had kicked me out of almost two months ago because I refused to go along with her plan for my life.

A decision I second-guessed more and more each day.

"This must be it." Cole shifted the truck into park, and we stared through the windshield, taking in the large building in front of us. For a moment, I thought about telling him to turn around, to take me back to Saint Stephen's Lake, that this city, no matter how wondrous it could be, would never be my home.

But as my hand reached toward the handle, I knew that wasn't an option. Even if I wanted to go back, there was nothing waiting for me at the lake but now-painful memories. If I genuinely wanted a fresh start, it needed to be somewhere new, somewhere I wouldn't always be Diane Winters' daughter.

Alex nudged my side. "Are you ready?"

I nodded, forcing myself to exhale. "Yup, I think I am."

As Alex and I climbed out with a couple of bags from the front seat, Cole called out from the driver's side window. "I'm going to circle the block and find somewhere to park. Let me know if there's a back alley or something we can use."

We nodded before walking inside the lobby bathed in white marble, leather couches lining the floor-to-ceiling, tinted windows. A large chandelier adorned the center of the ceiling, making it appear as if a thousand crystals rained down from the sky. It was gorgeous, a far cry from the rustic charm I was used to.

"Can I help you?" a voice called out from the other side of the lobby. I turned to find an older gentleman smiling softly at me, his brown skin lined with age, but there was still a youthful humor in his expression.

"Oh, sorry!" I moved over to shake his hand. "I'm Calla Winters. I'm staying with my sister, Devyn, in apartment 8B. She was supposed to leave a key for me at the front desk?"

"Ahh," he sighed, opening a drawer. "The younger Miss Winters. Your sister warned me you were trouble."

I rolled my eyes. "Devyn's one to talk."

"That girl needs to experience some trouble. Works harder than anyone else I know." He passed me the key across the counter. "Name's Harold. If you need anything, I'm your man." He winked at me. "Just don't tell my wife I said that."

I chuckled as Alex talked to Harold, asking about a place to park the moving van so Cole wouldn't be driving around in circles for hours. He offered to lead her to the service entrance as I grabbed the bags and walked toward the elevators.

My fingers shook as I pressed the button for the eighth floor, and the metal doors reflected my uneasy expression. *This is a good thing—it's the fresh start you so desperately needed.*

But now that I was here, it felt like the walls were closing in on me. This building reminded me too much of the apartment I'd escaped as soon as I could. All the cold, modern elements made me ache for the familiarity of the Isadora. Most people didn't understand the appeal of living in a hotel, but to me, it would always be home. My favorite memories took place on the grounds of the resort. While we'd always listed Manhattan as our official address, the moment school let out, my sister and I were bound for my grandfather's resort, spending every day at his side.

It was where I learned to swim and sail, spending as much time as possible in the water. It was where I had my first kiss and my only true heartbreak. It was where my family, the ones I'd chosen instead of the ones who shared my last name, resided.

Home would always be the Lake.

Maybe New York could be too. The city reminded me of bitter memories, of forced smiles and failed expectations. It might have been where I was born, where I'd grown up, but I'd left the moment I could. Perhaps now was my chance to experience the city on my own terms, to see if this place could help me carve out a future for myself. My best friends were all starting new chapters of their lives. Alex and Cole were getting serious, and Javi and his husband were trying to have a baby. Everyone was moving on, and yet, for the past four years, I'd been stuck. The lake was a haven, a place to hide away from pushing myself to try new things, to break out of my stagnant existence, but here? There was no safety net, no familial business to fall back on. I'd have to carve my own path. And even though it terrified me, it was also sort of exciting.

The elevator dinged, pulling me out of my haze. The doors opened, revealing a pristine, white marble hallway. Doors lined the halls, looking completely ordinary among the luxury of the building—like they knew what was hiding behind them.

As I shoved open the door to our apartment, I let out a little gasp. Pictures did not do this place justice. The entire back wall was made up of windows—the New York skyline was Devyn's backyard. While I loved living upstate, there was magic in the city nowhere else in the world could replicate. Looking around Devyn's home was almost eerie, a glimpse at what my life could have been if I had followed Winters family plan.

"Uggh." A groan crashed through the front door a moment

later. "How in the hell do you have this much clothing? There's no way all of this was in the guest room closet." Alex dropped the boxes in the entryway, joining me at the window. "Damn, Calla. This place is an *upgrade*."

I elbowed her in the side. There was no comparing this apartment to her cozy cabin. It would be like comparing apples and a tsunami. While this place might look like it was plucked from the pages of a magazine, it held none of the comfort and warmth Alex's place provided.

"Not an upgrade; just different," I said. "Plus, we both know you're going to need that guest room sooner rather than later."

Alex blushed but didn't refute my words. We both knew it was only a matter of time before Cole popped the question. He'd been dropping hints since the moment he moved to town to be with Alex permanently. He'd already promised I'd be the first one to know when it was time, wanting my help to make sure everything was perfect for Alex.

"You sure about this?" she asked, taking my hand in hers.

"Of course," I lied, blinding her with my best smile. My emotions were bucking like a see-saw, rotating between excitement and fear. I really wished my sister was here to greet me. At least then, it wouldn't feel like I was moving into a stranger's place. However, with her being up for junior partner this year, Devyn was always at the office. She gave new meaning to the word workaholic. She claimed it would all be worth it soon, but that was yet to be seen.

I tried to imagine myself in her shoes, spending my entire day surrounded by paperwork, buried deep in the latest case files. I shuddered at the thought. I might not know what I wanted to do, but that was definitely not it.

As if she could read my apprehension, Alex linked her arms around my waist in a sideways hug. "Say the word, and I'll be here."

"Don't you dare," I chuckled, laying my head on top of hers. "You've got so many amazing things coming, Alex, and you deserve every one of them. I'm so proud of you." I smirked down at her. "Plus, we both know you're going to be too blissed out from all the orgasms to think about anything else."

Alex rolled her eyes, but her cheeks heated at my words. I'd hate Alex if I didn't love her so much. First, she got to date one of the hottest actors on the planet, even if it was all for show. Now, she was madly in love with a man obsessed with her.

I was happy for her. I really was.

But there was also a part of me that ached with jealousy. My entire life, I'd been obsessed with love stories, from the fictional to the real ones like my grandparents. The idea of being wholly loved by someone was all I wanted, but I had yet to find in real life. Instead, I buried myself in romance books, soaking up as many endorphins as I could get.

Don't get me wrong—I wasn't giving up, at least not yet. But I also refused to settle for anything less than the real thing. Unless it was that can't eat, can't sleep, can't live without them kind of love, it wouldn't be worth it.

As if on cue, Cole walked through the front door, carrying all my heaviest boxes, the ones I'd marked pillows but filled with books just to mess with him. As he placed them next to the ones Alex dropped, he glared at me. "Not fucking cool, Winters. I'm sending you the bill for my chiropractor."

"Hey, you owe me after last year." I danced over toward the pile of boxes. "Who else could have pushed you to admit your feelings for Alex?"

Cole shook his head but didn't argue. Last year, when Alex was fake dating his best friend, it was painfully apparent that Cole was falling for her. But being the most stubborn man on the planet, he refused to act upon it. After a disastrous double date between the four of us, I gave him a heavy dose of tough love, trying to make him see the error in his ways. He wised up shortly after that, and I took the credit for it.

Alex and I continued to move my things into the guest room over the next few hours, only taking breaks to explore the stark white apartment my sister called home. There were no pictures, no art, no sign of the Devyn I grew up with. She was always the loudest of our trio. Our eldest sister, Laurel, was the quiet and reserved one, Devyn was the outspoken wild-child, and I was the peacekeeper between the two. Growing up, Devyn was always covered in paint, chalk, or some other art medium. Now, her home was the place where color went to die.

I shouldn't have been that surprised. Things had changed over time, especially when Devyn broke our pact and caved to our mother's demands. She'd transformed, losing so much of that vibrancy I loved about her.

Once my room was almost unpacked and the flattened cardboard boxes lined the hallway, Alex chewed on her lower lip, staring at her phone before she glanced up at me. "Are you sure you don't want me to stay? I hate the idea of leaving you alone here."

"I promise it's okay. Devyn should be here any minute." That probably wasn't true, but I wasn't going to tell Alex that. "Cole has to be exhausted, and I know you two want to make the most of your night away. You don't have to worry about me."

"Easier said than done," Alex mumbled, wrapping me in a tight hug. "I hate that you're not going to be there when I get home."

"Me too." I held her a little longer "But it's only temporary. I'll be back in a couple of months to help with the soft opening. Cole promised he'd send updates and photos of the Lodge. I can't wait to see it when it's ready for guests."

I linked my arm with Alex's, leading her to the living room. We could hear Cole's snores before we even got into the room.

He was sitting on the white leather sofa, his head propped up on the back cushions, his mouth hanging open. He was clearly exhausted after spending the entire day hauling boxes.

"I can never repay you guys for this," I said, dropping my head to her shoulder. "If you need a kidney, I'm your girl."

"Don't even joke about that!" Alex shifted to the front of the couch. She leaned forward on Cole's slumped shoulders, pressing a soft kiss to his nose. He stirred, opening one eye before beaming up at her.

"That's the best way to wake up, sweetheart," he teased, pulling her hand so she landed in his lap.

"And here I thought it was my mouth on your—-"

"Do not finish that sentence." I placed my hands over my ears. "This place is so clean, you'll sully it with your nasty words."

"Sorry, Mom," Cole joked, standing up with Alex still in his arms. Once his feet were on the ground, he placed her at his side, but not before dropping a kiss to the top of her head. "You sure you'll be okay?"

"Yes, *Dad*, I'm a big girl. I can handle the big, bad city. I swear."

"If you run into any trouble, give Adam a call." Cole shifted to take out his phone. My phone chimed with a text, and I looked down to see that Cole sent me a contact.

"What's he going to do from LA?" I asked, shoving my phone back into my pocket. There was no way I'd ever call him. Adam was the nicest person I'd ever met, but he was still a movie star. It was hard enough being in the same room as him without gawking. There was no way I'd work up the courage to ask him for a favor.

Cole shared a look with Alex. "He's not in California right now."

"Really?"

He nodded. "He's taking a break from movies. Theo's shitting a brick, but they're both staying here for at least the next six months. Adam wanted to try something new."

"Oh..." I say, curiosity piqued, but I shook it off before my mind could run away with any errant thoughts. With a glance up at the clock, I knew Devyn should be back soon, and I was looking forward to a few minutes to get my bearings on my own. "I'm not trying to kick you guys out..."

"But you're kicking us out," Alex chuckled, pulling me into one last hug. "Seriously, Calla. Any time you need me, I'm here. All you have to do is call."

"I know," I say, trying to keep my chin from trembling. "And same for you."

She squeezed me a little tighter before backing away, letting Cole give me a one-armed hug. "Take care of our girl," I whispered so only he could hear.

"With my life," he swore.

After one last look, they were gone, the elevator taking them back down to the lobby. I shut the apartment door behind me, setting my hands on my hips in determination.

This was it.

Time to figure out my life.

How hard could that be?

TWO

Theo

Do not murder your client.

Try your best not to murder your client.

Staring at Adam Rice across the table, I tried to calm my erratic heartbeat, repeating his words in my mind. His blue eyes were darting back and forth between mine and the script sitting in between us, the one I thought he'd happily scoop up, ready to jump headfirst into the next phase of his career.

But that was not what happened.

A break. My biggest client wanted to take a break.

Forget that he'd just become a household name, that his latest performance was garnering Oscar noise. No, none of that mattered to Adam. He wanted a break.

Fuck.

Maybe it wouldn't be the worst thing. I was just settling into life in New York, and the ink was barely dry on my new contract. When Wallace and Associates started talking about setting up a New York satellite office, everyone was determined to be the one leading the charge. I was honestly surprised I was the one chosen when there were so many people vying for the job.

Not that I'd let anyone know that.

It had taken a couple of weeks to convince a few key agents to make the move with me, and then I was on a plane, bound for a new life in a new city. It seemed fortuitous that Adam also wanted a change from life in LA, enjoying the East Coast when he filmed his last picture in a small town upstate. I was under the assumption this would be the moment he'd make his mark and take his career from booming to legendary. How wrong I was.

"I need this, Theo," Adam said from across the table, breaking me out of my thoughts. "I can't keep jumping from project to project. I need some time to figure out my life away from the cameras, away from the press."

Sinking back into the cool leather of my chair, I tried not to crush the ballpoint pen in my iron grip. It wasn't like I didn't have a heart, no matter what my ex-wife tried to suggest. As much as I cared about Adam's career, I reminded myself that I cared about him as a person more.

I sighed, regretting the words before they even left my mouth. "How long are you thinking?"

"At least three months."

My hand instinctively jumped to my chest, rubbing the knot of uncertainty that had settled there. As my biggest client, keeping Adam happy was one of my key responsibilities. With his latest movie in post-production, I was getting offers every single day. He'd put on a hell of a performance, and everyone wanted to work with him. But no matter how tempting the project was, Adam kept saying no, claiming that he was searching for the perfect role. I should have known something like this was coming.

We'd been working together for almost five years, and I knew Adam better than most of my friends. Truth be told, he was one of my closest friends. How fucking pathetic was that? I pulled myself away from that self-deprecating thought, forcing myself to focus on what mattered.

Adam's career.

Adam smirked at me. "Who knows? Maybe I'll sign up for one of those reality shows. Do you think I'd make a good suitor?"

The clear crystal pen snapped in my grip. "Shit," I hissed as the blue ink hit my skin. *Blue fucking ink.* How did these get into my office?

"Don't even joke about that," I sighed, rubbing my hand down my face. I stood up, discarding the broken pen in the trash before turning to stare out the window. My eyes couldn't focus on a single thing, my mind too wrapped up in problem-solving mode. I never thought I would say this, but I was sick of the gray weather already. Spring in New York was a crap shoot; there was no knowing if you'd have bright blue days or rain. Since the moment our plane touched down, it had been the latter.

I never thought I'd say it, but I missed our offices in LA. When they started to bring on more prominent clients, the owners bought a historic building with warm, Spanish-style accents that made it cozy without even trying.

But here, on the twenty-eighth floor of another glass-shrouded skyscraper? It was *lifeless*. The conference room was surrounded by glass-paneled walls, echoing the same elements as the rest of the office. A past tenant had doused the entire place in shades of gray. Would it have killed for my boss to spring for some color? Maybe a painting or two would make this place feel like less of a hospital waiting room. Shit, even those had mass produced paintings to give your eye something to look at.

"Theo," Adam called out from the other side of the table. "Did you hear me?"

"Yeah, I heard you." I ran my hand over my face, trying not

to let my irritation show. "Are you sure this is the way you want to play it? Walking away from these offers could be career suicide."

"I know," Adam answered, his voice quiet but determined. "I've been thinking about this a lot. I just..." He trailed off, scrubbing his hand over his jaw. "I've been trying to get my passion for acting back, and nothing's cutting it. I'm burnt out, man. Something needs to give, or I don't know if I can do this anymore."

My fists clenched. "Is this about Alex? You couldn't have known—"

I thought it was an easy decision to set Adam up with a contracted girlfriend last year. It seemed like a win-win situation after he was photographed with a local woman while he was filming. He'd get some positive press after a nasty break-up, and she would get enough money to get her out of her shitty job. It seemed ideal for both—at least until she fell for Adam's best friend, Cole. As far as I knew, they were still dating. Cole had even moved to the middle of nowhere to be with her.

When it all unraveled, Adam insisted he was fine and that there were no real feelings between him and Alex, but he had changed, becoming more guarded and jaded. Adam said a resounding no to every project I'd brought him over the past few months.

"It's not about her," Adam snapped. "This is about me!" He stood, pacing the space between me and the table. "I'm so sick of all the bullshit, Theo. I never know what's real and what's for my image. I need a break to be *myself*, to figure out who I am away from all the cameras and noise."

I took in his sagging shoulders, the tension radiating off him. The frustrated man in front of me wasn't the Adam I knew. Ever since we met at an industry party years ago, he'd taken fame in stride, grateful for every part he got to play. He never lamented the publicity or the cost of fame.

I clapped him on the shoulder, stopping his pacing. "Okay, Adam. I hear you." His relief was palpable. "Let me see what I can figure out, and we'll go from there."

"Thank you, Theo," he muttered, dropping back into his seat. He dragged his fingers through his shaggy blond hair.

"There's no need to thank me. It's why you keep me around."

WHEN I FINALLY UNLOCKED THE door to my new apartment, the world around me was dark. After dropping all my stuff by the door, I walked out to the balcony, opening the doors to let in the air, fresh after a quick rainstorm. The city lights sparkled around me, reminding me I wasn't alone. There were millions of other people in buildings just like this one, trying to make their way in a city that was so effortlessly taxing.

In the daylight, New York felt almost cold and cruel. But at night, the lights made it something exceptional. After getting my fill, I meandered into the kitchen, pulling a glass from the cabinet. Opening the fridge, I found it almost empty, save for a large bottle of vodka and a couple boxes of Chinese take-out. I pulled out the first box, taking an apprehensive sniff. Nope, no way that was any fucking good. Tossing it into the trash, I grabbed the vodka and poured two fingers into the crystal glass.

Dangling it in my hand, I stepped back toward the window, peering out to the world below me. With the patio doors now closed, the apartment was quiet, way too damn quiet. My head ran through the numbers, calls I needed to return, projects I needed my clients to sign off on.

This stress was what you wanted, what you signed up for. I'd fought tooth and nail to prove that I was ready for this step, that the partners could trust me to lead this expansion. I'd been at Wallace and Associates for over ten years, starting in the mail room right while I finished law school. Being a talent agent was never my dream, but it seemed like the best career for a lawyer with no desire ever to enter a courtroom.

I'd worked my ass off for the last decade, hustling my way up the ladder. I'd taken on *every* client, no matter how demanding or challenging. I never backed down from a scandal, always trying to find the best situation for all involved.

But it wasn't until Adam that people started to take me seriously. He was a relatively unknown actor when I first signed him. My gut hadn't failed me before, and I knew he was worth the risk. I just had no idea how much it would pay off. Not only had he become a star, but he catapulted me into the big league, suddenly grabbing lunch and golfing with the heads of the company. Lately, there was a lot of talk of me becoming a named partner. It was everything I had imagined for years.

And now, I was one mistake from losing it all. My biggest client was taking a break from acting, and I was responsible for making sure this office was a success. Anything less, and I'd be shipped back to LA.

It felt like a cruel karmic joke. I'd worked so damn hard to get my fucking foot in the door, and now my fate felt so out of my control.

Tomorrow, my mind screamed, trying to force me to relax. *Tomorrow you can stress about work.*

I almost had to laugh at the thought. My work-life balance was non-existent. I was available to my clients at all hours of the day, and when I wasn't working *with* them, I was working *for* them. Contracts needed to be written and emails needed to be drafted. There was a reason I turned the second bedroom into a home office.

I shifted to look at my new "home." It was a basic lease. Six months, and then I could re-up, or someone else would take it over. There was nothing personal, no items that made it mine. A place to sleep and maybe fuck if I found the time. I glanced around, taking in the spacious living area. It reminded me of our office space, even made of the same cold, dark materials and chrome accents.

In my everyday attire, I tended to favor blacks and grays, but my home was a different story. I liked to have some life in my home, even if I wasn't the one living it.

I set the empty drink down on the kitchen counter before strolling over to my briefcase. I looked over my notes from my meeting earlier, hating that my chicken scratch was so much harder to read than my assistant's. Marie was my lifeline, the closest thing I had to a long-term relationship. Of course, she was happily married to a wonderful woman with two chubby-cheeked toddlers waiting for her at home, but to me, she was family. She was the one who'd tell me I needed to get out of the office more, kicking me out to enjoy the sunshine on beautiful days.

Fuck, I missed her.

The next few hours were a blur, and my mind turned off as I worked through my list. Half of it was bullshit tasks, things I usually paid people to do for me, but Allen, my boss, and I agreed that we would start the New York office with a skeleton crew. A couple of other agents were making the transition with me, but they were flying out later in the week. Until then, it was just me and the damn janitorial staff in chrome city.

As my eyes started to blur from exhaustion, my phone blared to life at my side. I glanced down at the caller ID, and I saw Adam's name. Hopefully, that bastard had had a come-to-Jesus moment and realized he was risking everything for nothing. But as soon as I clicked on the call, I knew that was not the case.

"Before you ask—no, I haven't reconsidered. I'm staying in New York, and I don't want any scripts for at least six months." *Fucker.* This morning, it was only three. "But I need a favor."

"No."

"You don't even know what I'm going to say."

"Considering I'm neck deep in your last fucking favor, I'm sticking with that answer."

Adam sighed. "Look, it's not really for me. It's for Alex-"

"Not a chance in hell." I didn't have an issue with Alex, even going so far as to invest a large chunk of money to help her buy a hotel in her hometown. But I had a limited number of favors, and she already used up all of hers when I got her and Cole out of several messes when they were dating behind Adam's back.

"Theo..." Adam sighed. "This could be good for you too. Would it kill you to hear me out?"

Great question.

"Fine."

"Do you remember Alex's friend, Calla?"

I might have spent a month in that lakeside town, but the only person I got to know was the take-out man from its lone Chinese food restaurant. The name rang a bell—I had a knack for remembering those, a necessary evil in my career. But I couldn't place the girl's face.

"Not exactly."

"She just moved to New York, and she's looking for work. You said you needed some help around the office..."

I groaned, leaning back to squeeze my brow with my fingers. This conversation was not going to end well. From the limited information I had on Calla, she seemed flighty and more suited for a nightclub than a professional office. But before I could say no, Adam continued, "Look, I know this isn't something you'd normally do, but Calla, she's a good person. She's just down on her luck. She needs a break."

"If I do this, will you agree to read through the script I sent over?"

"Nope. I won't," Adam chuckled.

"Then I have zero motivation to help her."

"C'mon, man. What do you have to lose? Do me a favor and at least meet with her."

It was the last thing I wanted to do. I was already floundering, trying to navigate a role I barely knew how to play, and now, he wanted me to take on someone else who had no experience and potentially didn't bring any skills to the table?

But Adam never asked for favors, at least not personal ones like this. As much as I wanted to say no, I couldn't, not when he was the one reaching out. A thought tugged at the back of my mind, "Why?"

"Why what?"

"Why are you advocating for a girl you barely know?"

"Shit, Theo," Adam chuckled. "Not everything has to have some sinister motive. Calla's been dealt a shitty hand. I'm just trying to help her out, pay it forward or whatever you want to call it." He exhaled slowly. "Put her in the mailroom, have her answer phones. There has to be something she can do to help. You know you need it."

I groaned. "Tell her to be at my office at 9 am on Thursday."

"Thanks, man. You're not going to regret this. Who knows, you might love working with her."

Not fucking likely.

THREE

Calla

As the doors to the elevator closed behind me, I tried to catch my breath. Freaking public transportation. Even though I'd grown up only a couple of blocks from here, I'd never taken the subway much. The train had been late, and I'd ended up going in the wrong direction, meaning I had to get off at the next stop and try to find the right one.

I knew I should have sprung for an Uber or a cab, but with my bank account draining by the second, every penny saved was precious.

Thank goodness Adam pulled some connections to get me this interview. While I wasn't thrilled about the idea of working for his manager, it was better than my other job offers, which, for the record, were none. When you're a twenty-six-year-old with limited work experience, you're not anyone's dream candidate.

It was fine. It wasn't personal. None of these jobs knew me, knew what I could bring to the table. *Which is what?* The little voice in the back of my head gave life to the thought that had been plaguing me for almost a month.

Sure, I'd gone to one of the best universities in the country, but education and practical skills were two entirely different beasts. I shoved the thought down, smoothing my hands over my borrowed skirt.

Devyn insisted on dressing me for the interview, deeming my closet too bohemian for the Manhattan job market. So, instead of the floral, A-line dress I'd picked out, I was wearing a black pencil skirt with a green satin blouse tucked into the top. I finished the look off with a chunky white cardigan and some thin gold necklaces. Maybe Devyn would disapprove, but I firmly believed that how you dressed affected your mood.

When I pushed inside the lobby for Wallace and Associates, the empty white walls almost blinded me. The room was silent, which immediately raised all my red flags. I knew it was a new business, but this was not what I was expecting.

"Hello?" I called out, but my echo was the only response. *Perfect.* I didn't know Adam well, but I was pretty sure he wouldn't have sent me here if there wasn't a real job.

Not to mention, the office was *cold.* The temperature itself was fine, but the room held zero personality. Not only was there the white walls, but it was all bland furniture, obviously picked out from one of those bulk order catalogs. How could they host clients here if the room looked like it was more appropriate for murder than business?

I peeked down the hallway, hoping that someone would be out to greet me. Glancing at my watch, I grimaced when I realized I was exactly on time—so much for getting here early to show initiative. That was before the subway debacle forced me to sprint the last couple of blocks.

At least I wasn't the only one running late, if the lack of a greeter was any indication.

I sat down in one of the waiting chairs, smoothing my frizzing waves with my fingers. My breath pushed through my lips. It would be fine. It *had* to be fine. What was the alternative? Cowering back to my mother with my tail tucked between my legs and working at my stepfather's company?

I involuntarily shuddered. Trapped with David as a boss? No, thank you. There was no way I'd resign myself to that life. My shoulders shook, trying to force a false confidence. I was going to rock this interview. It was a little unclear about what the job entailed, just that I would be working for Theo, Adam's manager. According to Adam, he was one of the top agents at the firm. I guessed he would be out dealing with clients while I'd likely be answering phones and going for coffee runs.

As I debated looking around some more, the man of the hour stepped into the lobby, his eyes widening a little when he saw me sitting there. "Do you have an appointment?"

His voice was deep, almost melodic with its timbre, but that wasn't what stunned me the most. While Theo wasn't as tall as the men I was usually attracted to, he oozed confidence and power. No wonder he was so successful. His dark brown eyes held mine, and my hands shook a little, trapped under the intensity of his stare.

"Are you lost?"

I shook my head, forcing myself to my feet. When I stepped closer to him, holding out my hand, I realized he wasn't that much taller than me. At 5 foot 8 inches, I was almost six feet tall with my heels on. We were pretty much the same height, but he had such a forceful presence that my knees nearly buckled.

"Sorry, I'm Calla Winters. I think we crossed paths a few times when you were staying at the Isadora. I'm Alex's best friend." I beamed my patented smile at him. "I'm also your nine o'clock meeting."

Theo chuffed but placed his palm in mine. "Theo Ayad, acting Manager."

As our hands shook, he looked at me, his intense eyes studying every inch of my face. I could feel my cheeks flush, but

I wished the blush away, hating that he was already making me flustered.

"Follow me."

As he ushered me down the hall, which I assumed led to his office, I tried to remember everything I learned about him from my friends. While Adam spoke highly about his talents as an agent, Cole had called Theo an unbearable ass. Alex was on the fence, having spent a lot of time with Theo when she was posing as Adam's girlfriend. She said he'd been supportive. Even after everything that had transpired, Theo was one of the leading investors in her hotel back in Saint Stephen's Lake. Without him and the others, there was no way she would have been able to afford her property.

But there was also the part about Theo threatening to sue Alex multiple times, which gave him a black mark in my book.

We ended up in the corner office with, *you guessed it*, absolutely no personality. The only furniture in the room was a black leather couch and an oversized glass and chrome desk. It reminded me of the one in my mother's office. I never understood the purpose of desks like that. They didn't have any drawers, so where were you supposed to keep your things? My desk was stuffed, the surface covered with various colored pens and post-its, books and papers. *I probably should clean that...*

"So, Miss Winters. Tell me why I should hire you."

My eyes snapped to Theo's. So much for easing in slowly. Did I miss the small talk portion of our interview? I cleared my throat, taking a seat in the chair across from him.

"I think I'd be an asset to your company, Mr. Ayad," I started, trying to recite the words I'd practiced with Devyn this morning. "I'm, uh, a fast learner and enjoy challenges. I think I would be a great addition to your..." I glanced around the office, noting I was the only other soul on the floor. "Your team."

"Clever," Theo smirked, however the way he said the word showed that he thought my answer was anything but.

My smile wavered under the weight of his stare, and I waited for him to say anything else—to ask me a question, something other than stare at me as if I had three heads—but it only got worse when he sighed, tossing me the piece of paper in his lap. "You should know that I only took this meeting as a favor to Adam. Normally, I wouldn't have given you a second thought."

"Excuse me?"

"You've been out of school for almost four years and have barely any work experience."

"I was helping my mother—"

"Yeah, I know all about the hotel," Theo cut me off. "That was more of a hobby, right? It sounds like you assisted with organizing events, and that's it?"

Despite my best intentions, my mouth started to wobble, hating that he pointed out my insecurities so easily. When did everyone else get the memo that you had to know *precisely* what career you wanted the moment you finished school? So maybe I'd been coasting longer than most, but I refused to believe I was the only person who felt lost, who didn't want to pick a career just because it was easy or convenient. I wanted that drive, that passion, for what I did for the rest of my life. Apparently, I was the only one who thought that way.

My hands shook from sheer embarrassment. For the first time, I started to think that maybe my mother was right. Her words played out in my head again, reminding me that I was throwing my life away.

"It was more than that." I tried to force out the words, but they came out weak. "I helped plan and run many large events, sometimes simultaneous ones..." At the sound of my voice cracking, Theo looked up, his eyes widening. I brushed my hands on my skirt, trying to leave my nerves in the fabric. "I organized a lot of weddings and other milestones, moments people dream about. Making them happen..." I cleared my throat, offering him a half-hearted smile. "Maybe it doesn't seem like much to you, however it means something to me."

Theo leaned forward, propping his elbows on his muscular thighs. He exhaled slowly as his hand slid down his face, stopping to rub his jaw. "Do you have any administrative experience?"

"Excuse me?"

"Clerical work," Theo repeated. "Filing, setting up meetings, note-taking. Do you have experience in any of those skills?"

"Yes," I answered honestly. "I spent most of my summer and school breaks at the Isadora. I've been helping with the books and all the behind the scenes work for years. I might need some time to catch up on any newer systems. Otherwise, I can handle it."

"Good," Theo answered, talking more to himself than to me. "Look, you've caught me in a rough moment." He motioned at the empty office. "As you can probably tell, there's a lot to be done around here. I'm being pulled in a thousand different directions, and my head is spinning." He laughed, the sound dark and rich. "Which is why I'm unloading on you instead of being more professional. Please forgive me."

When my eyes met his, I suddenly noticed the dark circles that lined them. The man looked exhausted, as if he'd been killing himself to get everything set up. Maybe I should have done the smart thing and found a job where the boss wasn't giving me emotional whiplash, but I'd never been able to walk away from someone in need.

"Let me help."

"Excuse me?"

I steeled my nerves, trying to emulate my older sister's confidence. "You're right; on paper, maybe I'm not the right fit for your company, but my resume, as bare as it might be," Theo chuckled a little, "isn't the whole picture. Let me help, and then you can evaluate how I'll fit in here." I shrugged, trying to make my suggestion seem casual while my anxiety wreaked havoc in my chest. "Like an audition."

Theo stared at me for a long moment then leaned back into his chair and laughed. "You're serious?"

"What do you have to lose?"

He leaned back in his chair, weighing each of my words. I was used to being the one on the other side, the one trying to read people and their intentions. Theo watching me made me feel vulnerable. *Raw.*

He shook his head like he wanted desperately to say no. I closed my eyes, dragging in deep breaths to prepare myself for the inevitable rejection, but instead, he held out his hand. "Alright, Ms. Winters. You can start tomorrow."

"Are you serious?" I squealed, tempted to clap my hands, but I tucked them in my lap instead. "Thank you, Mr. Ayad."

"Thirty days," he said quickly. "You have thirty days to prove yourself, or I will fire you and find someone more capable for the job."

"I won't let you down."

FOUR

Theo

The following day, I still couldn't figure out why I had decided to hire Calla Winters. Maybe it was sleep deprivation; maybe it was stress-induced psychosis. Or perhaps I had just lost my mind. There was no logical explanation as to why I decided to hire a woman completely unqualified for working in my office. I ran my hand through my hair, trying to get the image of her out of my mind. I mean, she almost burst into tears in the interview. What were the odds that she'd last more than a day working with me?

Maybe it was the guilt that led to me hiring her. I was used to speaking to my grunts in a certain way, not caring what impression I left behind. My previous assistant was good about bringing me back down, calling me out when I got too stressed and short with others. She would have killed me if she saw how I acted with Calla.

My bad mood didn't even have anything to do with Calla's interview. That was courtesy of the back-to-back lousy news I'd received that morning. First, my ex-wife was contesting her alimony payments, claiming they weren't enough to support her in her lifestyle. *What fucking bullshit.* The excessive amount I already paid her was enough to take her latest boy-toy on a month-long tour of India, but what would I know?

But that call was expected. Anytime something positive came up in my life, Natalie decided to destroy it. The word vindictive wasn't enough to describe that woman.

No, that phone call wasn't the one to devastate me. That one was courtesy of my now-former assistant, who decided she wasn't able to make the move to New York after all. Now, I was stuck here, completely alone and hating every minute of it.

Maybe that was why I took Calla up on her offer. My initial instinct was to usher her out the door; there was no use for someone so green. But when her voice started to break, something in me did as well. It was odd; empathy wasn't one of my strengths. Maybe it was a result of working alone for the past few weeks. I was so desperate for human contact that I was willing to lower my usual expectations of my employees.

When I arrived at the office that morning, the elevator doors dinged open, and I was pleasantly surprised that I wasn't the first one in. Calla smiled brightly at me from the reception area, grabbing the two coffee cups waiting on the counter behind her.

"You look surprised," she smirked as she passed me one of the white and blue paper cups.

"I'm not used to seeing someone else here," I answered honestly. I took a long sip of the beverage Calla made for me, but my whole face contorted. "This is horrible."

Calla grimaced. "Sorry, Mr. Ayad. I wasn't sure what kind of coffee you liked, so I went with black."

My brow arched. "Is that the impression I give?" She shrugged, following me as I turned down the hall. "In the future, cream and sugar. Nothing over the top, but I need a little more than just plain coffee to start my day."

She pulled out a notepad from her cardigan pocket, quickly jotting down the order. I couldn't help but smirk. It reminded me of my mother, how she was always bringing home her check-book after long nights of waitressing. At the thought, my throat tightened, a wave of grief washing over me before I cleared my throat, willing it away.

I led Calla into my office, motioning for her to take a seat as I got settled behind my desk. She tapped her pen on the notepad. "So, boss. What do you need me to do first?"

I thumbed through my papers, reviewing the various stacks of documents I'd haphazardly piled there last night. I put my finger on the largest stack, dozens of file folders waiting to be looked through. "These are all the recent client intake files. The LA office sent us a bunch of people located in the city, and we need to start evaluating to see if anyone is worth a meeting. Scan each one of these and create some kind of document to help me wade through the requests."

Calla started to reach out to take them, but I shoved my hand on top again. "Normally, I'd make you sign an NDA, but I have too much to do to draw up the paperwork now."

"Ah, yes." Calla smirked. "I've heard all about your infamous NDAs."

"A requirement in this line of business, I'm afraid." I tapped the files with my thumb. "I'm trusting you, Miss Winters."

She shook her head. "Mr. Ayad, I promise that I do not have any intentions of betraying your trust. No offense, but I'm not really interested in your secrets." She winked. "Just the paycheck."

She slid out of my office, dropping the files on top of one of the empty desks outside. After leaning back in her chair, she pulled the top folder into her lap and started reading.

As the morning moved along, I tried to focus on my list of tasks, but for some reason, my eyes kept getting pulled back to Calla. It had to be a morbid curiosity, one that came when my initial impression was so off. I had doubts that she would even show up today, much less beat me to the office. It was only the first morning, but she was already defying my expectations. Time would tell if she would keep it up, but something told me she would.

During her interview, Calla tried to appear confident and strong, but there was a quiet doubt that filled her eyes, especially when I brought up her work history. She'd visibly flinched at my harsh words, a slight I'd regretted since they slipped out of my mouth. At first, I thought it was because she had little work ethic, relying on her parents' money to coast through life. But if this morning was any indication, Calla was a hard worker and wanted to prove herself.

As my mind wandered, wondering what had caused Calla to come to the city without a job, a voice called out from the other side of the doorway.

"Excuse me, Mr. Ayad?" I lifted my gaze away from my desk. Calla toyed with the end of her hair as she stood at my door, wrapping an auburn lock around her finger. "If you don't mind, I have a question." I nodded, allowing her to continue. Her nose wrinkled as she looked around my office. "Who decorated this place?"

"No one," I answered honestly. "Most of this furniture was left from the previous tenant. It was easier to keep it than to replace everything."

"Oh," Calla sighed, shifting her hands down to fumble with her dress pockets.

"You don't approve?" I asked, leaning forward in my chair.

"It's not that," she said. "It's just...."

"Stale?"

"Boring," she answered. "Looking through these files, I don't know—these are people chasing their dreams; they're bold and unafraid." She grimaced, looking around the room. "This place looks like the land where dreams go to die."

I chuckled at her words. "And what would you do differently?"

She smiled at me. "If I was the one in charge, I would start by adding some color to the walls. More artwork, maybe some candid photographs of different clients if they were willing." She shrugged. "Different things to make it cozier, more welcoming."

"I'll take it under consideration." I turned back to my computer, but something nagged at me as she turned back to leave. "Calla, wait," I called out. Sighing, I reached into my wallet, pulling out one of the corporate cards. "When you finish with the files, see if you can find some pieces to make this place feel less *boring*."

She tucked her lip between her teeth as she stepped closer to my desk. I pulled the card back before she could take it.

"Do not make me regret this."

Calla's lip curled into a devious smile. "Don't worry, Mr. Ayad. I have excellent taste."

***

"WHAT THE FUCK..." I whispered as I walked into my office a couple of days later. The room was unrecognizable. It looked like someone had broken in, but instead of stealing from me, they replaced all my furniture.

Gone was the black leather couch, replaced by a much more comfortable and warm-looking brown loveseat and two armchairs. There was even a new rug in the middle of my office, lines of dark red and brown weaved together in an intricate pattern. Framed artwork lined my walls, and my collection of signed photographs from my clients had migrated from a box in my apartment to a shelf on the far side of the room.

What the fuck had she done?

"Calla!" I yelled into the hallway. There was only one person who could be responsible for this: the woman who had somehow managed to convince me to give her the corporate credit card, as well as a key to my apartment and the office, within hours of working here. What the fuck had she slipped into my coffee?

Three days. Calla had worked for me for three days, and she was already causing chaos. Marie had asked to redecorate my office for years, and I always declined. I liked my things a certain way, needing order to function correctly. Now, it looked like Pottery Barn had thrown up in my space. When I told her she could buy some things for the office, I assumed she'd buy a couple of paintings, maybe some new furniture for the lobby. I didn't think she'd do *this.*

Calla stepped into my office and dropped into the armchair across from me. "Yes, Mr. Ayad?"

I stepped over to my desk, placing my hands on the cool, smooth surface. I tried to breathe to calm the fury inside of me. I wanted to scream. I wanted to fire her.

And with that smug smile on her face, I wanted to bend her over that chair and slap her ass until my handprint was branded on her skin.

What the hell?

I wished I could say this was the first time I'd had an inappropriate thought about my cheeky new assistant. I blamed the tight little skirts and dresses she insisted on wearing. Maybe I could convince her to try a new style, one that didn't make her subtle curves drive me to distraction.

I shook my head, trying to recenter. "What did you do?"

"It looks great, right?" Calla smiled. "Less sterile and more personality. It'll be good for your clients to feel comfortable here. How much do you love it?"

I rubbed the bridge of my nose. "Calla..." I sighed, drawing out each syllable. "I meant making sure we had enough computers, enough equipment for everyone, make sure that the conference room is good to go. Not redecorate my fucking office." Each word was a struggle, and I was barely keeping my temper in check. "I should fire you."

I swore she rolled her eyes. After a couple of days of working together, Calla had grown more comfortable around me, at least enough to give back some attitude when I said something she didn't like, which was apparently often.

"But you won't," Calla answered. "Because you know I'm right, and this place looks a million times better. If you're going to fire me, at least fire me for a real reason, Mr. Ayad."

She had me there. I ran my hand over my face. "Fine. For future reference, I like my space a certain way."

Calla nodded, her smile much bolder than when she first walked into the room. Without another word, she stood, heading back to the area she'd carved for herself. I felt a strike in my chest when I realized she'd barely done anything for her work area, focusing on my space instead.

I dropped into my chair, looking around at all the new items. This office *was* much more comfortable. Even I'd felt on edge working here before, hating all the bland colors and minimal furniture.

Now, it felt homey, like a place I could put in long hours. Calla matched everything she picked to my style. I had no idea how she knew what to look for, but everything was what I would have picked myself. Calla had done an amazing job. If she could do this to the rest of the office, people would be flocking from LA to work here.

If only my pride would let me admit it to her.

FIVE

Calla

I woke on Friday with a broad smile on my face. By some sort of luck, I'd managed to survive my first week working with Theo. It felt like a minor miracle that he hadn't killed me, or worse—fired me. After Theo calmed down about the redecorating debacle, everything had gone pretty smoothly.

The job itself was relatively simple. The biggest challenge was trying to read Theo's moods. I'd tried to get a sense of his needs and anticipate them the best I could. Some were easy.

A long client meeting: he'd need a glass and scotch and silence in the office.

A phone call with the main office back in LA: he'd want me to print out every single client list and take meticulous notes about their plans.

And anytime his ex-wife called: I should toss the message into the trash and never bother asking if he wanted to call her back.

Most of the time, Theo was a workhorse, constantly keeping himself busy, which in turn meant that I was always busy, but at this point, it was kind of a blessing. My usual social life was a joke, and most nights, the apartment felt more like a tomb than a home. Devyn was rarely around, and if she was, she was buried in briefs and other court documents.

And while I liked that work distracted me, I was also *exhausted*. The majority of nights, Theo worked until at least midnight. He'd often try to tell me to go home, I didn't feel right leaving him behind. Still, I drew a line at crashing at the office. There were a few times when I'd accidentally dozed off at my desk, but I refused to sleep there willfully, a sentiment that Theo did not share. I found him passed out on the couch twice already, his suit rumpled from his all-nighter.

At least he stopped complaining about his new furniture after that first night.

After getting ready and springing for a cab to the office, I shoved the door open with my hip, shocked to hear other people inside. After it being only Theo and me here all week, it was a little jarring to hear others in our space. I walked down the hall to find Theo in his office with six other men.

I looked around the room, taking in their designer suits and powerful auras. They must have been the other agents he told me about. I had the date marked on my calendar, making sure their offices were assigned and stocked before they arrived, but I forgot that they were getting in late last night.

As I stood in the doorway, none of them seemed to notice me. They were too focused on the documents, charts, and spreadsheets sprawled all over the coffee table. One of the other men, a younger guy with slicked-back blond hair, glanced up first, giving me a sideways smirk before standing. "And who do we have here?"

Theo rolled his eyes at him. "Jack Fischer, this is my assistant, Calla."

"Ah," the man—*Jack*—said as he walked over to me, extending his hand. "The new Marie."

"That's yet to be determined," Theo muttered, not even bothering to take his eyes off the paper he was studying.

Well, so much for him warming up to me. The words struck a nerve for a moment, but I quickly brushed it off. I straightened my shoulders, refusing to let Theo rattle me. It would take a lot more than that. My mother and stepfather had practically made it a blood sport. Theo would have to work harder if he wanted to get under my skin.

I placed my hand in Jack's, noticing the strength in his grip. "Don't mind Mr. Ayad," I winked. "He's not used to having someone call him out on his surly attitude."

Jack and the other men barked a loud laugh, and he smiled down at me. "I like this one, Theo." He lowered his voice, "When you get sick of his shit, come find me. I could use an assistant with some spark."

"Don't even think about it," Theo warned, finally looking up at us. *Please.* I rolled my eyes. With his constantly shifting moods and attitude problem, I should jump at the chance to work for someone else, but I felt a sick sense of loyalty to Theo. He was willing to give me a chance when no one else would even let me in the door.

But it was nice to have options.

I coyly smiled up at Jack, "Tempting offer, but I'm good right now." I winked at Theo, secretly loving how annoyed his expression had turned. "I can handle him."

Theo stood, placing his hand on my arm to steer me out of his office. He let the door close behind him, bringing me to my desk and depositing me into my chair. "Do I need you to reread the employee contract?"

I arched my brow. "What for?"

"There's a strict no-fraternization rule." He narrowed his eyes. "Jack is a shameless flirt, but he's also one of the best sports agents in the country. If you try—"

"I'm going to stop you there." I held up my hand. "First of all, this is the first and last time we will discuss my dating life. It's none of your business."

"It is if it affects this office."

"And second," I continued, matching his irritated glare, "that policy only applies to supervisors and their subordinates. And last: I have zero interest in dating Jack. That was a *conversation*, in case you haven't heard of those before. It's something two people do when they work together. Maybe you should go back to your makers and see if they can install a better social chip. Yours seems to be defective."

He paused, leaning away from me. "Because I'm a robot?"

"Now he's getting it," I teased, placing my hands down on my desk. "To make it clear, yes, I read the contract and know that interoffice dating is not allowed. Trust me, it won't be an issue."

Theo nodded slowly, apparently appeased by my words. He looked down at the calendar on my desk, studying the notes I'd left for the day. I'd already been planning on working late, trying to get a jump start for next week. Knowing Theo, he'd be working all weekend and have an endless list of tasks waiting for me on Monday morning.

He tapped his finger against the surface. "I need you to set up a dinner."

I nodded, grabbing my ever-present notepad. "For when?"

"Tonight."

I sucked in a sharp breath. "Unless you want fast-food, it's going to be hard to get a reservation with only a few hours' notice. How many people?"

"Six," Theo said with a disinterested tone, as if he hadn't just thrown me an impossible task with an even more ridiculous deadline. "Most of the department heads flew in last night, and I want to start this team off on the right foot."

"Sounds like a blast," I drawled, scribbling down ideas.

"Hardly. More like most of them will get hammered and stick me with the tab. But that's how things are done."

"Then maybe you should bring me along," I jokingly suggested. "That sounds like my idea of a good time." I stood, tapping him on the shoulder with my notepad.

His brow furrowed. "Assistants don't usually attend these events."

"I know." I smirked. "I was teasing, Mr. Ayad."

But he kept staring at me, those dark brown eyes breaking through all my defenses. Theo's stare worked right through to your soul, making you feel exposed and vulnerable. It took everything in me to keep up my calm façade.

I waited, assuming he would have a come-back, something to break the unnerving tension between us. But before he could, Jack poked his head out of the office. "Boss? We need you."

That snapped Theo out of his trance. He muttered a quick "get it done" before returning to his own office.

I turned over my shoulder, meeting his stern expression through the glass wall. While the rest of the room was watching him, his eyes never left mine, almost as if he wished he was sitting out here instead of stuck in there.

I shook my head. I was clearly going insane. Theo barely tolerated me most days. I'd lost track of the number of times he'd already threatened to fire me, but somehow, when I showed up the following day, he almost seemed relieved to see me.

Maybe I was seeing what I wanted, making up emotions that Theo lacked. He wasn't the type of boss who would ever give out pity praise or commend someone for doing basic tasks. The most I'd gotten so far was a brief head nod, confirming that I'd done the job accurately.

I was determined to impress him, to prove that I was more than my résumé. After years of failing to rise to others' expectations, working for Theo gave me a new purpose and a sense of ambition. This job would never solve world hunger, but I still wanted to do it well.

With that mindset, I turned back to my phone, scrolling through my contacts until I reached my sister's number. I doubted she'd answer, but it was worth a try. Devyn had been in New York much longer than me and had more connections than I could even imagine.

ME:

Any chance you can hook me up with a dinner reservation for tonight? Six people? Some place that will impress my new boss.

I chewed on my lower lip as the three dots appeared, keeping my fingers crossed until her response appeared.

DEVYN:

Done.

SIX

Theo

The cool spring air hit my lungs as I stepped out of the restaurant. A passing rainstorm had left the city covered in a shiny sheen, and the lights reflected off the water pooling on the streets. The other agents followed closely behind me, an excited chatter filling the air. Hands clapped my back as we hailed cabs, a good sign that tonight had been a success.

The entire evening felt like a test, the first opportunity I had to prove to the other agents that I was capable of leading our office. While internally, I knew I was ready for this challenge, looking out at six employees I respected made the doubts sink in. Hopefully, they didn't catch the shake of my hands or the crack in my voice.

The restaurant was a good choice. All my guests seemed enamored with the level of talent dining with us. Actors, athletes, and musicians filled the tables, most a respectable distance from the windows to avoid the flashing cameras. While the paparazzi might be a nuisance outside- *inside*, we were the sharks in the water, waiting for the perfect opportunity to strike.

At least, the rest of the group was acting that way, carefully assessing every person in the room.

Me? I was too distracted with thoughts of my assistant.

I had no idea how Calla managed to get us a reservation with such little notice. It was a dick move to ask her to try to fit us in somewhere, especially on a Friday night. Most high-end restaurants in Manhattan were booked out for months, only willing to fit in celebrities who promised clout and media coverage.

But Calla not only managed to get us in to one of the hottest restaurants in the city—she also got us a table in the center of the room. For a meeting with clients, this would have been disastrous, drawing too much attention. But for our group, it was perfect, making us seem like the most influential people in the restaurant.

After all, that was the goal.

If this task was a test, Calla aced it with flying colors.

She was different than I expected, so much more than the stories led me to believe. Her first day on the job, I stayed extra late at the office, trying to close a negotiation for one of my actors. It was practically morning by the time I wrapped up for the night. I'd assumed she'd gone home hours earlier, but instead, I found her at her desk, sleeping softly on the surface, her hands curled under her face.

I stared at her for a few minutes, taking the opportunity to study her. If she saw me watching her, she'd probably call me a creep, but I couldn't help it. Her auburn hair was falling all over itself, escaping the bun she'd twisted it into hours earlier. Her heels were tucked next to her desk, the soles facing up at me. She always had a youthful glow to her, but when she was sleeping, it was even more entrancing. It was tempting to touch her cheek, to feel if her subtle skin was as I imagined.

It took me a minute to snap out of my stupor and remember who Calla was to me. *Who I was.* She was young, vibrant, and full of life, and I was darkness, a shadow passing through the world without engaging with it. We were nothing to each other, just a necessary stop along the way.

I needed to remember that.

As a cab blared in the background, I snapped out of the thought in time to wave off several of the department heads. As they left, Jack stood at my side, tucking his hands into his pockets. "That seemed like a success."

"Yes, it was," I muttered, finally letting my guard drop. Out of all the people I'd dined with tonight, Jack was the only one I'd consider a friend, our bond forged by working side by side for years. "I'm waiting for Chuck to make a move to take me out."

Jack laughed, rubbing a hand over his perfectly trimmed goatee, "As you should. He's going to be watching you for any mistake." He smirked back at me, "Speaking of...what the fuck were you thinking, hiring that girl?"

My jaw tensed. "What do you mean?

"She's not your usual type."

"Which is?"

"Older, work-focused, *dull*." He emphasized the last point. "But Calla..." He sucked in a breath. "She's a fucking knock-out. How the hell are any of us supposed to get any work done with her in the office?" He shook his head, smiling slyly at me. "I forgot who the hell I'm talking to. You probably didn't even notice."

Oh, I'd noticed. I have to be fucking blind not to notice Calla's beauty. Between her long legs and a smile that lit up the world, it was impossible to keep my thoughts about her strictly professional.

Not that I would ever let Jack know that. I forced a scowl on my face. "Don't even think about it."

"What?" he chuckled. "I'm just saying that if the whole assistant thing doesn't work out, she'd make a great first wife."

"Like you'd ever willing tie yourself down to one woman."

He placed his hand over his heart like he'd been struck. "You wound me, my friend. Maybe I'm just waiting for the right one to come along."

"Just make sure it's not my assistant."

"Say no more; she's off limits." He winked at me. "How about we go for another drink and see what this city has to offer?"

I shook my head. "Another night. I have a meeting with a client tomorrow, and I need to make sure everything is good to go."

"Oh, c'mon, Theo. You know the saying about all work and no play."

"Makes me in charge of this office," I added solemnly. "A lot is riding on us bringing in new clients. I'm not going to fuck it up in our first month."

"Whatever you say, man," Jack joked, walking backward down the street. "Let me know if there's anything you need in the morning."

I waved him off, hailing a cab uptown. At the late hour, it didn't take long to get back to the office, but my eyes were already heavy. Most sane people were probably heading home for the night, tucking themselves into bed next to their partner, but I meant what I said to Jack. This office *needed* to be success-ful. There was no other option.

The rest of the building was quiet as I rode the elevator up, all the lights turned down low. While I enjoyed seeing more faces around the office, these were the moments when I thrived.

But as the doors opened on our floor, a strange sound echoed from the office—music. More specifically, someone was singing. I walked down the hall, following the noise. Maybe a janitor had left the radio on? One of the staff? When I turned the corner, however, someone entirely different came into view.

Calla was in my office, white AirPods tucked in her ears.

She swung her hips as she sang along with the words. She had twisted her hair up, and she'd kicked off her heels to the side of the couch. As she piled different file folders on my table, she sunk to the floor, twisting her hips as she rose back up.

What the hell was happening right now? I waited for a surge of annoyance, for my anger to rise at the sight of her desecrating my office, but instead, I found myself smiling, unable to look away. I lingered for a moment, just enough for the memory to implant itself right alongside the last one. Her hips moved in a seductive rhythm, as if begging for my palms to caress them, to hold her against my chest, letting her feel the effect she had on me.

I sucked in a sharp breath, trying to keep my dick in line. If she turned around and saw me watching her like that, it'd be a recipe for a sexual harassment case. This needed to stop. These daydreams about Calla were going to be the end of my career, and I couldn't allow that.

My jaw tensed as I walked into my office, taking her phone off my desk. After I pressed the pause button, Calla kept going, belting out the last few notes.

"What the hell?" she snapped, quickly turning around. "Oh shit." She ran her hands through her hair, rushing over to throw on her shoes. "Theo—I mean, Mr. Ayad, I am so sorry. I got carried away, and I just—"

"Thought you could perform a private concert in my office?"

She scrunched her face. "Sort of. It helps keep me awake during late nights."

"And why are you here so late?" I asked, suddenly desperate to learn more about her and her thoughts. "It's Friday night. Surely you have better things to do than collate my files."

"I wanted to stay," she admitted, a new blush filling her

cheeks. "I know you're really swamped next week, so I wanted to make sure I had everything prepared."

I nodded, thumbing through the documents she left on my desk. Everything was meticulously organized. Hell, she had even color-coded the folders based on the types of meetings. It was a simple touch, but one I appreciated.

But instead of voicing that thought, I said, "You can leave now. I'll take it from here."

"Oh..." Calla brushed a few strands from her forehead. "Are you sure? I have a few more things I want to get done." When I looked up, she snapped her lips closed. "Of course. I'll get out of your way, Mr. Ayad."

I watched as she gathered her things, a new ache opening in my chest. What was it about Calla that elicited this guilt? I'd been brash with assistants before, but it never caused any sort of reaction. I couldn't let her leave just yet.

"It's Theo." I waited for her to turn back around to face me. When she stopped, I continued. "You don't have to call me Mr. Ayad. Theo works just as well. And next time, you can use my office speakers." I pointed to the wall. "Much better sound quality."

"Next time?" Calla furrowed her brow.

"That you want to stay late." I glanced up at her. "But please, no more Ivy Abrams. If I never hear that song again, it'll be too soon."

"Oh, crap." Calla clapped her hand to her forehead. "I completely forgot. Listen, no offense to Adam, but this album is *amazing*. If she's looking for an agent, you should try to recruit her. The girl is blowing up."

"Oh, I'm aware," I groaned, sinking into my chair. "But I doubt after our last few conversations that Ivy would be interested in joining forces. Besides, I would never do that to Adam."

"Aww, Theo," Calla crooned, stepping to the other edge of

my desk. I hated how much I loved hearing her say my name. "There is a heart under all that Armani."

"They installed it with my software patch." I tapped my chest. "Just have to figure out how to turn the damn thing off."

"What?" Calla's mouth hung open in surprised delight. "A heart *and* a joke? Oh, Theo..." She shook her finger at me. "You're going to have the ladies lining up if you keep this going."

I shook my head. "Out, Calla."

She winked at me as she crossed the room, stopping in the doorway. "Don't worry, Sunshine. It'll be our little secret."

Calla

The past two weeks were a blur. Ever since the other agents started filling the empty desks, there was a life in the office that wasn't there before. While I was beginning to love the constant sound of ringing phones, the bustle that echoed through the halls, I had mixed feelings about their arrival. Many of the senior agents were intimidating, and the younger ones who filled the bullpen by my desk were looking to make a name for themselves. As the gatekeeper to the boss, they went out of their way to make a good impression on me, but with them constantly stopping by to "check in," it was hard to focus on my own work.

When I imagined my ideal career, being someone's assistant never crossed my mind, however, being here and watching how much went into starting this office from the ground up was a unique experience. I'd quickly gotten used to being by Theo's side, observing as he built his dream team. And although he never voiced it out loud, it seemed like Theo was beginning to trust me as well.

Last week, he hired a professional to finish what I started, but he pulled me into every meeting, checking if I approved before he signed off on any of her choices. It was nice to feel important, like someone valued my opinion. Slowly, the office stopped feeling like a dentist's waiting room and more like an actual, functional workplace.

I grabbed my files from the copier, stopping to greet Eloise, the new receptionist. I wasn't sure, but Eloise and I had to be around the same age. She was a recent transplant from the Midwest, following her boyfriend as he started a new career. Theo was against hiring her at first, thinking she'd be too soft to handle angry clients, but somehow, I'd managed to convince him to give her a chance.

Usually, we were very friendly with each other. However, today, the way she was looking at me made my stomach flip. Eloise grimaced as I reached her desk, and passed me a stack of pink messages.

"All Natalie?" I scanned the first one, matching her sour expression when I saw Theo's ex-wife's name on almost every single slip. "How many times did she call?"

"Twelve," Eloise answered. "And let me tell you, that woman has a mouth on her. I don't think I've ever heard anyone use the f-word so many times in one breath."

"Remind me to introduce you to my best friend," I chuckled. "Thanks for handling her. If she calls again, direct it to my line. I'll make something up."

I waved goodbye as I took the stack, oddly curious about why Natalie was so desperate to talk to Theo. From what I could tell, he never called her back, barely ever bothering to read her messages. As much as it was none of my business, I was dying to know what had happened between them.

But as I rounded the corner toward Theo's office, the sight on the other side of the room pulled all the thoughts from my head. Theo was standing in the middle of his office, stripping off his jacket. He then tossed it on the back of his chair before rolling up the sleeves of his button-up. If you looked up forearm porn in the dictionary, this scene would be a perfect example. My mouth ran dry as I scanned his body, wishing I could feel his arms around me.

I cursed the person who decided to make the walls of his office out of glass.

When it was just the two of us, I had free range to work wherever I felt like. But now that most of the other desks were taken, I was confined to the one right in front of Theo's office, which meant that, all day, I could see him as he worked.

Which was a major distraction.

No, Calla. Lusting after your boss is the worst thing you could do right now. You are just finding your footing in this city. I was also getting accustomed to having a paycheck and using it for luxuries like food and clothing.

This ridiculous crush needed to stop. Not only was the man my boss, but he was also a workaholic and cold—not my type at all. Maybe it sounded conceited, but I never went for guys who were hard to get. I liked my men to be obsessed with me, never making me wonder what they were feeling. Too bad no one had come close to meeting my ridiculously high standard.

The only one who had come close was my high school boyfriend, Gray. He treated me like a queen until the day he graduated, moving to Seattle to follow his baseball dreams. And while I could look back now and know that what we had was nothing more than puppy love, he'd set the bar pretty high.

Maybe that was why I hadn't had a real relationship in the past eight years. Sure, there had been plenty of short-term ones and a few situationships I wasn't exactly proud of, but there hadn't been anyone I'd let myself fall for.

It wasn't that I was opposed to falling in love, but also I wasn't willing to settle. With the little I knew about Theo, he'd never be able to give me what I wanted. He was too jaded, too set in his ways. Sure, he looked like he was carved out of my deepest fantasies, but having a fling with my boss would be a *terrible* life choice.

Trying to erase that thought from my head, I knocked on his door, clearing my throat to break him from his stare down with his cell phone. Was Natalie blowing up that phone as well? I shook my head. *It's none of your business, Calla. Professional. Be professional.*

Theo's lips curved into a half smile as I stepped closer, but as soon as I passed him the stack of messages, it fell. His jaw clenched tighter as he read each one. When he reached the end of the pile, he tossed them all on the coffee table. "This is fucking ridiculous."

I chewed on my lower lip, trapped between comforting him and backing quickly out of the office. I settled on the former. "Is everything okay? I know she's usually...persistent, but this seems excessive, even for her."

Theo sat up in his armchair, resting his elbows on his knees. For a moment, I thought he wasn't going to answer me or would toss me out of his office for prying into his private life. Instead, he exhaled slowly. "I have no idea. She's probably got it in her head that I'm not paying her enough alimony. Last time we spoke, she threatened to take me to court."

"Can she do that?"

"Probably not," Theo answered. "But she'll make my life hell until she gets her way. It's easier just to ignore her until she calms down."

I nodded, unsure what to say. "If you ever need a lawyer, my sister's a pretty fantastic one. She doesn't usually do divorce cases, but I'm sure she'd be able to help you out."

"Thanks, Calla." Leaning back in his seat, he ran his hand over his face. "This is why marriage is bullshit. Remind me never to do it again."

I smiled at him, but for some reason, his words stirred something in my stomach. I hated that Theo had given up on love after one bad experience. There were times I was tempted as well, especially after watching my mother's marriage ruin everything it touched, but I refused to let their toxicity ruin my view of love. Maybe I hadn't found the kind that existed in my books, but I refused to be cynical.

As I went back to my desk, I started thinking about my social life since I moved to the city. I'd only been out a couple of times with my sister, and both times had been cut short by a work call. I'd been too busy trying to figure out how to make money to even consider dating. But now that things felt more stable, maybe I should put myself out there.

I glanced down at my phone, wondering if it was time to reinstall my dating apps. While they worked, I hated swiping through photos to try and find my soulmate. Call me old-fashioned, but I wanted that movie moment, the one where the couple looks across the room, meeting each other's eyes, and they just *know*.

I pulled out my phone, creating a new group chat.

CALLA

Which do you think sounds worse: speed dating, or one of those single-and-mingle events?

ALEX

This feels like the start of a cry for help

DEVYN

I'd rather get a root canal than go to either of those

CALLA

Who said I was inviting you?

DEVYN

Please. I can feel the puppy dog eyes from here.

ALEX

You really shouldn't go to stuff like that alone

CALLA

...Fine

Any better ideas?

ALEX

For fuck's sake, go to a bar

DEVYN

I second that

And before you ask: yes, I will go with you. Case wrapped up today, so I'll be out at a normal time.

CALLA

Holy shit, this does call for a celebration!

DEVYN

Ha. ha. Ha. Just meet me after work

ONCE THE CLOCK STRUCK FIVE, I gathered my things and adjusted my lipstick in my compact mirror. I could feel Theo watching me through the walls of his office, but I didn't bother to turn around. He'd been brooding for hours, declaring that the whole day was shit. Between Natalie's relentless phone calls and the low-ball offer his client received, Theo was in a foul mood. It was tempting to try to break him out of it, but nothing seemed to help. I was quickly learning that on days like this, it was better to let him sulk and work out his problems on his own. Interfering only resulted in him snapping at me. Not because he was annoyed with me, but because sometimes, he acted like an overgrown toddler who had trouble handling his emotions.

As soon as I slung my purse over my shoulder, Theo called out for me. *Shit*. Maybe I wasn't in the clear like I thought.

"Yes, Theo?" I walked inside his office, propping a hip against the open door. His eyes scanned my face, snagging on my lips a little longer than usual.

His dark eyes narrowed on me. "Did you get those copies of the Peterson contract sent over?"

"Of course..." I drawled. He'd already asked me twice about this. "I sent a copy of the fax receipt to your inbox."

Theo nodded but didn't take his eyes off me, stuck on my lips. His darkened eyes made me want to squirm, but I stood still, refusing to admit he had any effect on me.

"Anything else you need?" I asked.

Theo just continued staring at me, as if waiting for something to happen. When he didn't speak for a few more seconds, I rolled my eyes and started to walk out of the office, but I didn't get far. A large hand gripped my elbow—tight enough to make me stop, but not enough to leave a mark.

I glanced down where Theo held me then back up to meet his eyes. They were alight with a new fire, one that made my thighs clench together. It was heady seeing this man stare at me like he wanted to consume me. It was terrifying, *exhilarating*. I never wanted this moment to end. But as quickly as it had started, it did. Theo dropped his arm and took a significant step back. He cleared his throat and crossed his arms over his chest. "I wanted to say...thank you."

I arched my brow at him. He had never said those words before. Usually, when I made changes, he'd mutter something about needing to fire me, but he never followed through on his threat. I was beginning to think threats were his love language.

"You've done a lot around here in a short time, and I... appreciate it." Theo steeled his gaze, staring at me with an intensity I'd never seen from him before. "I appreciate *you*, Calla."

I just gawked at him, unsure how to respond. His sincerity knocked me off guard. It took a moment for me to realize we were staring at each other across this small space.

"You're welcome." I cleared my throat and took a step away from him as I hitched my thumb over my shoulder. "But I'm going to be late for dinner. I'll see you tomorrow."

Theo only nodded, not saying another word as I headed down the hall.

EIGHT

Calla

"That's all?"

My sister, Devyn, stared at me across the table, nursing the martini she ordered when we arrived an hour ago. Her long blonde hair was fashioned into a picture-perfect chignon, aligning all too with her neutral, tailored suit. It was still hard to wrap my head around this version of my sister compared to when we were growing up. When we were younger, Devyn spent most of her days running wild through the woods or covered in paint in her makeshift art studio, the complete opposite of the corporate Barbie she'd transformed into. Even drinking, she was posed and perfect, as if she was in the middle of the courtroom, waiting for closing arguments.

However, I was on my third drink and starting to come apart at the seams. I'd never been very good at keeping my thoughts to myself, and with a bit of liquid courage, everything was starting to spill out.

"He said *thank you*." I waved my hands in the air for emphasis. "The man *never* says thank you. Maybe something is wrong, like, you know, when people get sick and start to appreciate things more? Or maybe it's like the calm before the storm." I gasped, grabbing Devyn's arm. "Do you think he's going to fire me this time? Like, for real fire me?"

"I don't know how to respond to that."

I lifted my thumb, nervously chewing on the cuticle. Devyn slapped my hand away, knowing it was a nervous tick. She held up her empty glass, summoning the bartender to bring us another round of drinks.

I was about to tell her to stop, thinking that I had to drive home, but then I remembered I no longer lived in a tiny town where the cabs stopped picking up at nine o'clock. That was one of the best parts about living in the city. I held up my hand. "And one more for me too."

As the bartender mixed our drinks, I looked around the bar. The lights were dimmed low, giving it a moody, trendy vibe. Most of the patrons were bankers and other Wall Street bros looking to network. It wasn't quite my scene, but it was only a couple of blocks from Devyn's office, making it less likely that she'd bail on me at the last minute.

She held up her drink to clink with mine. "To you overanalyzing and spiraling because your boss thanked you."

"I'm serious, Devyn. I'm just starting to stand on my own two feet." I chewed on my lower lip until a thought popped into my head. "That's it! My thirty days are almost up. He's just trying to butter me up so I don't flip when he lets me go."

As she took another sip, Devyn studied me before a smirk formed on her lips. "You like him."

"What?" I snapped, giggling at her insinuation. "Because I don't want to get fired? No. No, no. That's—*no*."

"Way too many nos to be truthful."

"Fucking lawyer logic," I grumbled into my drink.

"Fine, you *don't* have feelings for him." She rolled her eyes. "Even if you did, it's for the best that you don't act on them. He's your boss. That screams messy, even for you."

"Ouch." I smacked her thigh. "And that was never even an option. Sure, I enjoy looking at Theo, but *date* him? That would be a *disaster* waiting to happen." I started counting off my fingers. "He's a jerk incapable of saying anything nice, he's emotionally stunted, and he's way older than me."

"How much older?"

"Old enough," I answered. "At least in his mid-thirties. And he's got his life together, Dev. He would never be interested in someone like me."

She scrunched her face. "What is that supposed to mean?"

"Nothing," I sighed, needing to change the subject. "How's your case going? Is there any more word about when they're going to announce the junior partnership?"

Devyn lifted her drink, taking a large gulp. "I might kill my client, except she's not even really my client. She's his daughter. So now, I need to play nice with an eighteen-year-old who's determined to throw away her entire trust fund. It's *exhausting*."

"Sounds like it. And this will help you get the promotion?"

"That's the goal," she sighed. "There are three other associates who could get the job, but none of them can match my billables or wins. The only advantage they have is their penises."

I snorted, sending vodka through my nostrils. Devyn giggled, handing me a napkin. I was glad to know I wasn't the only one feeling the drinks. But just as her laugh started to fade, a cheer broke out through the crowd, all eyes glued to the no-hitter on the TV screen above the bar. Devyn sneered as she spotted the familiar ashen hair of number thirteen smirking on the pitcher's mound as another player struck out.

I jabbed my elbow into her side. "Gray's having a great season."

"He better," Devyn scoffed, taking another long sip of her drink. "They're paying him enough."

I arched my brow, debating how far to push Devyn on Gray. While we might have dated in high school, they were best friends for years before that. However, they had a falling out right before he left for college. No one knew what it was about, but Devyn rarely brought him up and snapped at anyone who tried to ask. Despite their rift, she never missed one of his games.

"You know you two live in the same city, right?"

"So?"

"Well...." I stirred my drink, weighing my words. "Maybe it's time for you to talk–"

"Hard pass."

"Devyn, I—"

"So, are you sure there's nothing going on between you and your boss?"

"Nice deflection." I rolled my eyes. "Yes, Devyn," I answered dryly. "I am sure that nothing is going on between Theo and me."

"Good," she answered, nodding toward the door. "Because I'm pretty sure Theo just walked in."

My eyes widened as I watched Theo shuffle into the bar, his eyes almost immediately finding mine. The corner of his lip picked up, as if it was all a big game. For a moment, I thought he was here for me, but I quickly realized that was ridiculous. In what world would my boss track me down to some corporate bar in Midtown?

But I couldn't lie—part of me wished he had.

As I tried to push that thought out of my head, Theo approached our table. Devyn smirked, turning to hide her smirk in her drink. "Okay, I'm starting to get the appeal. Pictures do not do him justice."

"Shut up," I hissed through a forced smile.

"Calla..." Theo greeted me as he reached our table, waving for his friends to find a spot without him.

"Theo," I answered back, unable to hide my grin. "I can't believe you're here. I was starting to think you never left the office, much less socialized with other people. That new software update is working wonders."

Devyn's eyes went wide, but Theo just stared at me, that same corner of his mouth quirking in amusement. "There's a lot about me you don't know."

"Care to share any more secrets?" I dared to ask, not sure why exactly I was openly flirting with my boss. Maybe in the morning, I'd regret my choices and realize I was toeing a very dangerous line. But three drinks in, reasonable, sensible Calla was nowhere to be found.

That version of me was delighted when Theo leaned forward, his lips brushing the shell of my ear. "That lipstick is very distracting. I can't seem to take my eyes off it."

My breath sputtered out, and I was unsure how to respond when Theo pulled back, winking at me before leaving our table. "See you tomorrow, Calla."

NINE

Theo

Despite saying good night to Calla right after I walked in, I couldn't stop watching her. My eyes kept drifting back to her table, as if pulled by some invisible force. It was slow torture, seeing her so at ease while different men gravitated to her, and all I could do was sit back and let it happen.

You're her boss. You're too old for her. You would both lose your jobs if you crossed that line. The words echoed in my head, becoming my newest mantra. But fucking hell, watching her was the purest form of temptation, and I was just enough of a masochist to indulge.

The men seated around my table continued laughing, utterly oblivious to my predicament. Outside of the office, I had no real ties to them; most were junior agents who asked if I wanted to join them as they celebrated a big win. Typically, I would have said no, but with Calla's perfume still lingering in the air and that red lipstick altering my brain chemistry, I agreed. I was in dire need of a distraction.

And, as luck would have it, they dragged me to the same bar as her.

I felt guilty about not introducing myself to her companion, too focused on the woman who plagued my thoughts. I watched their interactions, curious about how they knew each other. It seemed like they were related. They had the same smile and honey-brown eyes, but nothing about the blonde woman called to my soul like Calla did.

She was a balm to my banal world, igniting the shades of gray into vibrant hues.

"Theo?" one of the men across the table called out to me. I think his name was Harry? Maybe Hunter? I didn't care enough to remember, which probably reflected negatively on my leadership, but at the moment, he was nothing more than a distraction, taking my attention away from where it really wanted to be.

As I turned to him with an unamused look, he cleared his throat. "We're going to head out to another bar. You in?"

When I debated continuing my night, taking myself out of Calla's orbit, her friend's phone rang, and she hurried to take the call. She spoke in a hushed tone for a minute and then gave Calla an apologetic look. With a kiss on her cheek, the blonde rushed out the door.

I watched Calla for a moment longer, wondering if she would be leaving as well, but she surprised me when she called for another drink. With a smile on my lips, I shook my head. "I'm going to call it a night. Go have fun. I'll settle the tab."

With an excited cheer and many claps of thanks on the back, I was wonderfully alone.

But I had no intention of staying that way.

I slid over to the now-empty barstool next to Calla, watching as she swiveled her straw in her drink. She turned to me, the sly smile from earlier returning. It was different than her usual look, a wide grin that took up almost her entire face. Calla was not a person who gave out half-hearted smiles for the hell of it. When she was happy, it was obvious to the world.

But this look was even more intriguing.

"It's about time, Sunshine." Calla turned to face me fully. "I was wondering if you were going to come back over here."

"Were you hoping I would?" I asked, lowering my voice so she had to lean in closer to hear me. That same alluring scent overwhelmed my senses, shooting straight to my groin. Fuck, how long had it been since I wanted someone like this? Sex lately had become as much of a chore as everything else in my life—just a checkmark on the list of the things I needed to get done.

But sitting this close to Calla, her knee pressing up against my thigh, was enough to send me spiraling, a primal need taking over.

"Of course I did," she answered. "You never got to meet my sister."

"That's who you were with?" I glanced toward the door. "She left in quite a hurry. Something you said?"

"Nope," Calla laughed. "One of her clients has a crisis." I must have frowned at the statement, because she waved me off. "It's fine. She hung out longer than I expected. Usually, she doesn't even make it through the first drink before work calls her away."

"Are you close?" I asked, although I wasn't sure why I cared. There was something about Calla that made me curious, and I'd developed a need to know everything about her.

Calla shrugged, motioning to the bartender for another drink. "We used to be, but now it feels like we're ships passing in the night. It sucks because she's the only person I have in the city."

"Not exactly." Calla arched her brow at my words. "You have me."

She laughed, the sound light and ethereal—*intoxicating*. "No offense, boss, but it's not like I can call you to grab drinks if I'm feeling lonely."

"Why not?"

She shook her head. "Well, for one, I work for you. I think us becoming drinking buddies might raise some questions." *She had me there.* "And also, you seem to live in the office most nights. Even when you're not there, you're thinking about work."

"I'm not thinking about work right now."

"What are you thinking about?"

How your lipstick would look smeared on my cock. I reared back, trying to rein in those fantasies. Being this close to Calla was veering us into dangerous territory. My imagination was already running rampant before this moment. It would be even worse now that I was able to smell her shampoo, the subtle scent of wildflowers filling the space between us.

I shook my head, trying to get myself under control. This couldn't happen. Even if the office didn't have a strict no-fraternization policy, I'd never been open to those types of relationships—too close for comfort.

Steering the conversation back to neutral territory, I asked, "What brings you out tonight?"

Calla's face fell, playing with her fingers. "I'm trying to meet someone."

Fuck. I cleared my throat, wishing I had more than two drinks before coming over here. "Why?"

"I have no idea," she laughed. "If I tell you the truth, will you promise not to make fun of me?"

"Absolutely not."

"Theo!" she laughed, smacking me on the leg. "You're supposed to say yes!"

I shrugged, and my arm found itself on the back of her chair. For a moment, I thought she'd shy away or make a comment, but neither of us made any attempt to move. "You know I'd never lie to you, Calla. If you say something ridiculous, I can't promise I won't use it against you."

"That's it—now you'll never get to know."

I leaned in, loving the way she shivered when I spoke into her ear. "C'mon, Calla. You know you want to tell me."

"Fine." She pushed a breath through her lips and stared up at the ceiling. "I guess I'm tired of waiting for the real thing to show up, so I thought I'd try to put myself out there, see what the city has to offer."

"No luck?"

"None," Calla chuckled. "Honestly, if this is what I have to do to meet someone, I'd rather stay single forever." She sipped her drink. "What happened to that old-fashioned kind of love? You know, the moment—when you lock eyes across a crowded room and the world stops moving? And you just *know* that this is *your* person. That the universe has aligned for you two to find each other."

I snorted. "You've been watching too many movies."

Calla chewed on her lower lip. "Maybe."

I hated the look on her face and wished I had the words to make it alright, but we were on opposite sides of the coin. She was looking for true love, and I was pretty sure it didn't exist. Love was a series of choices, about hoping you'd find someone who best checked the boxes you needed most. There was nothing fated about it, just dumb luck and poor decision-making.

But instead of spewing my usual rant, I let down my walls a little bit, wondering what it would be like to see the world through Calla's eyes—to view each experience as an exciting possibility instead of waiting for it to fail.

"Have you been in love before?"

Calla scrunched her face. "Not really. I thought I loved my high school boyfriend, but it was more friendship than anything else. That's the closest thing I've had to something serious." She glanced up at me. "Don't get me wrong, I've dated. But I don't see the point in continuing something if it's not going to work. If you don't feel that..." Her voice trailed off, searching for the right word.

"Chemistry?"

"Yes!" she exclaimed. "But it's more than that. Your person should make you the best version of yourself, don't you think?" I grimaced, thinking back to my marriage. While it started great, we did the opposite, bringing out the angry, vindictive sides of each other. Hell, even two years after our divorce, we were *still* bringing out the worst in each other.

"I don't want to settle for anything less than that, so I guess I'll be waiting for a little bit longer." She nudged my side with her elbow. "Know anyone you could set me up with, boss?"

My fists clenched as I imagined Calla grinning up at someone else. I wanted to be the sole recipient, to hoard her smiles all for myself greedily. But as much as I was a selfish bastard, I would never drag her down to my depths. She was light, pure, and full of heart. I would never be able to give her everything she needed or deserved.

I shook my head. "No one who deserves you, Calla."

"Aww, Sunshine." She placed her hand on my arm. "That might be the nicest thing you've ever said to me."

I reached out, placing my hand on top of hers. A breath escaped me as I felt the softness of her skin, wondering what her hands would feel like on other parts of my body. "I mean it, Calla. You're right not to settle for something less than you deserve." I inhaled slowly. "I hope you find it."

"Theo..." Her eyes flicked down to my lips for a moment. Fuck, the temptation to claim her mouth was overwhelming, to taste the alcohol from her drink on her tongue, to swallow her moans of pleasure. As if able to read my thoughts, we both leaned in, our noses briefly brushing. My hand reached up, brushing an errant curl behind her ear.

Something about the move must have snapped the tether, because Calla jumped back, putting some much-needed space between us. She quickly gathered her belongings, throwing down a couple of twenties on the tabletop. "I, uh, should go. Devyn's probably home by now."

"Let me give you a ride." I stood at her side. "My driver can be here in a couple of minutes."

"No, no, thank you," Calla said, walking quickly over to the door. "I'll be fine. Just..." She sighed, staring at me for a long moment. "Good night, Theo."

The next morning, all I wanted to do was crawl back into bed. Maybe it was the three...no, wait, *five* drinks I'd downed before eventually calling it a night. But in reality, it was more like I was dreading coming face-to-face with Theo again.

I stretched out my arms as I got to my feet, heading into the shower before I could convince myself to call in sick. Even though I desperately wanted to, there was no way I could take today off. Theo had several important meetings scheduled, and with my day ending at a regular hour yesterday, there was a ton left to prepare.

Maybe his meetings would keep him out of the office and away from my desk. The thought brought a strange chill down my spine, uncertainty twisting my stomach into a knot. After last night, I had no idea if I wanted him close or as far away as possible.

What the fuck was he even doing at the bar? I would have been less surprised to see my mother standing there than him. Theo never went out. *Ever.* If he did, it was for business meetings disguised as a night on the town.

It must have been a cruel joke from the universe, sending

the one man I couldn't get out of my head to my side when I finally decided I wanted to give dating a real shot. Even if I had met someone, all hopes were dashed as soon as Theo walked in. His presence was like lightning in my veins, and I couldn't ignore it if I wanted to. This connection between us was becoming a real, tangible thing, and no matter what I tried, I couldn't seem to make it stop. The harder I tried, the more I wanted to give in, to learn what his touch would do to my body.

I twisted the shower handle, blasting myself in the face with ice-cold water. Maybe aversion therapy would do the trick. Even if Theo *was* interested, it wasn't an option. He would never risk his job for a relationship. He wasn't wired that way. He'd already made it clear that his career was his priority. I wanted the opposite, someone who preferred relationships, believed in love, and definitely someone I would not get fired for getting involved with.

All the things that Theo was *not*.

So, why couldn't I get him out of my head? At first, I thought it was all the time we spent together. I must have had some kind of deranged Stockholm syndrome where I developed feelings for the man I worked for every day. But the more time I spent with Theo, the more I realized it was just...*him*.

As I climbed out of the shower and started brushing out my hair, my phone rang on the counter, and I smiled when I saw my best friend's face shining back at me. "Hello, gorgeous."

"Hey, stranger," Alex said. "I was hoping to catch you before work. How's everything going down there?"

I shrugged. "It's going. I think I'm finally getting a handle on this whole working woman thing, although the hours officially suck."

"Devyn kept you out too late?"

"Nah." I placed the phone on the counter to run some

product through my long hair. "She ended up bailing, but luckily, Theo was there to keep me company for a little bit."

"Wait...*Theo* was there? At the bar?" Alex scrunched her face. "Did you invite him?"

"Nope." I shook my head. "He just happened to show up. We hung out for a little bit and then went home."

"Together?"

I glared at her through the phone. "Seriously?"

She laughed. "You never know!"

"*I* know." I shook my head. "He's my boss, Alex. We would never cross that line. Plus, you know I'm not looking for a fling, and that's all Theo's capable of."

She studied me, trying to assess the lies in my words. Even though I knew they were true, they still felt wrong. My head knew Theo and I would never work, but my libido had a different opinion.

"I guess," Alex sighed. "Look, I know Theo is a good guy, but I just want you to be careful. If something does happen, it's going to blow back on you, not him."

"What do you mean?"

"He's on track to be one of the partners in the firm, and you're his assistant. If anything happens south–"

"Which it won't."

"*If* it does," Alex said pointedly. "And if it doesn't work out, you'd be the one without a job—the one without a backup plan." She pushed her breath through her lips. "No matter what happens, I'm on your side, Calla. But if things start to change, promise me you'll think this through."

Her words struck true, battling all my inner defenses. They were the same ones I'd told myself a thousand times, but hearing them from someone else's lips made them feel more real. Alex was right—I had just started finding my place in this big, overwhelming city. Was I willing to throw it all away for a guy who could never give me everything I wanted?

I shook my head, forcing those thoughts away. "Alex, you don't have to worry. Nothing is going on between Theo and me. He can barely stand me most days. You should worry more about him firing me than fucking me."

She smiled knowingly back at me. "Maybe."

DURING MY ENTIRE ride to work, I thought about my conversation with Alex, wondering if she saw something I didn't. God knows I was able to see how she felt about Cole long before she owned up to it.

I closed my eyes, letting my head rest against the plush leather seat of the town car. My head was so confused, and all I wanted to do was erase last night from my memory, to pretend I'd never seen that side of Theo, never known what it was like to have his heavy stare weigh on me.

Would it be possible to pretend nothing happened, to go back to who we were weeks ago before the lines started to blur?

That was it.

I had to remember my first few days when the lines were much thicker and we hadn't torn down so many boundaries between us, when I thought I'd just be another girl at the desk and Theo was my asshole boss.

My resolve steeled as the driver dropped me outside of our building. It became stronger as the elevator climbed the floors and the door eventually opened to the Wallace and Associates lobby. I waved a quick hello to Eloise and some of the other associates before heading to my desk.

I peeked into Theo's office, letting out a relieved sigh that it was empty. He must have already taken off for his breakfast meeting. Now that I'd avoided *that* confrontation a little longer, I tucked into the kitchen, finding my favorite mug and brewing a coffee pod. Just as I did, the door swung open, and Jack strolled in, taking a minute to let his gaze drift down my body. I rolled my eyes. Jack seemed like a nice enough guy and a close friend of Theo's, but something about him didn't sit quite right with me. He walked up behind me, glancing at my coffee cup.

"Working for Theo requires a lot of caffeine?"

I barely contained my groan. "The morning requires caffeine for most of us, Jack."

He laughed but stepped out of my space, and I instantly breathed easier when he was on the other side of the room. "So, Calla, have you considered my offer?"

"What offer?" I turned, propping my hip against the counter. "About coming to work for you? I didn't think you were serious."

"Oh, I would never joke about that," he chuckled. "But I've seen your work, Calla. I think we could be a good team."

"Pass." I turned to the fridge to load my coffee with creamer. It was a common joke with my friends that my coffee cup had more cream than anything else. Sue me if I didn't love the flavor of coffee, just the happy little side effects. "Theo and I have a pretty great thing going."

"So I've heard." I looked up at him, noticing that the joking look had left his eyes. "Be careful, Calla. I know you're just getting to know him, but I've worked with Theo for years. He's one of my closest friends. I know he's a good guy, but when Theo wants something, he can be a little short-sighted. People who get close to him tend to get hurt." He stepped closer to me. "You seem like a good person, Calla. I'd hate to see that happen to you."

His words should have soothed me, serving as another reminder of the long list of reasons why Theo and I would never be anything more than what we were, but something didn't sit right with me, like he was alluding to a situation I had no right to know about.

"Thanks." I tightly smiled at him. "But I'm more than capable of handling myself."

"I know you are."

I tried to push past him to head to my desk, but he stopped me with a hand on my arm. He leaned in, whispering close to my ear. "Listen, I don't want to be the one to tell you this, but there have been some rumors about the two of you. Some of the other agents are wondering why Theo hired *you*, a girl with no experience, to help him run this place when he had his pick of assistants."

"And?"

"Just something to think about." Jack tried to inject some earnestness into his words. "In this business, sometimes a rumor is worse than the truth."

He walked through the opposite door, leaving me to ponder his warning on my own.

ELEVEN

Theo

Something was wrong.

Sure, it could have been one of the thousands of tasks piling up on my desk, or the fact that my phone had not stopped ringing all day. And those should have been my greatest concerns. However, today, my entire focus was on my assistant, the same one who was pointedly ignoring me.

Ever since I returned from my morning meeting, Calla had been acting off. There was none of her usual sass, no quips, no obnoxious nicknames. Hell, after five straight hours of "Yes, Mr. Ayad.", I was getting desperate to see one of her smiles, willing to do anything to get some of her usual spark back.

This job wasn't supposed to be complicated, just another steppingstone to getting my name on the company letterhead. The hardest part of this job was supposed to be managing the other agents, not my assistant who had invaded all my thoughts. I'd worked with my last assistant for years, and while I loved her like family, I never noticed what she did outside of my office. Calla's every action intrigued and ensnared me. With Marie, I never had to worry about her breaking into my office and rearranging everything. She wouldn't insist on using pastel legal pads, leaving stacks of varying hues all over my office.

I never found myself pausing at the elevator for her, waiting until the exact right second so we could walk into the office together.

At the thought, I glanced through the glass window, watching as Calla twisted her hair up into that intricate little knot. There was no question in my mind that last night was a mistake. We'd been playing with fire from our first glance, practically daring each other closer to the edge. All my common sense flew out the window when I saw that look in her eye, daring me to toe the fading line between us. I didn't know where it had come from, this odd need to be close to her, the overwhelming desire to see her smile curve just for me. It was all I could think about.

It was also the *last* thing I needed.

Christ, I needed to get myself together. I was leading a multi-million-dollar expansion, not getting my rocks off at a high school dance. I didn't have time to worry about other people right now, not when work was supposed to be my sole focus.

But with each day I spent with Calla, the boundaries between us blurred even more. It had only been a couple of weeks, and my attraction to her was driving me mad. What would happen if we kept working together? Would I be able to reinforce my walls, or were we inevitably going to crash into each other?

I forced myself back to my computer, pulling up an email thread between myself and a casting agent. Just as I started to tick off my checklist, Calla's laugh echoed through the walls. I instantly sat up straighter, my eyes darting to her desk. All I could see was the high back of her chair, her auburn hair tied up in some kind of fancy knot. But that wasn't what caused my grip to tighten.

No, that would be Jack perched on the side of her desk. He leaned over, brushing his hand on her forearm under the guise of showing her something on the computer. It was innocent enough, nothing I could condemn him for without drawing suspicion.

And yet, I was having a tough time not strangling him.

Before I could overthink my actions, I stormed out of my office, arching a brow at Jack and Calla. She immediately averted her eyes, suddenly preoccupied with the forms on her desk. Jack, however, just smirked at me. "How's it going, boss man?"

"Busy," I said, my tone laced with annoyance. "Maybe I should have delegated more tasks to your team."

"Oh, we're actually in the middle of that negotiation for–"

"Then get to it," I snapped, taking my suddenly sullen mood out on my friend. "I want that deal closed by the end of the day, contract on my desk in the morning."

Jack's brow lifted, but he didn't argue. Instead, he lifted off Calla's desk, squeezing her shoulder once. "See you later?"

"I'll think about it."

As soon as Jack disappeared down the hall, I stepped back toward my office, holding the door open. "Calla, a word?"

Tension immediately rippled up her spine at my request, but she stood, stepping in front of me to take a seat across from my desk—another inconsistency. When we worked in my office, Calla always chose one of the leather lounge chairs or sprawled out on the plush carpet, usually kicking off her heels and letting her red waves down.

But today, none of that happened. Instead, Calla perched on the edge of the chair, her hands crossed in her lap. I stepped behind my desk, settling into my seat, but I kept my eyes on Calla. She squirmed under my attention, and a strange sort of discomfort twisted in my chest. It wasn't the first time I put one of my employees on edge, and usually, it didn't bother me. At least, it never did before this woman started working for me.

Calla cleared her throat. "Is there something you need, Mr. Ayad?"

"Stop." I held my hand up. "Please, Calla. Stop with the Mr. Ayad crap. Stop with the cold shoulder." I leaned back, rubbing my hand over my jaw. "If I crossed a line at the bar, I apologize. I don't know what got into me."

Calla stared at me for a long moment. "There's no reason for you to apologize."

"I can admit my mistakes," I answered, almost too sharply. "And if I made you uncomfortable–"

"You didn't." My eyes jumped up, meeting Calla's soft expression. "I'm not upset with you, and you didn't do anything that bothered me. I'm just..." She looked up at the ceiling as if it held all the answers. "I'm confused, Theo."

Join the club. I'd been confused since I hired Calla, too wrapped up in worrying about her to make any logical decisions.

She sighed, then continued, "You made sure I knew about the no-fraternization rule. You almost had a coronary when you thought I was hitting on Jack. But then, last night, you were *flirting* with me at the bar." She arched her brow. "That was flirting, right?" I swallowed, debating between the truth and a lie for so long that Calla stopped waiting for an answer. "Either way, it didn't upset me. But it was a mistake to let things go that far."

I shook my head. "Nothing happened."

"But it could have," Calla cut me off. "You're my boss, Theo. Even if there wasn't a rule against us dating, it still would be a bad idea. We work too closely together. If we crossed that line and it all fell apart? I'd be the one left standing in the ashes." She placed her hand on her chest. "I'd be the one crushed."

"You wouldn't be–"

"Yes, I would." Calla stood, now pacing the floor of my office, almost talking to herself more than me. "And not to mention, we want completely different things out of a relationship. I'm looking for love, *connection*, and you're looking for..."

"One night."

She nodded. "I'm not wired that way. I mean no disrespect —I wish I could handle no strings, but I'm a relationship girl, and you don't seem like that's a priority for you."

For a moment, I thought about arguing and saying I was willing to try. But Calla's words hit home, and I knew she was right. There was little I could do to contradict her, not when I'd seen the rubble left behind in my last relationship. Calla deserved better than that, someone who could give her everything she wanted and more.

When I didn't respond, Calla crossed her arms around her waist a little tighter, almost as if she was disappointed. She breathed out slowly. "Jack mentioned that his new secretary wasn't working out, so if you don't think we can–"

"No." As I stood, Calla's wide eyes met my furious stare. Jack might be one of my closest friends, but his meddlesome ways were starting to outweigh his usefulness. I encroached on her space, making sure there was no question in my mind. "I want you here, Calla. Working with me. Are we clear?"

I expected her to back down, to look at me with the same uneasiness as others did when my anger reared its ugly head, but instead, she rolled her lips together, trying to hide her smile. "I thought..." Her whiskey-colored eyes met mine, filled with a vulnerability that almost broke my resolve. "I thought you'd be relieved to be rid of me."

"What do you mean?"

She motioned to her outfit, shaking her head. "I thought you wanted someone more professional, someone less...."

"Outspoken?"

"I was going to say enthusiastic, but I guess that works too." Calla shook her head. "You probably should find someone else. My job is to make your life easier, and I'm afraid I've made it messier." She dropped the smile, her face tensing, as if she was bracing for disappointment. "But I like this job. I like working for you. So if you want me to be more reserved and take a step back, I'll happily do it."

I lifted her chin with my fingers, making sure she was looking at me before I spoke. "Calla...I want you to be yourself." She chuffed, as if she couldn't believe the words. "Yes, your style is different from what I'm used to, but I think it's what I need." I motioned around the room. "Look what you've done with this place in such a short time. I'd be a fool not to see the effort you're putting into your job."

"Thank you, Theo."

"I mean every word."

The silence between us started to grow heavy, the tension building back to where it was before. Calla's eyes gradually lifted, meeting mine apprehensively. All the carefully practiced words fell at my feet, leaving me lost and adrift. All I could hold on to was her gaze.

But just as quickly as it started, it was dashed when Calla pulled away, shaking her head as if she was coming out of a daze. She tugged her hair out of the ridiculous top knot, shaking it out. "Thank God. That bun was giving me a migraine." She winked at me. "What's next on the agenda, Sunshine?"

And with one little word, my day instantly turned around.

"AND WERE you able to secure the deal?"

The voice droned on in the background as one of my agents

bickered with another on the phone. Apparently, they had differing views on how to get their client to commit to their current team. I'd lost track almost twenty minutes ago, unsure if we were still discussing the aging basketball player or the loose-cannon hockey goalie. It was all the same to me. I could fake my interest with the best of them, but sports had never been my specialty for a reason.

Three times a week, we had a phone conference with the LA office, and all the heads of the departments informed the partners of any major deals or upcoming events. However, ever since we branched into two offices, these meetings had devolved into a pissing contest.

As the two men argued, I sat back in my chair, steepling my fingers as I looked out onto the city. Were my days always going to be like this? Trapped in this office while the world hummed around me? Probably, but that was what I had wanted, what I had strived for.

So why the fuck was it bothering me now?

A sudden kick to my shin snapped me out of my thoughts, and my eyes narrowed at Calla, who was sitting next to me with an arched brow. She tapped her pen on the legal pad in her lap, her handwriting in the margin. *Something more interesting out there?*

I scoffed, not used to being called out in meetings. Marie would never be so bold. She'd be too focused on taking notes, beating herself up if she missed a single word.

Calla, on the other hand, had been drawing along the side of her paper, only noting what she deemed necessary or things I had to handle. I took the pen from her hand, scribbling next to her comment. *At least I'm not doodling all over my paper.* I drew a line up to a stick figure. *Anyone I know?*

She smirked before taking her pen back. *Just a certain boss who likes to make his employees pee their pants in terror.*

I was about to respond when someone else's voice broke through the conversation.

"That's bullshit!"

I snapped back to attention at the sharp curse, narrowing my eyes at Jack on the opposite end of the table. His fist was wrapped tightly around his pen, and he was glaring at the phone.

A chuckle broke through the line. "What can I say, Jackie boy? Ricardo wants to go with a real agent. He said you weren't able to secure a three-year deal. I got it in a week."

"Because you're a fucking sniveling–"

"Enough," I snapped, narrowing my eyes at Jack. "That's it for today. We'll meet again on Friday and discuss the matter further." I leaned forward in my seat. "I suggest your office read the agency bylaws before we speak again. Interagency poaching is frowned upon."

I asked Jack to hang back as the rest of the departments cleared the room. Calla got up to leave as well, but I placed my hand on her arm. "Stay. I need you to take notes."

She rolled her eyes, subtle enough that only I would notice.

Jack leaned back in his seat, running his hand over his face. "Sorry about that, man. You know how Logan gets–"

"What happened with the deal?"

"I told you, Logan's a snake."

"Not with Logan. With the team. You told me you were working on Ricardo's contract a month ago. Why couldn't you close it?"

Jack's jaw tensed, pissed I was questioning him. I would be the same way in his position. Usually, I'd be on his side, ready to seek revenge for the other agents stepping onto our turf, but I had no room for pleasantries and coddling right now. This office had to succeed, and we never would if the LA office vultured all our biggest clients.

"They wanted a shorter-term contract. One season only." Jack shook his head. "Ricardo wants to settle down, so that wouldn't work for him. I tried to make them extend it, but nothing worked."

"Find out what Logan offered them." I stood from my chair. "And we need to start looking for someone to fill his place—a bigger name, if possible."

Jack ran his hand over his brow, as if mentally filing through the players he knew. Suddenly, he snapped his fingers. "I heard a rumor that Anders is looking for a new rep."

"The player from the Rebels? The pitcher?" I asked. Jack nodded. "Get him onboard."

He shook his head. "Not that easy. He's notoriously private. He's not going to sign with us unless we jump through a lot of hoops. I heard his last agent only got the job because he was connected to Anders somehow."

"Figure it out, Jack." I gripped the back of the chair. "Or I'll find someone else who will."

Jack stared at me in disbelief, his mouth hanging open as if he didn't believe my words. But it was no idle threat. There was no room for dead weight on this team, no matter how close we once were. The partners warned me that this would change how others saw me, but I hadn't expected the shift to come so soon.

I sighed. "Get a meeting on the books as soon as possible."

Just as I thought Jack was about to lose his shit, Calla stood, smiling up at me. "Actually...I might be able to help you out with that."

TWELVE

Calla

"This is a terrible idea."

My eyes almost hurt from rolling them so much today. Leave it to my gloomy boss to take the fun out of everything. When I suggested we meet with Gray during an informal lunch, I thought Theo's mind was going to explode. It took almost an hour for me to convince him to change out of his expensive Armani suit. He was still plucking at the sweater I'd picked out for him as if he couldn't stand the feel of it against his skin.

He might not like it, but holy hell, it was making it hard to look away from him. Even though I repeatedly told myself that Theo was off limits, it was getting more and more difficult to remember why. Just seeing him dressed down made my imagination run wild. I was dying to know what he was like when he lost all that careful control.

Get it together, Calla.

For fuck's sake, we were on the way to meet my ex-boyfriend, a fact that *might* have slipped my mind when I sold Theo on this plan. However, Jack was right. Gray had been burned in the past by a shady agent. There was no way he'd go with our company just because Theo was the best. He needed that connection, someone he could trust.

As soon as we entered the diner, Theo curled his lip. He looked at the dated pleather furniture and stained walls with clear disgust. For someone who didn't dine anywhere without a Michelin star, this was probably his biggest nightmare.

While Theo stood in the doorway, I spotted Gray across the room. I waved in his direction until his steely gray eyes met mine, and he broke out into a broad smile, standing up to greet me. When he got close enough, he wrapped his arms around me and tugged me up into the air. "Hey, kiddo."

"Hey, Anders."

He placed my feet back on the ground, stepping back to take a better look at me. "Damn, Calla. The years have been good to you."

"Like you're one to talk," I teased, smacking him on the shoulder. "I wouldn't have recognized you if I didn't watch most of your games." In high school, Gray had been the quintessential golden boy, always clean-shaven with not a hair out of place. The bearded Viking who stood in front of me could not be more different, with his shaggy, dark blond hair tossed up in a bun. My eyes traced along his forearms, taking in all the brightly colored designs inked into his skin. A couple of the images looked familiar but not enough to place them readily.

"You watch most of my games?" Gray smiled. "I'm touched, kid."

"Not really," I laughed. "It's all Devyn. She never misses one."

As soon as the words left my mouth, I wanted to take them back. At the mere mention of Devyn's name, Gray's eyes went cold, as if he had seen a ghost. But unlike Devyn, whose expression always turned stormy at the mention of her former friend, Gray looked almost pained.

Before I could say anything else, Theo came to my side, clearing his throat. "Oh, I'm so sorry. Gray, this is my boss, Theo Ayad. He's the one we talked about on the phone."

Gray nodded, stretching out his hand. I waited for Theo to say something, anything, to show some of the usual charms he used on his clients. Instead, he just stared at Gray as if assessing a threat. I nudged him in the stomach with the tip of my elbow. "Theo, this is when you use your words." I rolled my eyes at Gray. "Sorry about him; he's not a diner kind of guy."

"I never said that," Theo answered, turning to stare at me. "But Calla's right. It's very nice to meet you, Mr. Anders."

Gray motioned to the booth, taking a seat by the window for himself. I started to join him on the same side, but Theo placed his hand on the small of my back, pushing me toward the empty side. As soon as I settled, he shuffled into the spot next to me.

I furrowed my brow, shocked at how close he sat. Sure, we usually stayed together during meetings, but that was because I took notes for him. Now, there was no reason for him to be hovering next to me. There was no reason for his leg to be pressed up against mine—his super muscular, strong thigh.

Shit. These were the exact thoughts I should *not* be having about my boss. I should be trying to distance myself from Theo, not snuggling up next to him in a teeny booth. Pushing a breath through my lips, I tried to get my head together. This meant nothing. There was nothing between Theo and me. The only thing I felt for Theo was lust, which was a perfectly natural reaction. I mean, the man looked like he was made of marble. If I wasn't attracted to him, I would be concerned.

Gray smirked at me, probably able to read the turmoil on my face. The bastard always knew what I was feeling before I could voice it. "So, Calla, you got me here. Now tell me, why should I hire this guy to be my agent?"

"Oh..." I smiled at Theo, hoping he didn't notice my nerves.

Yes, Gray knew me better than most, so it was easy to forget he was on the fast track to the MLB Hall of Fame. I shook my head. "I'm just his assistant. Theo is the one who should answer that question."

Theo's brow furrowed, but he didn't argue. Instead, he turned toward Gray. "Due to the informal setting of this meeting, I don't have our usual materials and numbers. I'd love to bring you into the office to meet the team and see how we can best suit your needs."

Gray shook his head, "No can do. Not interested in getting the sales pitch." He nodded back to me. "I trust Calla. If she says you're the guy, then I believe it."

I could feel my nerves start to take over, from my foot tapping on the off-white and black linoleum to my fingers twining together under the red lacquer table. This whole meeting might have been my idea, but what did I know about selling an agent? Shit, I barely even knew anything about baseball.

As my anxiety built, I felt someone's finger loop over mine and tug my hands apart. I glanced up at Theo, seeing nothing but faith in his gaze. Was it possible that he believed in me?

With that silent affirmation, I steadied my shoulders. "I know absolutely nothing about being an agent. Even after a month working for this guy, I'm still not entirely sure what he does." Theo choked on his water at my words. I gave him a smug smile, asking him to trust me. "However, what I do know is how much Theo cares about his clients. Since I started, I've seen Theo move mountains for them. His work is his priority." Theo stiffened at my side, but I continued anyway. "A lot of agents only care about their client's careers, but Theo looks at the whole person beyond just their stats, and he's building a team that feels the same way. If you decide to sign with Wallace and Associates, I promise that our team will respect you, and your voice will be heard." I leaned forward, placing my hand on top of Gray's. "This is the right move, Gray."

He shrugged. "Works for me."

Theo pulled out his phone and started typing a text. "Next time we meet, I'll bring Jack Fischer. He's the head of our sports department, not to mention one of the best in the business."

"Nope." Gray smirked, leaning back on his side of the booth. "It's you or the deal's off. I don't want to deal with another suit. I've had enough of those stalking the locker room. *You're* my guy."

Theo paused, steepling his hands in front of his face. Most people would think he was deep in thought, debating his next move, but I'd learned that this position meant Theo had already made up his mind but knew it would have consequences. I hoped like hell he wasn't going to let Gray down, not only because I knew he'd do the right thing for one of my oldest friends, but also because I'd stuck my neck out for him. If this deal fell apart, what would that mean for my job? Would Theo stop trusting me?

But my worries were unfounded. With a sudden, deep sigh, Theo reached out his hand. "Sounds like we have a deal."

Over the next hour, Gray and Theo discussed every aspect of his current contract, including what he wanted to change for the next season. Technically, because he was still under contract for another year, Theo couldn't talk to any teams on Gray's behalf. But knowing my boss, he'd find a way to work around the confines of the league's rules.

Not long after they drafted tentative terms, Gray took off, saying he had to meet with his trainer. We made plans to see each other soon, but I didn't know if we'd follow through on them—not only because Gray was ridiculously busy, but there was also the little matter of my sister. If she knew I was here right now, Devyn would probably ice me out for a month.

After Gray left, I waited for Theo to move out of the booth, but he stayed seated as he picked out one of the laminated menus and started perusing the options.

"What are you doing?"

"Ordering food," Theo answered plainly. "Are you hungry?"

"Are you?" I asked, confused at his casual demeanor. "No offense, but I don't think they have anything you like."

Theo placed the menu on the table, turning to face me fully. His dark gaze cut through me, making my heart beat a little quicker. "And tell me, Calla...why is that?"

I rolled my eyes. "Because everything here is full of carbs or fried in oil. No plain kale salads in sight."

"Are you making fun of my dietary choices?"

"Absolutely," I laughed, pulling the menu to me. My mouth started to water just looking at all the options. "I'm surprised you don't want to rush back to the office."

I glanced up just in time to see Theo smile, and holy hell, it was everything. It made the corners of his eyes crinkle, softening all his features. It took everything in me not to fall apart, desperately wanting to know how his lips tasted. I stared down at them until his voice broke me out of my daze.

"We're both full of surprises today."

"Me?" I squeaked. "How did I surprise you?"

"You never mentioned you dated *Grayson Anders*." His tone was a little bitter, mixed with something I couldn't quite put my finger on. He shook his head. "Many people in my business would have led with that fact."

"That's ridiculous." I rolled my eyes. "We dated when I was sixteen. It was hardly a deep love connection. We broke up right before he graduated high school—amicably. We've kept in touch over the years, but we're not nearly as close as we once were."

He nodded, weighing my words. He suddenly stood, and for a moment, my heart sank. I was giving him a little piece of me, and he was walking away without a word? My lips pursed together, hating how deeply his rejection stung. But as I started to climb out of the booth, he settled on the other side of the table.

"Better," he sighed. He looked up at me and smiled. "Hi."

"Hi." I could feel the heat rush to my cheeks. As much as I hated losing his warmth, hated losing the feeling of his leg up against mine, it was nice to be able to talk face to face. As he looked at me, a flush crept up my neck. What the hell was wrong with me? Guys usually didn't make me nervous. Maybe it was because I admired Theo. Perhaps it was because his presence demanded attention from everyone in the room.

Or maybe it was because he was looking at me like he did at the bar that night. Like he wanted me. And as much as I was trying to bury it, every moment I spent with Theo only made me crave him more.

When the waitress came back to fill our coffees, Theo leaned back, breaking the tension between us. "What did you mean earlier?"

"Huh?"

"When you introduced me to Grayson. You said I'm not a diner kind of guy."

"First of all," I said, "it's Gray. No one calls him Grayson except the media." I arched a brow at him. "And honestly, when was the last time you stepped into a place like this? You forget that I make your reservations."

"You're making a lot of assumptions about me."

"Maybe because you haven't let me get to know you better," I answered. "You keep everything very surface level. It's hard for us to become friends if you don't open up at all."

"Friends?"

"Yes, Sunshine. Friends," I over-enunciated.

"We're not friends."

"We could be." I shrugged my shoulders. "I've been told I'm a pretty good one to have, and we both could use more. Besides, it'll make me better at my job. The way I see it, the more I know you, the more I can anticipate your every need." I smiled obnoxiously at him. "And then I will be the best assistant in the world."

"Lofty goal." He smirked.

"*Confident* goal," I volleyed back. Leaning forward onto my elbows, I whispered, "Tell me another secret, something no one else knows about you."

"I hate peas."

"What?" I stared back at him. "That's your deep, dark secret?"

"You never said it had to be deep and dark, just something that no one else knew."

I shook my head and started to stand. "Fine. Don't open up. I understand, boss." Annoyance and shame washed over me. I was an idiot, thinking there was a bond forming between us, that maybe Theo was starting to warm up to me like I was to him, that we'd developed a tentative trust over the past few weeks.

But as I grabbed my bag, Theo's voice broke me out of my haze. "My mother worked in a diner."

I shifted to face Theo, but he was looking out the window, almost as if he was talking more to himself than me. I settled back into the booth as he continued. "I spent most of my child-hood in a booth just like this one. My mother immigrated here when she was pregnant with me, wanting to provide a better life for her child. She worked from sun up to sunset but still managed to come to every school event, every parent-teacher conference." He ran his hand along the seat. "After school each day, I'd go to the diner, order a milkshake, and split it with my mom while she helped me with my homework." He paused, smiling softly at me. "When we walked inside..." He sighed. "It took me back for a moment."

"You've never mentioned your mother before."

"She died." He dropped his gaze down to his hands. "About five years ago."

I reached out, placing my hand on top of his. "I'm so sorry, Theo."

He squeezed my hand for a moment, his thumbs brushing the ridges of my knuckles. It was a small moment, but it felt like more. For the first time, neither of us pulled away, content in the bubble we'd made for ourselves. And yes, when we returned to work, we'd have to go back to being only boss and assistant.

But here, in this aged diner, we could pretend for a few minutes that we were so much more.

Calla

"This feels like too much."

Devyn sighed as she looked in my full-length mirror. She tugged at the slit of her dress, trying to make the fabric pull closer together. I stared at my sister in disbelief, sure that she was not looking at the same reflection as me. With her long blonde hair swept to the side in elegant finger waves and her vintage-style maroon silk dress, she looked like a movie star ripped from the golden age of Hollywood.

Digging through my closet, I found two clutches, holding them up so Devyn could pick. As she pointed to the one on the right, a wave of nostalgia washed over me. Growing up, some of my favorite memories were of helping my sisters dress up for special occasions, especially Devyn. While Laurel lived in dresses, she'd always leaned toward jeans and sweaters, favoring practical over pretty. She was still that way, especially because she was determined to make partner. It was rare that I caught her out of her power pantsuits. The temptation to break into her closet and burn them all was intense.

As she toyed with the bust line, I slapped her hand away, shaking my head at my phone propped up on the nightstand.

Alex smirked at me on the screen, relaxing on her couch back home in Saint Stephen's Lake. Even though he was out of the frame, I could tell Cole was sitting at her side, occasionally toying with the ends of her hair. It made my heart squeal to see my best friend so blissfully in love. I missed her more than anything, but I was proud we were both making strides in our new lives.

Well, more her than me, but I was getting there.

Most days, I felt like a rockstar, like I was crushing my job, but there were still moments when I was more like a hamster spinning in a wheel, trying to keep up with my boss' incessant demands.

However, something had shifted since our lunch earlier in the week. Theo was smiling more readily, letting me in a little more each day. During one of our late work nights, he ordered Chinese food and told me all about his early days in Hollywood while I talked about my grandfather and our adventures on the lake. Yesterday, he grabbed me a coffee on the way in, and we spent the morning trading music recommendations.

Seeing Theo let his walls down made it harder to maintain rigid professional lines between us. What I initially thought was only an attraction had developed into something so much more, a connection I was getting desperate to explore. And from the looks Theo kept giving me, he felt the same way.

Some nights, the tension was so thick between us that I could barely breathe in his presence. The only thing that kept me from crossing the line was that stupid freaking no-fraternization rule. I swore that if I ever met the person who put that in place, I'd give him a piece of my mind.

I shook my head, trying to focus on why we were going out tonight. With award season in full swing, several industry parties were popping up around the city. Theo managed to get an invite to one of the biggest, hosted by a fashion magazine I'd studied since I was twelve. It was a once-in-a-lifetime experience, and I was dying to make the most of it.

When the invite first came, I assumed Theo would want to attend with the other senior agents. Instead, he only asked Jack and me to tag along. Theo claimed it was because he needed my support to make it through the evening, but I knew the truth. He wanted me there, wanted *me* at his side, and that was the best feeling in the world.

Devyn flopped onto the bed, glaring at me. "Remind me why I need to tag along with you?"

Because I need a buffer so I don't jump my boss' bones.

I kept that thought in my head.

I sighed, running my fingers along my expertly curled strands. "Because Jack needs a plus-one, and I refuse to spend an evening stuck next to some stranger. This way, while the guys are off networking, we can dance and have a good time."

Devyn rolled her eyes. "Fine. But I still don't know why I couldn't have worn something from my closet. I'm pretty sure this dress costs more than my car."

"First of all, I refuse to let you attend one of the hottest events of the year in one of your work suits. I would rather swallow a handful of fire ants. And second—I told you, it's on loan. Jack has a connection with a designer, so she lets us borrow dresses in exchange for some publicity. Besides, you look amazing." I stared at the phone. "A little backup, please?"

"You do look gorgeous, Devyn." Alex smiled at the screen. "But I have to admit—I'm glad you found someone else to play dress-up with."

"Hey!" I objected. "Tell me one time I made you look anything less than beautiful."

"She doesn't need to dress up to be beautiful," Cole called from her side.

"Okay, if you're going to start spouting that nauseating

lovey-dovey stuff, I'm making Calla hang up," Devyn groaned, running her hand through her styled hair. "I could be curled up in bed with my Kindle right now."

"Please." I rolled my eyes. "We both know you'd be at the dining room table scouring through your client's financial records. You've been living at the office for the last week, Dev. Have some fun tonight. If anyone deserves to let loose a little, it's you." She flatly stared at me as I wiggled my brows. "There'll be an open bar."

That got her up and moving. "Enough for me."

Alex giggled at something Cole said. "I've, uh...gotta get going."

"Seriously?" I smirked. "Can't keep it in your pants for twenty minutes?"

"No can do," she teased, her voice speeding up. "Okay, I gotta go. I love you!"

I shook my head as she ended the call, tossing the phone onto the bed. Glancing in the mirror, I smiled at my reflection, pleasantly surprised at how well my make-up was holding up. If I wasn't already on cloud nine, Theo had arranged for a team of stylists to help Devyn and me get ready. It was one of the best days I'd had in a long time, getting to laugh with my sister as experts made us look our best.

Glancing over to my closet, I stared at the gown hanging against the door, covered in a plastic bag. The theme for tonight was the history of American fashion, and Devyn and I were determined to look the part. While Devyn was dressed like a siren from the Golden Age of Hollywood, I'd decided to go for more of a nineteen-twenties theme. The deep navy gown shimmered with dangling gems, making it sparkle with every step I took.

An alarm blared from my phone, alerting me to how late I was running. I pulled the dress off the satin hanger, savoring the feeling of the silk lining as it slid along my body. Once the straps were in place, I zipped up the back, turning to look at myself in the mirror. With all the details in place, it was hard to recognize the woman staring back at me. Nerves rattled my confidence, suddenly unsure if this was a good idea. Not only was I walking into a world I didn't belong in, but I would also be spending the night on Theo's arm. There would be no way to avoid him. While I was getting better at denying my feelings for him at work, every day felt like standing on the edge of a precipice. One wrong move, and everything would fall to pieces. As much as I knew it could be a disaster, it was only a matter of time before we combusted.

As my anxiety rattled my confidence, a loud buzz echoed through the apartment, alerting us that Theo and Jack were on their way up.

"I've got it," Devyn called out.

This was it—there was no more time to hide. As much as I wanted to take off the dress and fake a fever to get out of going, I also couldn't wait to be by Theo's side all night. With one more long look in the mirror, I pushed out a long breath and walked out of my bedroom, unsure of what the evening would hold.

FIFTEEN

Theo

Standing at the edge of the large, open foyer, I watched as Hollywood elite mingled with New York's power players. No expense had been spared to make tonight memorable. The museum playing host had pulled out all of the stops to transform the space to fit the event's theme. The decorations were lush and lavish, the food served from top-tier chefs. It was the kind of party most people would give anything to attend once in their lives.

Yet here I was, unfazed by any of it, too focused on the other side of the room.

"Drink."

As he approached me, Jack practically forced the glass of champagne into my hand. Not that it took much convincing. I'd been on edge all night, and it was only getting worse. Taking the crystal flute, I downed the champagne in one sip, not bothering to savor the taste. It wasn't enough. All the alcohol in the world wouldn't be able to soothe me tonight, to take this weight off of my chest.

I should have known that bringing Calla here was a mistake.

Not because she wasn't doing her job beautifully. From the

moment she entered the room, almost all eyes were on her. How could they not be? I'd barely been able to tear my eyes away from her all night. From the moment she stepped out of the hallway in her navy-blue gown, I was bewitched. Calla would be beautiful in any situation, but she looked like she was born into this world. She was the most captivating woman in the room.

Unfortunately, it was clear I wasn't the only one who felt that way. People had been coming up to her all night, pretending to talk to Jack and me but keeping their attention on her. After the fifth monotonous conversation, I excused myself, sure that Devyn would keep Calla away from any harm. But even as I made my way to the bar, my eyes remained fixed on her.

Jack sighed at my side, dropping his elbows on the bar. "Do you know what you're doing there?"

"I don't know what you're talking about."

I could practically feel Jack's eye roll. "I know I gave you shit before, but that was because I just thought this was a hit-it-and-quit-it kind of thing." He shook his head. "But the way you're looking at Calla right now?"

I shook my head, waving my hand to signal the bartender. "And how exactly is that?"

"Like you want to rip the face off every guy who talks to her."

I exhaled slowly, scrubbing my hands over my face. He was right. I could feel tension ripping through my veins every time Calla smiled at anyone else. Tonight was a test of my self-control, and I was failing. From the moment I arrived at her apartment, I wanted to pull Calla into my arms and never let her go. She wore a dress that clung to her delicate curves, the material glistening with every step. The plunging neckline also did nothing to help my resolve. I sighed, leaning against the bar counter. "It doesn't matter. You know the rules, Jack. I can't—no, I *won't* risk both of our careers." I lifted my head, turning to meet Calla's sweet grin once more. "No matter how tempting it might be."

"Fuck that," Jack scoffed. "You think half the partners haven't slept with their assistants? And that's just because they're looking for some excitement. You have feelings for Calla." He shrugged, like it was the easiest decision in the world. "I say go for it."

"It's not that simple."

"If everything else went away tomorrow—the job, the stress, your whole world—would you regret not telling her how you feel?"

Yeah, I would. I wanted to see Calla's smile every morning, and not behind a pane of glass. I wanted to be the one who earned all her laughter, to be the cause of her best days. I wanted to have so much more than stolen moments, ones we both knew couldn't last long.

I wanted Calla Winters more than I'd ever wanted anything else in my life.

As if he could read the resolution written on my face, Jack grabbed his glass and clapped me on the shoulder with his free hand. "That's what I thought."

CALLA BRUSHED her hair behind her shoulder, politely chuckling at the C-list actor in front of her. As much as it was driving me mad, at least she was making an attempt to be polite with potential clients. Her sister, on the other hand, looked like she'd rather be sipping cement.

Turning over my shoulder, I located Jack in the crowd, using his support to my advantage. I touched Devyn's back, making her flinch before turning toward me. She just arched a brow, her expression as cold as ice. I did my best to smile at her, but it came off forced and unnatural. "Jack wants to dance with you."

Devyn rolled her eyes. "And why didn't he come over himself and ask like a big boy?"

"You scare the shit out of him," I blurted out, sure that my friend would punch me in the balls the next time he saw me. "He's intimidated by you, but he thinks you're beautiful and would like the chance to get to know you better."

Devyn stared at me for a moment, debating the validity of my lie. But eventually, she placed her champagne on the high-top table next to her and took off in Jack's direction. Now, hope-fully, his charm would be enough to keep her occupied for a while.

I placed my hand on Calla's forearm, pulling her attention away from the group. "If you would excuse Ms. Winters, we have a few matters to discuss."

As we walked away from the rest of the group, Calla tilted her head toward me. "What exactly is this super important matter?"

"I wanted to spend some time with you without having to compete for your attention."

She let out a little laugh. "Theo Ayad, are you jealous?"

"Desperately," I answered honestly.

As she stared back at me in surprise, I led us out of the ball-room and into the museum's hallway. We walked down through the gallery until we approached a set of velvet ropes blocking off one of the minor exhibits. Calla scrunched her face as I ducked underneath, holding it up so she could join me.

"What do you think you're doing?" she hissed as she climbed next to my side. "We're not supposed to be back here."

"Live a little, Calla," I chuckled, taking her hand so I could lead her through the maze of artifacts. The lights were dimmed, but luckily, it was bright enough to see where we were going. Not that I had any clue where these halls led. All I could hope was that security would be at the party, guarding the most valuable exhibits and high-end clientele.

When I pulled her into an alcove, Calla tugged my hand, forcing me to stop. "Theo, wait. What is this?"

"I told you." I stepped into her space. "I needed a moment alone with you—away from clients, away from the other employees, away from everything." I sighed, lifting my fingers to brush her cheeks. "I can't stop thinking about you, Calla."

She sharply inhaled, her eyes widening at my admission. She slowly shook her head. "We can't do this, Theo."

"Then tell me you don't want me. Tell me you don't think about me." I placed her hand over my heart. "Because all I can see is you, Calla. Every time I close my eyes, there you are, tempting me to the brink of insanity, and I'm so fucking tired of trying to pretend otherwise."

She chewed on her lower lip, her eyes frantically searching mine. After the longest moment of my life, she shook her head. "You know how I feel about you, Theo. But the rules—"

"Fuck the rules."

As soon as the words left my lips, I crashed them against Calla's. She let out a little gasp when I kissed her but then instantly melted against me. Getting a taste of her was better than any drug, better than any high. Nothing else could ever compare. Calla's hands reached up, pulling on the short hairs at the back of my neck as if she needed me even closer.

I was all too happy to oblige, trailing my hands down her hips to her thighs, lifting her off the ground. Her back softly collided with the wall, and her legs wrapped tightly around my waist. Fuck, her mouth was heaven. It was probably a mistake, because this one kiss would never be enough. Now that I'd felt Calla's lips on mine, there was no way I'd be letting her go.

As if she would feel the possessive turn my thoughts had taken, Calla pulled back slightly and let out a quiet laugh as she touched her fingertips to her lips. "I can't believe that just happened."

"It was a matter of time." I kissed her once again, and she sighed as my tongue brushed against hers, stirring up another wave of need. But when she tensed in my arms, I paused. "Are you having second thoughts?"

"Not at all," she sighed. "Not about you. It's just..." Her bright eyes met mine. "Are you sure this is what you want? You're not into relationships–"

"I wasn't into relationships with anyone else, Calla." I pressed my lips to her forehead. "Being with you is a different story. I know this is complicated, and we're going to have to figure out what it looks like outside of this room." I lifted my hand, brushing the hair away from her face. "But I don't want to miss out on this, miss out on *us*, because of what might happen. So, for tonight, let's stop worrying about tomorrow's troubles and focus on what we both want. What we both need."

She stared at me for a long moment, and my heart stilled in my chest. I meant what I said, but in truth, my feelings were already so much more profound. It had been a long time since I felt the pull to someone like I did with Calla. She was quickly becoming my reason for getting out of bed in the morning, the reason my smiles came easier. She'd brought joy back into my life, and I'd fight like hell to keep it.

After the longest pause of my life, she leaned forward, claiming my mouth once more. But before we could deepen it too much, she uncrossed her legs, dropping them back down to the ground. As she took a step away from me, she held out her hand. "My place or yours?"

After bidding a quick goodbye to Jack and Devyn, feigning some kind of headache, Theo and I ducked out of the party. He waved over his driver, helping me inside the car with a new sense of urgency. I'd never felt this level of need before, almost unable to inhale because of the mounting tension between us. The moment the door closed, Theo told the driver my address. As the car pulled into traffic, Theo pressed a button, lifting the partition between us and the front. With the rest of the city cloaked in darkness from the tinted windows, I turned, feeling the weight of Theo's stare on me.

His eyes dropped down to my mouth as his hand reached out to tug me closer. When I nestled into Theo's side, his lips found mine again. One brief touch, and I was lost. This powerful, intoxicating man had been burrowing under my skin for weeks. Kissing him felt as natural as breathing, like I would need it to survive. I never wanted it to stop, no matter the consequences.

Those could wait until tomorrow.

Theo pulled back, pressing his forehead against mine.

"Fuck, if I knew it would be like this, I would have kissed you the moment we met."

"You've seen nothing yet," I teased before claiming his lips once more. As we moved together, Theo's hand slid along the slit of my dress, softly caressing my thigh. I sucked in a sharp inhale as he moved closer to my core, brushing the soaked center of my thong with his finger. Now, it was his turn to curse, letting his finger drag lazily against me.

"Is this all for me, beautiful?" he asked, his voice several octaves lower than usual.

"Always for you," I gasped as his fingers teased the lace edge of my thong.

"Right answer," he groaned as he leaned forward, capturing my lips at the same time as he ripped the fabric off me. I yelped at how the strings nipped at my skin, all too aware of how exposed I was.

"Theo," I gasped, hoping the partition was also soundproof. "We can't."

"Fuck that," he muttered. He turned toward my ear, his teeth grazing the shell as he whispered, "I've had enough of people telling me I can't have you. The only person who can tell me to stop is you." He leaned back, smirking down at me. "Is that what you want, Calla?"

I should have told him to do just that, to show some of that decorum ingrained in me for years, but the desire coursing through my veins was too strong. I shifted my legs, parting them a little bit more to give him better access. "Touch me, Theo."

His lips brushed my neck. "Say please, beautiful."

"Please, Theo. Touch me."

Without another word, he tucked my ruined thong into his pocket. He pulled at the split in my dress, pushing the fabric up until I was exposed to him. He cursed lightly under his breath, licking his lips as he looked at me, and I'd never felt more wanted in my life. I was about to beg, to plead with him to touch me, when his fingers grazed my core. My hips instinctively shifted closer to him, needing more pressure. He chuckled against my skin. "Patience, beautiful. I'm going to make you feel so good."

I leaned into the seat as he continued his ministrations. His touches alternated between soft and greedy, making my head spin. When one of his long fingers entered me, I had to bite back a gasp, covering my mouth on his shoulder. Every thrust left my body aching, needing more, desperate to feel all of him. All my clothes felt too tight, and the air in the car was too warm.

"Theo..." I called out, my voice a needy, desperate thing.

My moans echoed through the car as his lips dusted the hemline of my dress, coming so close to my breasts that I wanted to rip it off. But the fit barely allowed him access, and if I took it off now, we'd be fucking in the backseat of this car. As much as I wanted to explore my newfound exhibitionist kink, I'd rather not be interrupted the first time Theo was inside me.

My thoughts quickly became more jumbled when his fingers curled along my walls. "Oh my God," I muttered as Theo hit the exact right spot, making my vision go hazy. With a few more thrusts and circles of his thumb against my clit, my walls were *crumbling*.

"That's it, Calla," he murmured as another one of his fingers joined the other. "Show me how good it feels. Come for me, beautiful."

As I cried out his name, my nails dug into his arm, holding him in place. Pleasure washed over me, stronger than I'd ever felt before. If Theo was able to elicit this much of a reaction from just his fingers, what the hell would happen next?

Theo held onto me as my body stopped pulsating, dusting his lips across my face. He smiled as he pulled out his fingers, sucking them clean with a wink. My face burned with the audacity of this man, but he just kept grinning, leaning forward to press his lips to my neck. "I think I found my new favorite flavor."

Before I could even respond, he pulled open the door, letting the humid New York air greet us. I'd been so wrapped up in the moment with Theo that I hadn't even noticed the car had stopped.

The moment my feet hit the sidewalk, it felt like our bubble had popped. We stood there, staring at the entrance of my building. We both knew the moment we crossed the threshold, there would be no going back.

Theo turned to me, brushing my hair behind my ear. "It's not too late." My brows furrowed. "I can call back the car and go home to my apartment." He smiled down at me. "But I can't promise I'll ever forget what happened tonight."

I leaned forward, pressing my lips to his all too briefly. When he exhaled slowly, as if a weight had been lifted from his shoulders, I took his hand in mine. "Come inside, Theo."

THE MOMENT the door shut behind us, we collided. There was no trepidation, no asking what the other wanted. We joined together as if we needed each other's touch more than we needed our next breath.

Theo pushed me against the door, my arms clinging around his neck as his lips found my skin, leaving a trail from my collarbone to my jaw. I tilted my head to give him better access, twisting my fingers into his hair. When I tugged a little, he let out a growl. "Bedroom. Now." He nipped at my exposed skin. "Or I'll fuck you right here, against this door."

I let out a little giggle, pointing him down the hallway. Theo didn't waste a moment as he carried me down the hall, kicking open my bedroom door. As soon as he placed me back on the ground, he spun me around, shifting my hair over my shoulder. He toyed with the zipper of my dress while pressing soft kisses to the top of my spine. "Is this okay?"

"Yes," I breathed, reaching behind me to press my hands into his thighs. After imagining it for weeks, I couldn't believe I could touch him. His stiff muscles tensed under my grip, his cock straining against my backside.

When the cool zipper hit the base of my spine, I turned around, letting the dress slide down my arms to pool at my feet. Due to the design, I'd forgone a bra, and my thong was still tucked in Theo's pocket, so I was entirely exposed in front of him.

Theo sucked in a sharp breath as he took me in, studying like he was committing me to memory. I reached out, toying with the knot of his tie. "Are you alright, Mr. Ayad?"

"No." He shook his head. "I'm pretty sure I've died and gone to heaven. If I did, don't revive me." His hand reached out, pulling me closer to him. "I need to taste you, beautiful."

I chuckled, stepping out of his grip. "Didn't you have your fill in the car?"

"Not even close," he growled, watching as I lowered myself onto my bed. "That was barely an appetizer."

He started to lean forward, but I lifted my foot to his chest, stopping him from getting any closer. His eyes flared with a primal force. "I'm begging you, Calla. Let me taste you."

"I don't know if I'd call that begging." I smirked up at him. "You never even said please."

He glared down at me as I repeated his words from the car, clearly not used to having someone else challenge him. I stared back at him, matching his intensity. This man might have the power in most aspects of our relationship, but in this room, we'd both be in charge.

Without another word, he sank to his knees in front of me, his hands massaging my thighs. I propped up on my elbows to get a better look at him. "Calla," he breathed heavily, as if each word pained him. "Will you *please* let me taste you?"

I sighed, leaning back onto the bed. "If you'd like."

Theo instantly dragged me forward, positioning my pussy right in front of his face. His tongue consumed me, licking the entire length of my seam before finding my clit. He groaned against my sensitive skin as if this was more for him than it was for me. If this was what he wanted, I'd gladly let him taste me any time. Because the sight of this man on his knees will be etched into my memory forever

"Fuck," Theo mumbled. "You taste even better than I could've imagined."

Words didn't come to me, not while his tongue and fingers were playing my body like a well-practiced melody. It was all I could do to hold onto the bed, to not lose my mind before we'd even begun. But when his tongue started fucking me, my body erupted. By the time his tongue moved back to my clit, I'd combusted around him, my screams filling every inch of my bedroom.

"That was..." I panted, placing my arm on my head. "Holy shit."

I'd barely caught my breath when Theo slid up my body, bringing his lips around one of my sensitive nipples. He lavished the one with attention before moving to the other, and I squirmed underneath him, already desperate for more. As my hips shifted underneath him, Theo leaned up and claimed my mouth, the taste of me still lingering on his tongue.

"Good." Theo traced my nipple with his thumb. "Because you're not done yet, beautiful. By the time I'm finished with you, the sun's going to be up."

SEVENTEEN

Theo

Calla's eyes widened at my words. I might have gotten on my knees for her, but I wanted to claim all of her now. Not that I minded licking her perfect pussy. I'd gladly worship her all hours of the day if she'd allow it, but if I didn't fuck her soon, my dick was going to combust.

As I crawled over her, I paused, searching her gaze for any sign of hesitation. There was none—only raw need peering out from her honey eyes. My thumb brushed her lower lip, smudging the remaining lipstick. God, I wanted to see that smeared along my cock. Too bad it would have to wait. I'd never last if she took me in her mouth right now, but there would be other nights. I'd make sure of it.

Without any instruction, Calla's hand lifted, cupping my cock through the fabric of my dress pants. As she slowly stroked me, I leaned back onto my haunches, staring at the gorgeous girl at my mercy.

"Take me out, baby." I lifted her other hand to my belt.

Calla nodded with a gleeful smile, rushing to remove my clothing. As she worked on my pants, I shucked my jacket and dress shirt off, grabbing a condom from my wallet before tossing them onto an armchair in the corner of the room.

"Holy crap," Calla whispered, leaning back a little further on the bed. Her hand tentatively gripped my dick as her mouth widened in surprise.

"Good enough for you?"

"Too much." Calla shook her head as her hand worked the length of my cock. "There's no way... It can't. It *won't–*"

"Hey." I reached down to stroke her cheek. Her eyes found mine, still holding onto that apprehension. That wouldn't do. "You want to stop, we stop. No questions asked."

She swallowed, glancing down once more before shaking her head. "I don't want to stop. I want to feel you." Calla chewed on her lower lip. "What if it doesn't fit?"

I placed my hand on top of hers, stroking me together. "We'll make it work, baby. There's no way you and I won't fit perfectly together."

She nodded, sliding further back on the bed so I could join her. Any thought of punishment or testing her limits left my mind. Tonight would be all about us, about this overwhelming connection between us. I meant what I said: we'd fit together perfectly. I refused to accept any other option.

I nestled in the cradle of Calla's thighs, hating the nervousness now radiating from her. I smiled down at her, kissing her lips one more time. "We'll take it slow."

She nodded her head, lifting her hips to allow me easier access. I ripped open the foil packet and sheathed myself, unsure how much longer I could hold out. Calla was temptation in human form, and I'd never wanted someone more.

As I slowly pushed inside her for the first time, my head fell back in bliss. Her tight walls constricted around me, not allowing me much further. Calla shuddered, so I ducked my head to her chest, taking one of her tight nipples into my mouth. As I sucked and lavished both of them, Calla started to relax, her body accepting more of me. The moment I finally bottomed out inside her, Calla's mouth formed a wide circle, her eyes darting between my eyes and the place our bodies joined together.

I kissed her lightly, smirking down at her. "Look at how well we fit together, beautiful."

"You were right," Calla chuckled, her laughter causing her to tighten even more around my cock. Fuck, this would not last nearly as long as I wanted. It felt too good, felt too right with her. She reached up, tugging my face close to hers. "Theo, move. I need you to move."

Without waiting another second, I followed her command, slowly thrusting in and out of her. Calla's eyes never left mine, her face showing all her emotions. As her walls started to constrict around me, she cried out. "Oh, shit, Theo. I'm so close."

"Me too, baby," I promised, gripping her hips with my hands. Her nails dug into my back as she cried out, her release triggering my own without much warning. We came together, our hands linked together, holding on as we both crashed over the edge.

When the pleasure faded and my vision returned to normal, I placed my hand on Calla's cheek, relieved to find her smiling at me. I kissed her lips before I pulled out. "Please tell me I didn't hurt you."

"Not at all," she sighed. "I'm a little sore, but in the best way." She stretched out underneath me. "So tell me, old man: how much time do you need before we go again?"

I smiled broadly back at her, feeling more content than I had in years. "Don't worry, beautiful. I plan on making good use of that smart mouth before the night is through."

EVEN WITHOUT AN ALARM SET, my eyes opened at four in the morning. It took me a moment to get my bearings, unsure why I was in a room surrounded by color and clutter rather than my own bedroom. But when I turned, finding a sweet, slumbering redhead tucked into my arm, all felt right in the world again.

Typically, when a hookup was over, I was out the door as quickly as possible, but the thought never crossed my mind last night. When Calla asked if I wanted to stay over, I nodded, unwilling to waste a single moment of the night. But as much as I wanted to keep fucking her until the sun rose, my body had other plans. After several rounds, we'd passed out, our naked bodies wrapped together.

Calla nestled closer to my chest and let out a small, satisfied sigh. It brought a smile to my face. There was a part of me worried that last night was a dream, that I was going to wake up in my bed alone, still yearning for the woman I wanted most in the world.

But here she was, sleeping soundly in my arms, a fact I vowed never to take for granted. With a soft kiss on her forehead, I started to climb out of bed to start my day. However, before I could get too far, Calla's grip tightened around me, anchoring me close to her. I pressed my lips to her shoulder. "You should still be sleeping."

"So should you," Calla mumbled. She opened one eye and smirked up at me. "You didn't get enough of a workout last night?"

"It was one of the best of my life," I mumbled, shifting to hold her tighter in my arms. "But I need to get going. I have a session scheduled with my trainer. He's already going to be pissed that I'm moving slower than normal." She chuckled as I kissed her neck. "And I should get out of here before your sister wakes up."

Calla smiled, lifting onto her elbows to kiss me once more. It was slow and lazy, the kind of kiss that promised more in the future. I'd never been a man to need a send-off. Hell, when I was married, days would go by without checking in with my ex-wife. But now, I knew I never wanted to start another day without Calla's lips on mine.

She looked down at me, and then her face shifted, apprehension now layering her features. "So at the office..."

I exhaled, shifting to sit up but bringing her with me. "We need to act like nothing has changed." Calla nodded, her eyes falling to her fingers. She started toying with the edge of her comforter, the nervous tick meaning she was holding something inside. I held her a little tighter. "Talk to me, baby. What's going through your head?"

"This... We aren't over, right?" She sucked in a sharp breath. "Not that we are *anything*, but whatever is happening between us, please tell me it wasn't a one-time thing."

I shifted, capturing her underneath my frame. Her lips fell open, staring up at me with those wide eyes I adored so much. "Absolutely not," I said, my tone firm, leaving no room for argument. "Did you really think one night with you would be enough? I'm already plotting all the ways I want to take you tonight."

"Tonight?"

"Come to my place after work." I sweetened the offer with a kiss. "I'll cook for you, and we can talk about what comes next."

Her brow furrowed. "You can cook?"

"I can try." I smiled, unsure where this odd sense of confidence came from. It had been years since I had spent any real time in the kitchen, but something about this girl made me want to spoil her, made me want to see that sparkle in her eyes.

"Tell me you'll be there."

"Nothing could keep me away."

EIGHTEEN

Calla

In the morning, I woke up with a delicious ache all through my body. Last night felt like the best dream. Even after weeks of pining for Theo, he exceeded all my expectations. A shiver rolled down my spine as I thought of how easily he switched from domineering to gentle, checking in with me every step of the way.

It was hardly my first time, but it almost felt like it. In the past, being with someone new filled me with anxiety and nerves. It took me a few times to fully let go, to let myself be completely vulnerable. But with Theo, it was almost innate. Before our lips even touched, I trusted him, wanted him to have every part of me. He'd made me feel beautiful- *cherished*. All I wanted was him, unable to have enough of his body moving against mine. Even though we'd only been apart for a couple of hours, I was already counting down the minutes until I could be with Theo again.

I reluctantly climbed out of my bed, hating that I had to wash Theo's scent off my skin. But trying to pretend it was a typical workday was already going to be difficult. I didn't need a constant reminder of last night surrounding me all day.

Stepping into my bathroom, I turned on the shower, shifting to study my reflection while the water warmed up. There was a flush to my cheeks and a slight stubble burn on the curve of my neck. My lip tucked between my teeth as my fingers ran over it, loving that Theo had left marks on my skin. It'd take a lot of concealer to cover it up, but I'd know it was there. Normally, I'd wear his marks like a brand, proudly declaring I was his. Now, though, there was no way that was possible. Not when it could jeopardize both of our jobs.

While my job wasn't my dream career, it was working out better than I ever could have expected. All my bills were paid, I was able to contribute to Devyn's rent, and I could put a good amount in my savings. Not to mention, I really enjoyed working with Theo. Even before things shifted between us, I admired him, loving watching how he commanded rooms and drew others to his presence. I didn't have much work experience, only working for my family, but I could see that Theo's management style was different. My stepfather watched over his company from afar, barely bothering to interact with his subordinates unless they made him look bad.

My mother, on the other hand, ruled her domain with an iron fist, refusing to let anyone question her ways. She preferred fear over any sort of loyalty. While Theo had his moments, it was clear that his employees respected him.

I knew I did.

My hands scrubbed through my hair, trying to plan out how I would act when I got to the office. It would probably depend on Theo. My stomach lurched a little; it was going to sting when he acted like nothing happened. Even though we said it wasn't a one-night stand, a part of me feared that Theo could have changed his mind. A lot could have happened since we parted earlier this morning.

When we first met, Theo was adamant he didn't want to be

in a relationship, that all he was looking for was a hook-up. And while I was confident in our connection, it wasn't enough to convince me that I was enough to change his mind.

You weren't even enough for your mother, who is supposed to love you unconditionally.

I groaned, hating that this was the moment my brain decided to remind me of that fact. In the months since I left home, I tried to keep thoughts of my mother to a minimum. It was too painful otherwise. Honestly, there was a large part of me that thought she would have cracked by now, calling me or doing *something* to show that she missed me.

But there had been nothing—no calls, emails, or even messages passed to me through Devyn.

Climbing out of the shower, I stared at the mirror again, but the reflection wasn't the same. Gone was the blissed-out woman, replaced with the sour expression of a girl who'd never been enough—one whose worth was determined by how she could complete a pretty, perfect picture.

My hands wanted to reach out and smash the mirror so I wouldn't have to see the words written on my skin. Worthless. Unwanted. How long would it be until Theo saw the same things?

I pulled my shoulders back, refusing to let my thoughts go down that road. For today, I'd have to do my best to keep those thoughts at bay. Instead, I'd focus on tonight and the man who made me feel like I was everything.

"MISS WINTERS?"

Theo's voice cut through the fog, my brain almost numb after staring at scheduling documents for nearly an hour. With the partners coming in a few weeks to check out how the office was functioning, all hands were on deck to make sure they went home with a favorable report. For me, it meant coordinating their schedules and making sure I accounted for every minute. Sure, it was necessary—at least it was to Theo. This visit should tip the scales in his favor, the final success he needed to become a named partner, but holy hell, was it boring.

I glanced up at him, trying not to smile too wide. "Yes, Mr. Ayad?" I turned back to my computer screen. "I've coordinated almost all of the flights and drivers."

"That sounds great," Theo said absent-mindedly as he scrolled through his phone. "I need to speak with you in my office."

"Now?" I shifted toward him. "I was just about to finish–"

"Yes, now, Miss Winters. It's time for your thirty-day evaluation."

I arched a brow, unsure where he was going with this. Not to sound too cocky, but I was pretty sure I was killing it at this job. That, coupled with last night, made it a little surprising that Theo would be pulling me in for a meeting right now.

But I followed him, not bothering to ask any questions. The furrow between his brow told me I wouldn't get any answers. I plopped down in my usual spot on his couch, waiting as Theo sat across from me, lifting a pad of paper from the coffee table. He tapped a pen against it, not bothering to look up at me. "I have to say, Miss Winters, I am very unsatisfied."

"Excuse me?" I squealed as I sat up, looking at him dumbfounded. *Unsatisfied?* My mind raced, picturing ever moment he'd threatened to fire me over. They never felt sincere, like they were a private joke between us two. Maybe I'd mistaken him. My teeth bit into my lower lip, forcing it not to wobble. This was precisely what I'd feared. The moment we crossed that line, Theo would realize he wanted more than me, and I'd be heartbroken.

"Yes." Theo smirked. "I haven't tasted you on my tongue in hours. It's deeply troubling."

"You're the worst!" I gasped, tossing one of the throw pillows at him. "I thought you were talking about my work performance!"

Theo smiled as he leaned toward me. God, that look could make me melt. His smiles were so rare. It felt like I won the lottery every time it appeared. My fingers ached to touch him, but the hum of people outside his office reminded me we weren't alone.

"In case it wasn't obvious, Calla, I think you're amazing. You are everything I needed in an assistant and so much more." My cheeks filled with color, unable to hide my blush. To hear that I was doing a good job was rare, something I never knew I needed. "I don't think I could do this job without you."

My heart sank at his words. While I loved hearing his praise, it also nudged that insecurity in my mind, wondering if he had only cared about me because of how I made him look, because I was there to help him.

Theo must have sensed my mood change, because he stood up and moved to the spot next to me. "What did I say?"

"Nothing," I answered quickly, shaking my head. "I'm fine. Thank you, Theo. That means a lot to me."

"Calla," Theo whispered, placing his hand next to mine. His pinkie traced mine, the contact too little and just enough at the same time. "This can't work if we don't talk. If I said something to upset you, I need to know." He leaned closer. "Please, beautiful, talk to me."

I exhaled slowly, staring up at the ceiling. "I don't know how much you've heard about my family, but our relationship is... complicated. It shifted after my mother married my stepfather when I was a teenager. Our lives changed a lot. Our family became more about appearance than anything else. I've always felt like their love was conditional, like I needed to meet their expectations to matter." I let out a sardonic chuckle. "Which was cemented when I got cut off for refusing to go along with my mother's demands. My value to my family has always been about how I can make them look better." I glanced up at him. "So I can't help but wonder if you really like me, or if you like a certain version of me. If you wouldn't be interested in me if I wasn't your assistant."

Theo's eyes blazed into mine, almost knocking the air from my lungs. I waited for him to say something, but his jaw just ticked—as if he was weighing every single one of my words. All of a sudden, he stood, motioning to the door. "Come with me."

"What?" I asked, shifting further back on the couch. "Why?"

"Trust me, Calla." Theo held out his hand. "There's somewhere I need to take you."

Maybe others would have paused, would have questioned their blind faith in a man they'd only known for a month, but not me. Without a second thought, I placed my hand in Theo's, knowing I would follow this man wherever he led.

NINETEEN

Theo

I had to get my anger under control.

My self-control was never one of my finer traits. My words were often too brash, my actions too harsh. I refused to show Calla that side, not when she'd just started to peel back that mask she loved to wear so much.

I was almost ashamed of how long it'd taken me to notice it. There was a lot she hid behind that bright smile, and now that she'd started to let me in, I'd never let her bear that burden alone again. There had been comments in the past about Calla's mother, and we'd had a few brief conversations at the Isadora that raised red flags. But without hearing it from the source, I didn't want to make assumptions. I didn't want to guess what had transpired between Calla and her family, to make her end up in the city without a penny to her name.

We briskly walked through the halls until I stopped outside the furthest office. I pulled out my keys from my pocket to unlock the door and pulled Calla inside. Once the door closed, I let go of Calla's hand, letting her look around the room.

The office was pristine from being cleaned regularly, even though no one had claimed it yet. With it being so far away from the rest of the agents, no one wanted to take it, so we agreed it would stay empty until we either hired someone else or found another purpose for the space. It was significantly smaller than my office, and the walls were made of wood paneling instead of glass. Almost all the furniture was the same as what was in my office when I first arrived, before Calla changed it all to make the space more stylish.

In my office, it was easy to take for granted how much had changed in a short amount of time. But this space felt lifeless and stale, much like my world before Calla stepped into it. She'd opened my eyes to the beauty of life, bringing color into my sea of gray. I wanted to do the same for her, to be her safe space to land.

But none of that could happen if she didn't realize what she meant to me.

Calla turned back to me. "What is this place?"

"An empty office."

She glared at me. "No kidding, Sunshine. But why do you have a key?"

I smirked at her. "If you haven't noticed, my office is a little like a fishbowl. It can be hard to focus when there's so much going on right outside." I leaned against the wall, crossing my arms over my chest. "Also, there is a gorgeous woman who sits only a few feet from me. I can't count the number of times I've lost track of time because I'm too busy staring at her, wondering what it would be like to make her mine." She smiled at me as I continued. "I kept the key to this office so I could have a spare place to work. It helps when I have a deadline or can't afford to be distracted. It's my little secret."

"And now you're sharing it with me?"

"Calla, I'd give you everything if it made you smile. All you ever have to do is ask." I twisted, turning so I could wrap my arms around her. Today was torture, being close enough to see her, to smell that blend of wildflowers from her shampoo, but not able to touch her. "I'm sorry for what your family put you through. If you ever want to talk about it, I'm here." I tilted her chin up to meet my eyes. "But know this: how I feel about you has *nothing* to do with your work. I see you, Calla—the real you. I care about you. I love your smile and the way your nose crinkles when you tease me. I love that you never hesitate to call me out, and see the best in every situation. But most of all, I love that you have the most incredible heart, and I hope one day, you'll share it with me."

She nodded slightly, her eyes a little glossier than they were a minute ago. However, no matter the truth in my words, history was a beast to overcome. The thoughts that plagued us at night had teeth, and I knew better than most how difficult it was to silence them. However, I was determined to help Calla move past the harm her family caused.

Calla attempted to smile, but it was weaker than her usual expression. That didn't work for me. Nothing less than my beautiful girl's wide grin would suffice. I glanced over her shoulder, a plan forming in my mind. With a wicked smirk, I let go of her, walked toward the door, and twisted the lock.

Her eyes widened. "What are you doing?"

"Does this room remind you of somewhere?" I arched a brow, ignoring her question. "Maybe before you decided to upgrade everything? I looked around the room, realizing what she must have seen on that first day. "It was a little boring, I suppose."

"A little?" Calla laughed, walking over to the desk and propping herself up to sit on top of it. "You can admit it, Sunshine. You like the changes I made."

"Maybe. But you know what I like even more?" I stepped between her legs, playing with the silk ties at the top of her blouse. "The sight of you on top of this desk. It makes me furious that I can't have you on mine right now."

"Then pretend it is." She pressed her hand to my chest. "Mr. Ayad, I don't know what you've heard, but I am willing to do *whatever* it takes to get the job."

I pulled back, sure for a moment that Calla lost her mind. But when she mouthed *play along*, the scene suddenly clicked, making my dick harden in my slacks. My fingers danced along her collarbones, pushing the fabric away to inhale her scent. "I'm not sure, Miss Winters. I need someone willing to put in the work. It'll be long hours, and I'm known for being very demanding."

"I can handle it," she said breathily, her hand drifting down to cup me. "Let me prove it to you."

She started to slide off the desk, but my hands gripped her hips. "Don't even think about it." I gently pushed her backward until she was flat against the desk. "I've been craving a taste of you since I left your bed. I'm done waiting."

Calla let out a little giggle as my hands drifted to the hem of her skirt, pushing it up until it was over her ass. Her panties were already drenched. "You need this almost as much as I do, don't you, beautiful girl?" She nodded. "This all because of me?"

"Yes," she sighed. "You don't know what you do to me, Theo."

"You do the same thing to me." I pulled them down her legs, exposing her to me. "Now, be a good girl and come on my face. I need another taste of this perfect pussy."

SOMETIME LATER, Calla and I headed back to my office, hoping no one noticed our absence. While my schedule was flexible enough that I could come and go without much attention, Calla was another story. By the time we'd made it back to my office, five people had stopped her, asking where she'd been, apparently needing her input on different projects.

It made my chest fill with pride, seeing how far she'd already come here. Her opinion was invaluable to me, but now, others were seeing it as well. I never could have predicted this when she showed up at her interview, but I was incredibly grateful.

The new receptionist, the one whose name I could barely remember, came dashing out to meet us before I could even open my office door. "My apologies, Mr. Ayad," she rushed out, looking between Calla and myself. "But I've been trying to get in touch with you. Adam Rice is here for his meeting."

Shit. This meeting had been marked on my calendar for almost a week, and yet the moment Calla needed me, it was a distant memory. I should have been annoyed at myself; I should have *hated* that I put someone else's needs above my career. But as I searched for that seed of self-doubt, it was nowhere to be found.

"Sorry..."

"Eloise," Calla answered for me, shooting me a glare.

"Yes, Eloise. Please tell him that one of us will be there to greet him in a moment. I'll apologize to him then."

She nodded and walked away, but not before shooting Calla a look, one I'd seen a million times before. The one that relayed the boss was an asshole without the words. As soon as Eloise was a safe distance away, I stepped closer to Calla. "I don't think she likes me very much."

"Remembering her name would be a good place to start." She turned to look at me, her brow furrowing. "Everything okay with Adam?"

I nodded. "It's my monthly pitch to try to get him back into acting. That, and I want to make sure he's doing alright. He hasn't answered my last few calls, and that's unusual for him."

She studied my expression. "You're worried about him."

"It's my job to worry about his career."

"No," she said. "You're worried about him. Not because of work, but because you care about him. It's okay to admit you're worried about your friend."

I ducked my head. I was willing to admit that to myself, but I'd never voiced it out loud. Admitting that I was worried about Adam, was the same as admitting something was off with him. It made little sense, but in my mind, if I never said the words, it wasn't serious. That Adam was having a normal rough patch-like many other creatives did. It would quickly pass.

But of course, Calla was able to read through my silence. Even though it wasn't the first time she'd seen through me, it made me shift uncomfortably. I felt unnaturally exposed under her watchful eye. Calla was one of the few people who took the time to look beyond my usual asshole outer shell. While caring was a positive thing in most businesses, in my line of work, it could be dangerous to get too invested in a client.

As she went down the hall to grab Adam, Calla offered me a soft smile, one that made the weight in my chest instantly lessen. I might not know what the future might hold, but I knew one thing: I wanted this woman in it, no matter the consequences.

TWENTY

Watching through the glass, I grimaced as Theo paced his office. Whatever was happening in his meeting with Adam was *not* going well. It had been almost an hour since they walked in together, leaving me out here to wonder what they were talking about. I knew that Theo needed to be in there alone, dealing with Adam as more of a friend than an agent.

But Adam's posture was so different than usual, and it made me edgy. We'd spent a good amount of time together back at the lake due to our close friendships with Alex and Cole. As far as I knew, Adam was always calm, cool, and collected. The stress of his life would leave most people in shambles, but he seemed to take all of it in stride.

Until today.

Every muscle in his body was tense, and he was leaning against the wall the furthest from Theo's desk. Adam crossed his arms around his chest, and if looks could kill, my boss would be a pile of ash on the floor. The peacekeeper in me wanted to bust in to soothe the mounting tension, but it wasn't my place, no matter my role in Theo's life—especially not here.

As my eyes darted between the two of them, someone

stepped up to my desk, dropping a folder on top of my keyboard. "Holy shit," Jack whispered. "What I wouldn't give to be a fly on that wall."

My annoyance reared up. "What do you want, Jack?"

He tilted his head at my words before barking out a laugh. "Easy there, Calla. I was just dropping off Anders' contract. Theo wanted me to take a look before they started discussing next season."

After the gala, I talked with Devyn about Jack and how something about him unsettled me. However, instead of agreeing, she *defended* Jack, which was odd. Maybe she was right; because I was so protective of Theo, I was seeing threats that didn't exist.

But something about his words and actions still didn't sit right with me. I took the folder, holding it close to my chest. Maybe it was old insecurities. Perhaps it was the look that Jack got when Theo led a meeting. But my instincts weren't usually wrong, and they were telling me to be cautious with this man.

I tried to hide all my suspicions behind a smile. "I'll let him know. Thanks for dropping it off."

Without another word, I pushed back from my desk, beelining straight to Theo's door. Maybe I should have let them continue their argument, but my desire to get away from Jack won out. There was also a part of me that wanted to protect Theo. The entire office's eyes were trained on the glass walls, watching their boss argue with his biggest client. I knew if he wasn't so preoccupied with Adam, Theo would hate that they were seeing him like this.

I knocked lightly on his door, and when Theo called out, I stepped inside. "Sorry to interrupt, but Jack dropped off this contract, and it seemed urgent." Theo motioned for me to hand it to him. While he looked it over, I offered Adam a half-smile.

He did the same, running his hand through his shaggy blond hair.

Seeing him up close, it was clear that Theo was right to worry. Adam didn't look like himself at all. Typically, he was very put together, closely shaved, his hair sculpted to the point of perfection. Today, he looked like he'd just climbed off a barstool, the faint smell of scotch surrounding him.

Theo's eyes met mine for a brief moment before I stepped closer to Adam. "It's good to see you again."

"Same," he sighed, a little bit of that light entering his eyes again. "I'm glad the job is working out for you."

"Yeah, thank you so much for setting up my interview," I chuckled. "Sunshine over there took a little bit to get used to, but he's grown on me. He cares about the people he works with, you know?"

Adam swallowed, looking down at his feet. He stuffed his hands in his pockets. "I should get going. Thanks for the heads up, Theo." He placed his hand on my arm and squeezed lightly. "Hope to see you again soon, Calla."

"You got it. If you need anything, let me know."

He nodded, barely looking at Theo as he crossed the room. But before he could open the door, Theo called out. "Think about what I said."

Adam didn't respond, leaving before either of us could say anything else. The moment the door closed, Theo collapsed in his chair, tossing the contract across his desk. His head dropped into his hands. "Fuck!"

All I wanted was to crawl into his lap, to make him feel better. However, with the entire office on the other side of the wall, it was impossible to do anything but stand there awkwardly.

Theo shook his head then finally glanced up at me. "If you couldn't tell, that did not pan out the way I was expecting."

"What happened?"

"Wish I fucking knew." Theo rubbed his eyes. "I tried to talk to him about what's been going on, but the guy's a fortress. He wouldn't tell me anything, just that he's not ready to take any more jobs." He laughed, but there was no warmth in it. "Shit, Calla. What the hell am I supposed to do? It's like he's self-destructing in front of me, and all I can do is watch."

With one glance through the glass, I moved over to Theo's desk, pretending that I was showing him part of the contract. My hand briefly found his, offering him a comforting squeeze. "Give him time," I whispered. "Keep letting him know that you are there for him as his friend, not his agent. When he's ready, he'll open up."

"And if he doesn't?"

I wanted to make the moment better, to make promises I knew I couldn't keep, to tell Theo that everything would be alright when we had no idea what the future would hold. But all those words were out of reach, so I did what I could for him in this dark moment. I stood with him, waiting with him for as long as he needed.

As his breath started to even out, Theo looked up at me, an apprehensive smile gracing his features. "I'm sorry about that, Calla. You said Jack wanted me to look through that contract?"

"Oh, yes!" I jumped up and settled back on the couch. "He was going to drop it off later, but I thought you and Adam could use a little break from your conversation."

"Always looking out for me." He smiled before glancing over the documents. As he read through the text, I sat back, toying with the idea of saying something about Jack. Even though Devyn had dismissed my concerns, something about Jack still bothered me, like when he tried to warn me away from Theo.

"I can practically hear the gears turning in your head." Theo closed the folder and looked up at me. "What's going on, Calla?"

I sighed, toying with my bracelet before deciding to speak. "So Jack... You guys have known each other a long time?"

Theo nodded. "Over a decade. We started at the agency within weeks of each other. We've been a solid team ever since." He tilted his head. "Why do you ask?"

"I don't know how to take him," I answered honestly. "He's made a couple of comments that haven't sat right."

Theo sighed as he sat back on his chair. "Do you want me to talk to him?"

"No, nothing like that!"

"Calla, I'm serious. If he's making you uncomfortable in any way, I will handle it. Immediately."

"Theo, I promise. He hasn't said anything like that." I chewed on my lower lip. "But you trust him, right?"

"With my life," Theo answered. "He's had my back for years, Calla. There aren't many people I truly trust. Jack is one of them." He smiled at me. "You're another."

And with that simple admission, my heart started to beat a little faster, knowing I trusted Theo just as much. If he put his faith in Jack, I would have to as well, even if it seemed like the wrong choice.

LATER THAT EVENING, I stood in the middle of Theo's elevator, twisting my fingers together. I pushed my breath through my lips as I stared at the rising numbers, my anxiety growing as we got closer to the top.

Even though we spent last night together, this felt different. That was a collision, an inevitable conclusion to the tension between us. But being here tonight—this was a choice. I was walking into his apartment with no pretenses, no pretending that this was strictly a work relationship.

My nerves started when I arrived at his building, lying to his doorman about my visit. Thomas was a good man, one I'd gotten to know well during my frequent visits as Theo's assistant. I probably could have told him the truth, but after hiding our relationship from everyone else, it felt easier to continue the ruse.

I closed my eyes to push away the guilt, focusing on what was important. Even though I was anxious about taking this next step, I was dying to spend more time with Theo. I told Devyn I was going out with a few girls from work and that I was crashing on one of their couches for the night. She'd just nodded, barely looking up from her pile of paperwork as I ran out the door. Eventually, I'd have to come clean with her and the other people in my life, but for now, I wanted to enjoy my time with Theo without anyone else's input.

When the elevator door dinged open, I stepped inside his foyer, lifting my hand to knock on the door. Before I could, though, Theo ripped it open, pulling me into his apartment. The moment I saw his face, all my earlier nerves disappeared, and I was finally at ease now that it was just us.

"Thank God you're here," he called out as he rushed back to the kitchen. "I screwed something up, and I don't know how to fix it."

I chuckled as I followed him into the kitchen. The smell of burnt food invaded my nostrils the moment I walked inside. Covering my mouth, I stepped closer to his stove, lifting a pan lid to see a pile of black mush. "Do I even want to know?"

Theo ran his hand over his face. "I was trying to recreate one of my mother's recipes—this chicken stew she'd make when I was younger. She called it moghrabieh. Safe to say, I have no clue what I'm doing." He peeked over my shoulder. "Is there any way we can save it?"

"Nope." I chuckled in his arms. "Do you have any more ingredients? We can try again, together this time."

"Not really. To be honest, this was attempt number two. The first one was even worse." He grimaced as he looked inside the plan. "I wanted to make tonight special for you."

I leaned back, pressing the back of my head into his chest. "You don't need to do anything for me, Theo."

"I know, but I want to." He kissed my forehead before walking over to grab his phone. "Take out it is. What's your preference?"

"I can always go for pizza."

With a few clicks of the phone, edible food was on its way, and I helped Theo clean up the rest of his mess. Moving around his space should have felt awkward or foreign, but we moved in sync, like always. It was weird; I'd never had a connection like this one before. It was so natural that I almost didn't believe it was real.

Once his pans were scorch-free, Theo checked his phone, frowning. "Still another 30 minutes until the food gets here." He came closer to me and tugged me into his arms. "However will we pass the time?"

I leaned forward, capturing his lips with mine. "I'm pretty sure we can think of something."

TWENTY-ONE

As my eyes opened the next morning, I was greeted with my new favorite sight. Theo slept on the pillow next to me, softly snoring in my direction. My hands reached out, tracing a line along his cheek. I could get used to this. It was rare to see Theo so relaxed. When we were at the office, he was always dealing with a million things at once. While he tried not to show it, I could tell how much the pressure was getting to him.

But these moments, when it was just the two of us? It was like we could block out the rest of the world, leaving our problems and concerns behind.

When the early morning light started to stream in through his window, Theo groaned, tossing an arm around my waist and pulling me to his side. He kissed the side of my hair. "What time is it?" he groaned, his voice scratchy from sleep.

"A little after six."

Theo sat up, looking around the room as if he'd never seen it before. Then, he let out a surprised chuckle. "Shit, I can't believe I slept in."

I groaned, ducking under his arm. "Only a true monster would think this counts as sleeping in."

"When you usually get up at four, beautiful, it counts." He leaned down, pressing his lips to mine. "Are you hungry?"

A growl from my stomach answered his question. He chuckled, kissing me again before climbing out of the bed with invigorated energy. I leaned up to watch him, chuckling to myself as he winked at me over his shoulder. Who was this man, and what happened to the grouch who interviewed me weeks ago? If I'd known mind-blowing sex was the key to getting him to smile, I would have ripped off his clothes on day one.

I kept staring at him as he walked into the bathroom, unable to take my eyes off his perfectly sculpted muscles. Last night, I'd happily discovered that Theo slept shirtless, only liking to wear his boxers to bed.

As I heard the shower trickle on, I slipped back into his bed, snuggling further into Theo's pillow. His smell still clung to the fabric. I was addicted to this man, needing to have him around me in some capacity. It was tempting to steal a bottle of his cologne, keeping that leather and pine scent with me at all times.

I must have dozed off, because when my eyes opened again, I was alone, and the sun was fully shining. Without him distracting me, I took the chance to look around his room. I'd been to Theo's home a dozen times before, but I'd never made it back here. Last night, I was too focused Theo to take in the space. The room was bright due to the large windows, but almost all the design features were dark. The walls were lined in stained wood panels, and the bed frame was covered with thick, rich leather. The entire place was masculine and tailored, just like the man who owned it. It was a far cry from my cluttered, disorganized room, but I felt comfortable here, more comfortable than I expected.

Reluctantly, I climbed out of Theo's bed, stretching out my

aching body. Despite the limited amount of sleep we got last night, I felt more rested than I had in months. What the heck was Theo's mattress made of? I needed to find out. Compared to his, my mattress felt like something from the Stone Age.

After grabbing a shirt from his drawer, I padded over to the bathroom, laughing when I caught my reflection. Yup, I looked well and thoroughly fucked, and I had no regrets. With it being the weekend, I'd hold onto this look for as long as possible.

As I stepped out of Theo's bathroom and into the hallway, I studied the photographs that lined the walls. They were clearly stock photos; nothing was too personal about any of the images. How had I never noticed that before? His home reminded me a little of Devyn's, how it was beautiful in its design but lacked any sort of personal touches.

When I moved out of my stepdad's apartment, I'd claimed one of the Isadora rooms for myself. My grandfather had stipulated in his will that a wing would always be kept for his family, and I was more than happy to fulfill his request. The first thing I'd done was make the space my own, adding as much life and color to it as possible. I wondered what it looked like now. Had my mother stripped the walls, painting over the blue I'd spent hours debating, making it the same shade of beige as everything else?

I pushed the thought away as I stepped toward the kitchen, letting the sight of Theo shirtless distract me. Propping my hip against the wall, I watched as he worked, jumping between a couple of different pans on the stove. As he bent down to open the oven, a whiff of bacon reached me, and my stomach let out an embarrassingly loud groan.

He peeked over his shoulder, a smirk forming on his lips as I came closer. He stood up fully, rubbing his mouth when I stopped in front of him. Theo's hand toyed with the hem of his shirt against my thighs. "Could get used to this sight, beautiful. It's making me feel all sorts of things."

"Put a pin in that. I'm starving," I chuckled, lifting to kiss his cheek. "I need food before I can think of anything else. Consider this your warning: I am the *worst* when I'm hangry. You won't even recognize me."

Theo smacked my ass before he got back to work. "Haven't seen a side of you I don't like yet, Calla. Besides, after you've dealt with me at my worst, only fair I do the same." He reached down and pulled out a tray of bacon. "But I'll do my best to keep you fed, beautiful."

"Good answer." I kissed his bare shoulder. "What are your plans after breakfast? I can head home if you need to get some work done."

"Nah, I left everything at the office. I'll get to it on Monday."

My thoughts spluttered to a sudden stop. What did he just say? It was official: last night, Theo really had murdered me with orgasms. It was the only explanation as to why my workaholic boss just casually mentioned he took the whole weekend off.

As my mind melted down, Theo plated our food and nodded toward the table in the corner of the room. As soon as we sat, Theo dove in, not noticing the strange expression on my face. I just sat there, anxiously analyzing his words. My thumb jumped to my mouth, and I started to chew on the cuticle, unable to take a bite with my stomach swirling with nerves. But after a couple of seconds, Theo reached out to me. "Calla, why are you upset?"

"I'm not upset," I said quickly. "Just trying to figure out what's going on. Have you had a stroke? Is this a case of body snatchers? Because I can't think of a single other reason why you, of all people, would take an entire weekend off."

He put his utensils down, joining his hands together to look at me fully. "Calla, I want to spend the weekend with you. Just you. Not working, not worrying about clients." He reached out and intertwined our fingers. "I want us to have a chance to spend time together without any distractions."

"I like the sound of that."

"Good." He smiled, lifting my hand to kiss my knuckles. "Then eat."

AS I POLISHED off the last bite of my breakfast, I stood to place the plate in the sink. At least I did before Theo snatched it away. "I can do that." He nodded to the couch. "Go relax. It's your day off too."

"No way." I reached up to steal the plate back from him. "You cooked, I clean. I'm not going to let you do all the work around here."

As I squeezed some soap on a sponge, Theo wrapped his arms around my waist. He leaned down, pressing a kiss to the crook of my neck. "I like taking care of you, Calla. And during the week, I don't get to do it nearly enough." I leaned back into him, soaking up all his warmth, so I didn't even notice when he took the sponge out of my hand. "Now, get your ass on that couch and relax, and I'll reward you later."

I chewed on my lower lip, looking at the sectional along the far wall. It did look comfortable. I glanced over my shoulder, "Are you sure? I really don't mind helping."

Theo shook his head, leaning in to softly kiss me. "Let me take care of you, beautiful."

Okay, this relaxed, happy Theo was breaking my brain. Every moment I spent with him, I could feel myself falling for him a little bit more. It was fast—too fast to be thinking this way. We'd only started seeing each other a couple of days ago, and I was already falling hard, but it was useless to try and fight it. Every moment I spent with Theo, he laid a little more claim to my heart.

Before I could spiral completely, I moved over to the sectional couch, sinking into the plush cushions. It looked so familiar, but it took me a minute to realize it was the same brand as the one I'd picked out for his office—the one he spent *days* complaining about. *Jackass.* I knew he loved that thing.

Reaching for the remote, I scanned through his selection of apps, hating how few he had. I made an executive decision and downloaded Netflix, typing in my account info. Scrolling through the first row of shows, I mentally crossed out all the ones I'd watched before. Hmm, documentary? No way in hell. But as I reached the last group, my eyes widened in excitement.

"Score," I whispered as Theo lowered himself into the spot next to me, pulling my legs into his lap. My head fell back as his thumbs dug into my calves.

He shook his head when my show loaded, and a bunch of housewives instantly started screaming at each other. "I can't believe you watch this crap."

"How dare you, sir," I teased. "They are the new American masterpieces."

"No wonder we're a nation in decline."

"Have you ever watched it before?"

He snorted. "No. I don't waste my time watching a lot of television, but if I do, it's not for mindless dribble."

"Then you can't talk." I smirked at him. "If you're going to form a strong opinion about my taste in tv shows, then you have to have first-hand experience." I leaned into his side, letting his warmth surround me. It felt right, being in his arms like this. For so long, I'd been searching for a place I belonged, and nothing had ever felt like this, like I could live a thousand years, and I'd never feel more at peace than when Theo held me. "Give it a chance." I batted my eyelashes at him. "For me?"

"Devious tactic," Theo groaned, kissing the top of my head. "But fine. I can't bring myself to say no to you, beautiful." He nodded to the television. "Let the torture commence."

TWENTY-TWO

Hours passed, and we remained on the couch. Every time the option to continue watching came up, I'd look over at Theo, and he'd nod his head. I was shocked that he was still sitting here. After each episode, I waited, sure that this would be the moment he would break from this weird trance, desperate to bury himself in work. Considering that I kept his schedule, I knew how Theo spent most of his time, and curled up on the couch wasn't it.

I mean, the man barely ever took a lunch hour, much less an entire day off. But he made no effort to leave, only holding me closer and kissing me every chance he got.

As another episode started playing, his phone rang out in his pocket. Pulling it out, we both looked at the screen and saw Jack's name. I expected Theo to take the call, especially considering this was not the first time Jack had reached out today.

I hugged him a little tighter. "You should answer it. He could have an emergency."

"He can handle it." Theo kissed the top of my head. "There's a reason why he runs his department. Besides, if I can't trust the agents to handle their own crises, what use are they to me?"

Makes sense to me. But I didn't have long to mull it over. After silencing the call, which was a rare enough treat, Theo actually turned his phone off. My jaw dropped to the floor when the screen went black; I was pretty sure Theo had never shut it off before.

I smiled to myself, tucking closer to Theo's side. As much as I loved watching Theo work, knowing he was putting aside time to spend with me meant the world. He was the kind of person who never took a day off, never bothered to do anything for himself. So the fact that he was here with me meant more than I could put into words.

Theo sighed, tucking me closer to him. I looked up at him, studying his expression. It was content, more than I'd ever seen before. It was refreshing to see this side of him, to see him finally let the stress wash away. I made a silent promise to myself to make more time for moments like this, to pull Theo out of the fray every once in a while and remind him that he needed time to recharge as well.

The rest of the day passed by quickly. Theo ordered enough food to feed a small army, including all my favorite candies, the ones I'd hoard in my desk drawers at work. Little moments like this showed how much he paid attention, even when I didn't realize it.

Around five, as I chomped down on my third bag of Swedish fish, my phone chimed.

DEVYN

Just checking in. Are you coming home tonight? Send a sign of life, or I'm calling the cops.

I paused, staring at her message. Lying to my sister was difficult, especially after everything she'd done for me over the years. Glancing up, I found Theo in the kitchen, pouring me a glass of wine. I could go home and explain everything to Devyn, but Theo had blocked out the entire weekend to spend with me, and there was no way I'd end it early.

ME

All good, but I'm not coming back tonight. Girls night turned into girls weekend. I'll be home tomorrow night.

DEVYN

Have fun. Don't do anything that would require legal assistance.

After casting my phone aside, Theo settled back onto the couch, passing me a glass of red wine. He flinched as one of the main cast members on the show tossed her drink in another woman's face. He just shook his head. "She deserved it."

"Right?" I chuckled. "Never bring up children. That's a low blow."

Theo rubbed my arms, noting the goosebumps that had broken out along my skin. "Cold?" Theo asked, grabbing a controller to turn down the air conditioning.

"A little." I shrugged. "Can I borrow a pair of sweatpants? Maybe a hoodie."

"Nope," Theo chuckled, grabbing a blanket from the other side of the couch. "As much as I love the idea of you stealing my clothes, covering up these legs is a crime." He lifted his arm. "Get closer, baby. I've got you."

I smiled as I settled into his warm embrace, a rush of happiness washing over me as he draped a blanket across our laps. An immediate sense of warmth and safety engulfed me, settling deep into my tired bones. "Has anyone ever told you you're like a furnace?" I joked, letting my cheek rest against his chest.

"My ex-wife used to say that all the time," Theo laughed. "She'd complain that she couldn't sleep next to me because I always run so warm."

My mouth dried out at the mention of the woman he married. After speaking to Natalie a couple of times on the phone, their relationship made no sense. Theo might have flaws, but he was inherently kind and cared about the people closest to him. Natalie, on the other hand, was rude and demanding. I tried to empathize with her and tried to figure out what made her so cold, but with so many pieces of the puzzle missing, it was a mystery I could never solve. I cleared my throat, forcing myself to bring up the subject, no matter how uncomfortable it might make me. "Natalie, right? If you don't mind me asking..."

"What happened between us?" I nodded. Theo sighed, and for a moment, I thought he wouldn't answer. Maybe it was wrong to pry, but I wanted to know everything about him, what had happened in his life before we crossed paths. After weeks of watching the aftermath of their conversations, my imagination had made up all types of scenarios. The first couple of times, I was convinced that Theo was still in love with her. But now, it was clear there was no love lost between them.

Theo lifted his arm, leaning forward to rest his elbows on his knees. "Natalie and I were together for two years," he said slowly, as if pulled into a memory. "It was a whirlwind from the start. We met at an industry party, one my company was throwing for some of the new, up-and-coming actors. At the time, Natalie had just signed with us. She'd acted on a few television shows and claimed she was looking to break into movies."

"She didn't?"

"Maybe for a time, but it was clear after we got together that she wasn't really interested in acting, more the connections that it afforded her." Theo's hand found mine, and I laced our fingers together. The urge to comfort him was overwhelming, but I stayed quiet at his side, letting him decide how much he wanted to share. "We never talked about marriage before we eloped. We were in Vegas, celebrating my first major deal, and there was a little chapel..." He sighed. "After, I think Natalie thought I would change, that I would make her the priority. But if anything, it made me work harder. I had a wife and wanted to have a family someday. I needed to prove I could provide for them." He scoffed. "She gave it 18 months. Eighteen months and then decided that if I wasn't going to put in an effort, then she would find someone else who would."

"Shit," I sighed. "That's so messed up."

"I don't blame her," Theo quietly admitted. "She was right. I barely spent any time with her. I was a ghost in our own home, only there when we were entertaining and networking with the other agents." He sighed, rubbing his hand over his face. "She might not be my favorite person, but I'm not blameless either."

"You made a mistake."

"I made a *choice*," Theo answered, shaking his head. "It's why I don't want to repeat the same actions with you, Calla. For a long time, my work was my whole life. It was my wife, mistress, and everything in between." He gripped my hand a little tighter. "I don't want to make that mistake twice."

"You won't." Theo might doubt himself, but if he'd proven anything to me, it was that he was capable of amazing things when he put his mind to it. "I'm sorry you went through that. It sounds lonely."

"It was," Theo admitted quietly. He held me a little tighter. "But lately, it hasn't felt like that at all. You've given me so much more to look forward to. It feels like, before you showed up, I was just coasting, letting my life pass me by." He looked up, his dark eyes boring into mine. "Now, I want to experience the world, and I want to experience it with you." He dropped his gaze, vulnerability seeping out of all his pores. "If you'll let me."

"I want that too," I admitted. "But I also don't want you to feel like you have to change for me, Theo. I care about you because of the man you are, not this picture-perfect version of you. I don't want you to feel like you have to choose between me and your career. Even though–" I chewed my lower lip, not wanting to finish my thought.

"I might have to," Theo answered quietly. He ran his hand over his face. "Calla, if our relationship isn't worth the risk to you, I understand. I'd never fault you for that. But I made my choice when I first kissed you, and I'm not going back on it now." He leaned forward, pressing his forehead to mine. "I'm all in, beautiful."

I swallowed slowly, hating that my eyes were filling up with tears. "Before you decide you want this, you should know—my life is a *mess*. I'm still trying to figure myself out, and it's probably unfair to drag you into it. My mother and stepfather..." I sighed, hating that I was bringing them up again. Every time something good happened in my life, memories of them were there to sully it. "I've already told you that they're manipulative, but I didn't fully explain how controlling they can be. For years, they've tried to dictate who I should be. What I wore, who I hung out with, what I said, what I studied. It was suffocating." My body shivered, remembering how many times they broke my heart when all I wanted was to be enough for them. I shook my head. "Now that I've finally gotten some distance from them, I'm realizing I've never had the opportunity to choose anything for myself." I leaned back, brushing my fingers over Theo's cheek. "But if you're willing to stick with me while I figure my life out–"

Theo cut me off with his lips on mine. It was bruising, possessive, and everything I needed in that moment. He pulled back but kept his face close to mine, his hand cupping the back of my neck. "I meant what I said, Calla. My choice isn't contingent on you changing. I want you just as you are. If this is you as a mess, I'll happily stand with you as long as you'll let me. But you have to *let me*, beautiful."

I smiled up at him. "Okay."

"Okay?"

"I'm all in."

TWENTY-THREE

Theo

The weekend ended far too quickly. Calla and I spent the whole time together, not bothering to leave the apartment at all. And even after forty-eight hours together, the moment she walked out of the door to return home, I wanted her to come back.

It had been years since I took any time off from work. Even if I managed to pull myself from the office for a day, I would always sneak away to send some emails or check in with my clients.

However, when Calla was in my arms, I felt none of that. Instead of stressing about my constantly vibrating phone, I was annoyed—irritated that people were invading my limited time with Calla. We spent almost every day together, but I wasn't able to touch her or hold her. I wanted to savor every minute together, to pretend that nothing else mattered but the two of us.

However, as soon as Calla left, the reality of our situation started to sink in. Last night, I'd gone over every possible option, trying to figure out how we'd be able to stay together and keep our jobs, but nothing seemed to work. Not without Calla quitting or me resigning in disgrace.

Maybe it was selfish of me to pursue this relationship when it was against our company's rules, but I couldn't bring myself to feel guilty about it. As long as it didn't negatively impact Calla, I never would. I meant what I said—I chose her over the job, over the fear, over everything else. I wouldn't let her go without a fight.

When Monday rolled around, I got to the office before dawn. The city around me was still sleeping when my car pulled up to the front of the building, only the security guard around. He waved as I walked inside, familiar with my ridiculous schedule. Most days, when I arrived early, it was because I had a million projects I needed to wrap up. But today, I was because all I could think of was Calla and how we'd get out of this mess. Not to mention, my bed felt too big and cold without her lying next to me.

As the elevator doors opened, my heckles immediately rose. I was used to this building, and I knew its sights and sounds in the early hours. So when our office doors were open and all the overhead lights were on, I knew something was wrong.

The smell of coffee filled the air as I walked inside. Glancing at my phone to check the hour, I debated calling security up to our floor. But there was no sign of a break-in, and most burglars didn't stop to brew a coffee pod when they were trying to rob a place. More than likely, a junior agent had bribed a janitor to let them in, something I'd done many times when I was starting out.

But as I turned the corner and saw movement in my office, my blood pressure started to spike. I stormed inside, ripping the door open. A man jumped at the sight, sending files and folders into the air.

"Jesus Christ," Jack screamed. "Are you trying to give me a fucking heart attack?"

My jaw tensed, staring at him in my space. "What the hell do you think you're doing?"

"Seriously, man?" Jack asked. "You told me I could use your office on days you weren't here. I've been working in here all weekend."

I stared at him, trying to recall the conversation. It was a blank, but then again, that wasn't an uncommon occurrence lately. Between trying to keep my relationship with Calla a secret and awaiting the partners' visit in a few weeks, I was having trouble keeping track of non-essential things.

Dropping my briefcase at my desk, I dropped my head into my hand. "Shit, sorry." I sat down on the couch, looking over the papers he'd compiled. "I saw the lights on and thought someone was trying to break in."

Jack chuckled, grabbing the last of the fallen papers. "Shit, what did you think they were going to take?" He nodded at the fall behind me. "Although you could probably get some good money for those footballs online."

"Don't even think about it." I nodded at the papers. "Remind me why you wanted to work in here and not your office?"

He shrugged, "Your set-up is better than mine. I can't fit a full-sized couch in my office. You think Calla could hook me up too?"

"It's worth a shot. But I've got her working on the partners' visit, so she might not have time until after they leave." I took the file in front of him, twisting it so I could read the top of it. "The McManus contract? Why are you staring at that old thing?"

Jack rubbed his hand over his eyes. "Trying to think outside of the box for one of my guys. GM's trying to screw him over after they heard other teams were pursuing him." He leaned back on the couch. "Information you would know if you'd answered the phone this weekend. Where the hell were you? I thought you died or something."

"Thanks for the concern," I said sardonically, "I needed to clear my head, take a few days away."

Jack kept staring at me as if he knew there was more to the story. As if he could read the guilt on my face, he suddenly smirked, pointing at me. "You fucking dog. You were with a girl, weren't you?" When I didn't respond, he continued. "Please tell me you finally got over your shit and made a move on Calla. That girl is way too hot to wait around for you."

"Nothing happened."

Jack leaned back, studying me. "That's good. A lot of the guys in the sports department want to make a run at her. Maybe I'll pass along her number."

"Watch it," I bit out.

"Damn, I never thought I'd see the day." Jack chuckled. "Good for you, Theo. About time."

I smiled to myself, thinking of my weekend spend wrapped up in Calla. But being in the office poured cold water over my elation. My jaw tensed. "But listen, Jack. You can't–"

"I gotcha, buddy. Your secret is safe with me." He sighed, his face suddenly turning serious. "Just make sure you're careful, okay, man? I'd hate for this to mess up how hard you've worked."

I nodded, trying not to let his words get to me. They were ones I already knew, ones I'd told myself so many times that they were tattooed on my heart. But hearing them from someone else? Someone who had been by my side since I started working at Wallace and Associates?

That made them even more real.

I dropped my head into my hands. "I know. Fuck, I know.

But I'm falling for her, Jack, and I don't know how to get us out of this. It's either we stop seeing each other, or one of us loses our job. And as much as I want her, can I really start all over? I've been here for ten years. Ten *long* fucking years." I stood and walked over to my desk. "Forget it. This isn't your problem. Let me know if you have any more issues with that contract negotiation."

"Yeah, no," Jack chuckled. "I'm not leaving you to mess this all up. If you care about this girl, which I know you do, we're going to figure something out."

I rubbed the bridge of my nose. "I've been thinking about it all night. There's no good solution."

Jack paused, leaning on the back of an armchair. "What about transferring her to another department?"

"Fuck that."

"Listen," Jack held up his hands, "I know you don't want to hear it, but maybe it'd be better. Then you wouldn't be her supervisor."

"Jack, I'm the head of this office. I'm technically *everyone*'s supervisor."

He cursed under his breath. "Okay, that's valid. But this might be a good temporary solution. If the partners get wind of what's happening, at least she's not working directly under you. It might help soften the blow a little bit."

His argument made sense, even if it made me a little nauseous. It was selfish of me, but as I looked out at Calla's empty desk, I hated the idea of anyone else sitting there. We were such a good team, and I knew I'd already gotten lucky twice with assistants. Who the hell knew who'd walk in next?

But that was a small price to pay for some peace of mind, to know that I could hold onto Calla a little longer.

I turned to the window. "Okay, I'll think about it."

TWENTY-FOUR

Theo

Later that day, all thoughts and worries about Calla and myself were pushed aside, courtesy of all the shit that had landed on my desk. With many television shows on break for the summer, there were always a lot of movements. Still, lately, it felt like every one of my remaining clients was up for a contract renewal, all seeking more money or producer credit, things that the studios were always reluctant to give.

Sending off one last email to the studio, I leaned back in my chair, needing a break to clear my mind. It wasn't that I didn't enjoy my career—for the most part, I did—but I'd be lying if I said that was why I did it. When I first graduated, I took the job in the mailroom to get by, needing something to keep me occupied while I searched for a full-time gig. But watching how the senior agents garnered so much power and respect, not to mention the outrageous paycheck, I was sucked into this world.

And for ten years, I never thought about it.

I stared out toward the rest of the office, and it was another cold reminder of how much of my life I'd wasted trapped behind this desk, helping my clients achieve their goals while holding none of my own.

The only thing I wanted now was Calla.

The more I thought about Jack's idea, the more it made sense. Even though it was still technically against the rules, it was a much less flagrant violation. And we'd get to see each other every day, even if it wasn't like before.

Before I could make up my mind, I had to talk to Calla. The shift would impact her more than me, and I refused to choose on her behalf. I'd tried to bring it up when she arrived this morning, but I couldn't bring myself to do it. Every time the thought of her leaving came up, the pressure in my chest increased, and the words refused to leave my mouth.

As my mind wandered, a knock came on my door, pulling me back into the present. Calla smiled at me, her pale pink legal pad clutched in her hands. "Do you have a few minutes to go over some details of the partners' trip?"

"Of course, come on in."

She settled into the seat across from me, nervously toying with her pen. I stared back at her, trying to read her mood. She must have noticed, because she gave me a half-hearted smile. "It's nothing, just ignore me."

My jaw instantly tightened; I hated that she was trying to hide from me again. A knot formed in my gut. Had Jack already talked to her? I'd kill him if he did. I did not doubt he would try to poach her if she left my desk, but I explicitly told him I needed more time. "What's going on?"

Calla shook her head. "It's fine, just some family stuff. You have enough to worry about. I can handle this on my own."

It was so tempting to pull her into my lap and hold her until she felt better. Instead, I leaned forward, lowering my voice. "Talk to me, Calla."

She inhaled as if trying to keep her emotions at bay. "Devyn called. My mother is coming into town next month for some business dinner with my stepfather. We're expected to attend."

She rolled her eyes. "The woman hasn't even bothered to call me since she kicked me out, and now she's demanding my attendance at some bullshit family dinner?" She shook her head. "Never going to happen."

I nodded, not wanting to show my annoyance. My hands clenched under my desk. While I'd never understand how she could have treated her daughter so poorly, a selfish part of me was glad for it. Because of her mother's actions, Calla was here with me now, and I would never make the same mistake. The darkest part of her life had led to the best part of mine, and all I wanted was to return the favor.

She brushed her hair away from her face, shaking her shoulders as if pushing away the negative feelings. "It's fine, I'm fine. Like I said, it's nothing for you to worry about. We have a visit to get ready for, and that deserves all my attention. I've got several reservations lined up–"

"Calla." I stood up to approach her before thinking better of it. "You don't have to put on an act in front of me. I want to see you, all sides of you, even when you're upset."

"Fine, you want to know how I feel?" She let out a half-hearted laugh. "I'm so fucking *pissed*, Theo. I'm finally doing something with my life, something that I actually enjoy, and then, with *one* phone call, my mother brings me right back down." She scoffed as she stood, walking over to the window. "My entire life, I've never been enough for her. But there was a small, probably naive part of me that thought she still cared about me and wanted me to be happy." Calla turned to lean against the ledge, crossing her arms around herself. "When she kicked me out, it was like the dam broke, and all the insecurities and pain she'd caused over the years came rushing out. The mask was off, and I finally saw the real her. And the worst part? I still want her approval. I want my mom to be proud of me. Does that make me pathetic?"

"No, baby, it makes you human. If you're not ready to see her, don't." I reached out to place my hand over hers. "But if you decide to go, I can go with you."

"I'd never ask that of you."

"I'm offering, Calla. Think about it. No matter what you decide, I'll be there with you."

Calla smiled back at me. "You have no idea how good that sounds. But I'm not sure if I'm willing to subject you to my family. Devyn is the friendly one."

"You know I don't scare that easily, beautiful. Besides, if it's a night that ends with you at my side, it'll be a good one, no matter what happens."

Calla smirked as if she didn't quite believe me, but I was telling the absolute truth. I'd walk through fire for this girl. Hopefully, dining with her family wouldn't be as painful.

But with the look Calla was giving me, it was probably going to be worse.

She wiped her hands over her eyes. "Sorry. This was supposed to be about work, and I've unloaded all my crap on you again. Oh, and I forgot. Jack said you have something to run by me?" She leaned back in her chair, hurt lurking in her light brown eyes, but at least it was less than before. "Everything okay?"

My stomach churned, trying to find the words to explain this plan without hurting her more. After everything with her mother, could I honestly push her away, even if it was what was best for the both of us?

I cleared my throat, unable to force the words out. I'd tell her later. In the grand scheme of things, would a couple more days together make a difference? Maybe it made me selfish, but I wanted all of her. I wanted Calla in my home and bed at night and by my side during the day. Not only because she was good at her job, but because it made me the best version of myself.

"Yeah." I rubbed the back of my neck. "Just wanted to check in on the dinner reservations. Did you set up the ones Allen requested?"

"Of course." She smiled. "You know I've got your back, Theo. We're a team."

At her words, I knew I couldn't tell her, not yet.

TWENTY-FIVE

"Oh my God!" I screamed as I glanced down at my phone. A gorgeous diamond ring filled up the whole screen. I jumped up and down, happy that I was alone in my bedroom so no one else could witness my freak out.

Although, honestly, I didn't really care. My best friend was about to get engaged to the love of her life, so some celebration was *absolutely* necessary. I resisted the urge to call her, to revel in the secret only I knew. I chewed on my lower lip, holding my finger over her contact. I dropped the phone. There was no way I'd be able to play it cool right now. I was pretty sure if I ruined the surprise, Cole would hate me forever.

Speaking of Cole—now that my heart rate was back to normal, I texted him back.

COLE

What do you think?

ME

ARE YOU KIDDING? ITS PERFECT. SHE'S GOING TO CRY

COLE

You think so?

ME

Yes, trust me. Alex is going to be a MESS. I'm so happy for you guys!!!

COLE

I'm doing it during the soft opening next weekend. Alex doesn't know you're coming, right?

ME

She has NO idea. I blamed Theo and said he needed me in the city for the partners' visit in a couple of weeks. She didn't even blink.

COLE

Sounds good. Remind him he's expected to show up too.

I laughed, sure that Theo had completely erased the event from his mind. It had been a draining, laborious six months renovating the Fox Creek Lodge and Campgrounds, but Alex and Cole were finally ready to show off their hard work. They'd asked all their friends and family to come for the weekend to help them work out the kinks before paying guests arrived. When I showed Theo the invitation, he scowled at me, not understanding why they expected him to attend. Apparently, he intended to be a silent investor—emphasis on the *silent* part.

I wasn't about to let him out of it that easily. Besides the fact that I was ecstatic to see my friends after being gone for so long, I was excited to show Theo more of my hometown. He barely left the hotel the last time he visited, and it was time we changed that. As much as it shouldn't matter, I wanted him to love Saint Stephen's Lake as much as I did.

Just as I started to make a mental list of things to show him,

Devyn stormed into my room, her arms crossed around her chest. "You can't be serious."

"What?" I asked, toying with my cuticles. *Maybe* I had also implied that Devyn would be coming with me, even though she hadn't been to the lake in over five years.

"Don't play dumb with me, Calla," she sneered. "I just got an email from Alex's boyfriend, filling me in on all the details of this weekend."

I shrugged. "You and I both know you need a weekend away. Besides, Alex is my best friend, so according to sister law, you need to support her too. This soft opening means the world to her. Please come with me?"

She tapped her long nails against her arm, suddenly looking a lot like our mother. I didn't dare voice that out loud, not if I wanted to see tomorrow. After a long stare down, Devyn finally rolled her eyes. "Fine."

"Really?" I squeaked, jumping up to hug her.

"But I have ground rules." She pulled back to look me in the eye. "We go to the lodge, and that's it. No Isadora, no wandering through town, and sure as fuck no Lost Tavern."

I gasped and dramatically hit my chest as if she'd struck me. "That is so rude. You know I always need a burger when I'm home."

Devyn narrowed her eyes at me. "Fine. *You* go. But you better bring back one for me too." She tapped on her phone. "Did you order a car yet?"

"Not yet." I shifted on my feet. "I was thinking...what if we drove up with Theo?"

"Your boss?"

"Yeah..." I tried not to give away anything. I knew I had to tell Devyn what was happening *eventually*, but right now, I was living in my blissful ignorance, pretending that nothing could go wrong. The moment I told her, she'd voice all the reasons it was a bad idea. No, thank you. I wanted to hold onto this moment a little bit longer.

"He's heading up for the weekend too, and you know he's got a couple of nice cars hidden away." I toyed with a sweater on my bed, avoiding her stare. "It could be fun."

Devyn narrowed her eyes at me, trying to decipher the true meaning of my words. Maybe it was a bad idea to put all three of us in an enclosed space, but I didn't care. I wanted more time with Theo.

It had been almost two weeks since our incredible weekend together, and we'd barely gotten any time together since. I'd spent a couple of nights at his place while Devyn was pulling all-nighters at her office, but even then, he'd been so stressed about the partners coming that we talked more about work than anything else.

As much as I admired his work ethic, I was also greedy for more of his undivided attention. Maybe this weekend would give us that chance, away from the city and all the pressure of hiding our relationship at work.

Devyn shook her head, walking back through my door. "I hope you know what you're doing there."

"PLEASE EXPLAIN to me again why you're picking all the music when this is my car?"

Theo tilted his head, smirking at me as he pulled off onto the highway. I shrugged. "It's not my fault you have horrible taste in music. Even for an old man, this stuff is terrible."

"It's classic rock," Theo argued.

"A nice way of saying *old*."

"Children," Devyn called from the backseat, lifting an AirPod from her ear. "Some of us are trying to nap back here.

Both of you admit that you have terrible taste and drive in silence for a while."

I rolled my eyes as Theo chuckled. Somehow, I'd convinced both Theo and Devyn to take Friday off so we could get to the Lodge a little earlier. The sooner I got to Alex, the better I would feel. I could only imagine what Cole was going through. Even though we all knew Alex would say yes, it had to be nerve-wracking.

When the three of us loaded into Theo's SUV this morning, I wasn't sure what to expect, but we'd struck up a comfortable camaraderie. Devyn and Theo got along well, bonding over their mutual workaholic tendencies. Seeing Theo laugh with the only member of my family I liked made his place in my heart solidify a little bit more.

I turned, staring out of the window, wondering if I should try to get some sleep as well. We were only about an hour into our hours-long drive, and from here, it would mostly be empty highways and stretches of land, but I was too excited to close my eyes. It was sad. I'd spent years away from the city and never really missed it. Take me out of Saint Stephen's Lake for a couple of months, and it was like I was missing a limb.

"What's going on in your head over there?" Theo asked, keeping his eyes on the road.

"I miss home," I admitted. "Don't get me wrong; New York is great, but it doesn't fit quite right—like wearing a shoe that's two sizes too small."

"Do you think you'll move back?"

He asked the question casually, but I could see his grip tighten on the steering wheel. I'd been living moment to moment for so long that I never gave it much thought, but the idea of leaving Theo behind suddenly soured my stomach. "I don't know," I answered honestly. "Part of me would love to. But I also don't know if I could."

"What do you mean?"

"I've always loved being at the lake," I answered, turning back toward the window. "But I don't know if it's where I see my future. So many of my memories are at the Isadora. If I couldn't be a part of that..." I shook my head, cutting off that line of thought. "Let's just say I'd be starting all over again. And considering I'm doing that right now, I'm not looking to do it again so quickly."

"I remember that feeling. I left home as soon as I graduated high school," Theo quietly admitted. "Got my diploma, and the very next day, I packed up all my stuff and started my college courses early. I never even thought about going back."

"Really?" I asked, turning toward him. "What about your mom?"

He chuckled. "She was all for it. My mom wanted me to have every opportunity. She risked a lot to come to America. She was barely an adult herself, but she sacrificed everything to make sure I had the best life possible." He cleared his throat, twisting his hands on the steering wheel. "Every time I reach a new goal, it's because of her."

"You miss her."

"I do." Theo's voice was tight. "Every day. I hate that I wasn't there for her at the end, but I hope she's proud of every-thing I've accomplished."

"I think she is."

He turned, smiling softly at me. "One thing I know for sure? She would have loved you. She always liked calling me out when she thought my head got too big."

"Oh, so all the time?" I chuckled.

I reached out and took his hand, letting the comfortable silence take over, not caring if Devyn saw. So much of Theo made sense now, knowing more about his mother and how hard she had worked to prove a good life for him. Clearly, to him, it was a debt he'd never be able to repay.

I wondered what that was like to have a parent support your dreams, to give up everything to ensure you could lead whatever life you wanted. I hadn't spoken to my mother in *months*, and while part of me missed her, there was an even larger piece that felt relieved, as if a weight had been lifted off my chest. No more bowing down to her commands, no more fear of saying the wrong thing and being cut off.

Theo exhaled slowly. "All of that to say, I don't have much experience with the concept of home. But if something calls to your heart, don't ignore it." He squeezed my hand. "You are tenacious, Calla. If you decide you want something, the world better get out of your way."

I looked down at our joined hands, at how perfectly they fit together. Theo had no idea, did he? That home had been a foreign concept to me until he crashed into my life. And while I'd always loved Saint Stephen's Lake, I was starting to realize that I'd be happy anywhere, as long as I got to be at Theo's side.

And that scared me most of all.

TWENTY-SIX

Theo

After we settled in at the Fox Creek Lodge, Calla ran off to surprise Alex, and Devyn locked herself in her cabin, citing a work-related emergency. Left to my own devices, I decided to take a look around the property to see what my money had helped develop.

I'd only seen a few pictures from before the renovations started, but it was easy to see how much blood, sweat, and tears Alex and Cole had poured into this place. Each of the twelve cabins were pristine, a well-blended mix of rustic and luxury. Holding up the key to cabin nine, I walked inside, immediately taken aback by the craftsmanship. The cabin itself was small, only made up of a cozy sitting area, a king-sized bed, and a bathroom to the side, but the elements instantly soothed me. The walls were made of natural wood plank, and all the linens were white and airy. The back wall had been blown out, covered in a large picture window that offered a view of the surrounding forest. Even with other cabins surrounding mine, it felt isolated, but in the best way.

I forced myself out of my cabin, resisting the urge to scour my inbox and check in on the office. While the rest of the guests settled in, I took a walk to the main lodge, stopping to admire the view of the lake from the bottom of the hill.

Staring out at the picturesque scene, I closed my eyes, inhaling the clean mountain air. I'd lived in cities all my life and preferred the hustle to the quiet, but I was starting to understand the appeal of places like this. As I turned to face the lodge, I found Calla coming out, a broad smile on her face. To my delight, it only got wider when she saw me staring at her.

"Running for the hills already?" Calla asked, bumping my hip as she walked to my side.

"Not yet," I answered. "Give me a few more days, and that might be a different story. Did Alex like the surprise?"

"She was very excited." Calla grinned up at me. "Although I think she's starting to suspect something is going on. I had to bite my lip so hard to keep from telling her." She pulled my arm out, checking the time on my watch. "I only have to keep the secret for...five more hours. How hard can that be?"

"For you? Excruciating," I chuckled. "Let's get out of here, keep you from blurting out Cole's plans."

"I don't know..." Calla glanced between the lodge and the gravel driveway. It was as if she had to physically stop herself from heading into town.

I rolled my eyes, taking her hand without thinking. "C'mon, we'll be back in plenty of time."

"Are you sure?" She chewed on her lower lip.

"Dinner's not for a couple more hours. Alex can manage without you for a little bit, and we both know I saw the notes you were taking on your phone about places I needed to visit." I paused, pulling her to my side. Even though there were other people around, I couldn't bring myself to care. She stared up at me in surprise, her honey-colored eyes searching all my features. Before I could think any better of it, I leaned down and kissed the shock from her lips.

"Theo…" she said, trying to sound serious but failing miserably.

"I know." I wrapped my arm around her waist. "But I've missed you, Calla. Even with you right next to me most days, I've missed being able to kiss you when I want, to hold you like I'm always dying to." I pulled back to look into her eyes. "So just indulge me for a few more seconds, okay?"

She nodded, finally relaxing into my embrace. As more people decided to venture out to check out the view, I reluctantly released her, taking her hand instead. Leading her to my SUV, I opened the door for her and helped her climb inside. The second she climbed into the passenger seat, Calla grabbed the aux cord without asking for permission. I didn't mind, loving that she made herself comfortable in my space, in my world. I wanted more of it.

Driving around the minuscule town, she pointed out all the buildings and told stories of the various other residents. It was insane to me how much history she knew and how many of her former neighbors she could name on sight. Even after a decade in LA, I didn't know any of the people who lived near me. Neighbors came and went, and my life remained the same. For a long time, that was the exact way I wanted to live my life.

But the idea of making connections and creating roots wasn't as terrifying as it used to be. Even when I was married, I was so resistant to change. Natalie had moved into my home, learned my routines, followed my lead on most things, and all I gave her was my last name and heartache.

As we hit one of the main roads, Calla let out a little squeak. "Turn! Turn here."

I followed her directions mindlessly, letting her lead me to a small restaurant at the edge of a strip mall. From the outside, it looked like nothing. All that I could see was the front door and a small window with etched with a logo.

"The Lost Tavern?" I read aloud, waiting to see if this was some elaborate prank.

When I pulled into a parking space, Calla hopped out of the car, barely waiting for me before barreling inside. After following her, I pushed the front door of the restaurant open, finding her in a tight embrace with an older blonde woman.

She pulled back, placing her hands on Calla's face. "Gosh, look at you. I'd heard you weren't coming, but I told Curt there was no way you'd miss this."

"Of course I was coming," Calla giggled, pulling the woman in for another hug. "Can you believe the *surprise* is happening?" She wiggled her eyebrows along with the word.

"About damn time," her friend chuffed. "Told that boy months ago he needed to give her a ring." Her eyes found me waiting behind Calla. "And who is this?"

"Oh!" Calla squawked, turning around to pull me forward. "This is Theo, my..." Her nose scrunched as she tried to find an appropriate label. "My friend. He's friends with Cole, too." *Debatable.* "He drove up with Devyn and me."

"It's lovely to meet you." She reached out her hand. "Marta Anders. I hope you're taking care of our girl here. We've known Calla since she was in diapers."

"Don't you dare."

"Oh, hush, you." Marta swatted her arm. "All these kids are like our family, so if you ever want to see some incriminating photos, I have the best ones."

"Look at the time," Calla joked, looking down at her empty wrist. "We really should get going."

"Don't even think about it." Marta pushed us toward a bar-top table. "I promise, no more embarrassing tales. Let me feed you." She passed me a menu, not bothering to hand one to Calla. Marta's eyes dropped down for a moment. "Devyn came with you too?"

Calla's lip tucked between her lips, but she reluctantly nodded. Marta exhaled slowly, and a sadness flitted over her features. There was a story here, one I was not privy to, but I could tell that Calla felt uncomfortable.

"What would you recommend?" I asked, needing to break up the tension.

"Everything," Calla answered, smiling back at Marta. "You already know what I want."

"Smothered burger, hold the mushrooms." Marta chuckled. "What about you, handsome?"

There were too many options to choose from. I shook my head, holding it out to Marta. "I'll take what Calla's having, thank you."

As Marta darted to the back to put in our order, I leaned in toward Calla. "Please tell me the food here is edible."

"You bite your tongue," Calla tsked. "This will be the best burger you've ever had, I promise."

I almost snorted. "Calla, you do realize we live in New York, right? Walking distance to some of the best Michelin-starred restaurants?"

"I said what I said."

I smirked back at her. "Care to make things interesting?"

MY STOMACH ACHED as we left the Lost Tavern and headed back into the heart of the town. Calla must have felt the same, because she let out a loud groan next to me. "How could you let me eat that much?"

"Let you?" I scoffed, hitting the blinker to turn back onto Main Street. "If I've learned one thing working with you, no one *lets* you do anything."

"Truth." She nuzzled her head on the passenger seat. "But you need to admit that I was right, that I won our bet."

"And have you decided what you want from me yet?"

Calla pursed her lips, tapping them like she had to think hard about what prize to claim. With every touch, the need to claim her got stronger, wanting to fuck that pretty little pout the way I knew she liked.

"Not yet," she answered. "But next time we come up, remind me to get the wings. They're *almost* as good as the burgers."

My hands tightened on the steering wheel as my thoughts fixated on one little word in her statement. *We.* When we'd be back here. It was ridiculous how much I liked the sound of it, imagining long weekends spent just like this with Calla on my arm. Maybe it was a pipe dream, imagining a life this simple. With the partners coming soon, if the visit went well, there was a strong chance I'd be promoted. And with that, there would be even more work to be done. As it was, my phone had almost broken with the amount of texts pouring in while we were eating. I wouldn't know exactly how many, however, because about halfway through our meal, Calla snatched it away from me, putting it on silent and stuffing it in her purse.

"I'm holding this thing hostage." She smirked. "You've survived one weekend without jumping every time it rang. You'll survive this one, too. Besides, if any emergencies come up, Jack knows to call my cell now."

I hated to admit it, but she was right. That weekend had been the first time I turned my cell off in a long time, and as surprising as it was, the world didn't stop. When I got back to work on Monday, everything was still operating as it should, and any client concerns were handled that day.

A wave of guilt consumed me for a moment, thinking of how

many times I refused to put my phone away before. Dinner with Natalie, marriage counseling sessions. For fuck's sake, I was texting about a contract at my mother's funeral. Work-life balance was never my strong suit, but for Calla, I was willing to try.

I needed to try.

She motioned up ahead to an empty spot along the street. "Stop here, and we can walk around for a bit. Help my stomach from exploding."

I swiftly pulled the SUV to the parking space, shuffling to the other side to hold the door open for Calla. She took my extended hand, smiling brightly up at me. "Look at you, Sunshine. Who knew you were such a gentleman."

"You bring it out in me, beautiful."

She tucked her chin, trying to hide the flush on her cheeks. I wanted to run my thumb along it to trace its shape, to see how far the blush ran, explore the expanse of her bare skin with either my fingers or tongue. At this point, I didn't care which one. If we didn't get some time alone soon, I wouldn't be responsible for my actions.

Calla pulled me down Main Street, leading me into different shops and greeting almost everyone we met by their full name. She knew all their stories and which questions to ask. She was the most genuine person I'd ever met, and it was clear that this town loved her. It almost made me jealous, made me long for a place that never existed.

However, everything came to a screeching halt when we reached the florist shop. As soon as the door flung open, Calla's face paled, and she took a step closer to me. Instinctively, I reached out my hand, capturing hers, not caring who saw us. But the whole time, Calla stared at the woman leaving the shop carrying a bright bouquet. Her voice wobbled a little when she called out, "Mom?"

The woman froze, staring at Calla like she was a ghost.

Upon further inspection, it was no shock that these two women were related. It was like looking at Calla in thirty years. The same red hair that haunted my dreams was streaked with shades of gray. The same whiskey-colored eyes were lined with creases.

"Calla." Her mother opened her mouth like she wanted to say more before dropping her gaze down to our joined hands. I started to disentangle our hands, but Calla held firm. Her mother let out a disappointed sigh. "What are you doing here?"

"Does it matter?" Calla said, trying to appear strong, but I could hear the hitch in it, feel the way her hand trembled in mine. "It's not like you have any interest in seeing me."

"I told Devyn that I expected you–"

"At your dinner party. Right," Calla scoffed. "Because now you want to be a family? What is it? David needs to impress some clients, some deal he needs help securing?"

Her mother arched a brow. "Don't make a scene. If you had something to say to me, you could have called."

"So could you."

Sensing the tension echoing off each of them, I held out my hand. "Theo Ayad, Mrs. Winters. I believe we met last year when I was staying at the Isadora."

"Yes, you were with Mr. Rice's party." Her eyes narrowed at me. "How do you know my daughter?"

"We work together," I answered. "I suppose I should thank you for that."

"Excuse me?"

I smiled, but it held no warmth. After bearing witness to the damage this woman had done to her daughters, I had zero desire to play nice, not when it was her voice in the back of Calla's mind, telling her that she wasn't enough. "Your daughter is one of the smartest, hardest-working people I've ever met, and you were too stubborn to notice. So, yes, thank you for refusing to see her worth." I held Calla's hand a little tighter. "Because now I have the chance to make sure she never forgets it."

With that, I spun Calla around, leading her back to the car. She met me step for step, not saying a single word. A single tear ran down her cheek, and it hit me—I fucked up. Shit. The words poured out of me, and not once did I think that it would affect Calla. After a few more steps, I could apologize in private. I'd do whatever it took to erase that look from her face.

As soon as we were in the car, I turned, an apology already waiting on the tip of my tongue.

But Calla had other plans.

I could barely comprehend it when she launched herself from her seat, sealing her lips over mine. After a moment, she pulled back, resting her forehead against mine. "I've never had someone stand up for me like that. Thank you, Theo."

The relief crashed through me, hating that Calla had felt so alone before now. I took her hand, bringing her knuckles to my lips. "You never have to thank me for that. If I have my way, you'll never have to deal with anything alone again."

TWENTY-SEVEN

"Are you fucking serious?"

Alex's eyes widened almost comically, leaning against the outside wall of the main lodge for support. As her hands flew to her mouth, my gaze immediately darted to her new ring. I had to give Cole credit. The beautifully set diamond band looked like it always belonged on her finger.

Maybe I should have felt bad about pulling my best friend away from her engagement celebration, but I needed to talk to her. All night, my day with Theo had been playing through my head, his words on an endless loop. My entire life, I wanted a partner at my side, someone who'd stand up to my mother on my behalf. While I was capable of fighting my own battles, I was exhausted from having to fight her. Theo stepped in without being asked, saying exactly what I needed to counteract her. If I wasn't falling for him before, that would have pushed me over the edge.

Alex stared at me, trying to read the emotions on my face. "I can't believe you're dating Theo. *Theo.*" She shook her head. "I have to say, I did not see this coming when you started working for him."

"Neither did I!" I protested. "This was not part of my plan, Alex. It's not like I woke up and said, you know what sounds like a great life choice? Developing feelings for my older, much more jaded boss, especially considering I could get fired for it." I groaned, dropping my head into my hands. "It just kind of...happened."

Alex laughed. "Yeah, I know exactly what you mean." She took my hand, leading me over to a porch swing tucked in the corner where no one else could see. She sat down at my side, pulling me into a sideways hug. "Are you in love with him?"

"I'm getting there," I answered quietly. "But there's a part of me that's holding back. And as much as I tell myself it's because of work, I think it's more than that."

"What do you mean?"

"I keep wondering: when will he realize he's making a mistake? That I'm not worth the risk to his career. Things are going great with us right now, but what if this is all we're meant to be? Stolen moments away from the rest of the world?"

"What does Theo say about it?"

"He says he wants to be with me," I sighed. "But it doesn't change the facts. Something is going to have to give. I can't be his girlfriend *and* his assistant. Eventually, we're going to have to decide. And as much as I want him to choose me, I also don't want to be his downfall. He's worked too hard to lose it all for me." My lower lip started to quiver. "I have so many questions, Alex, and I'm petrified that it's going to scare him away. The guy hasn't been in a relationship since his marriage imploded. What if this is all too much?"

"You're never going to know unless you ask," Alex said. "Sure, he might not be able to overcome his fear, but it's better to know that now, before you fall any deeper." She held me a little closer. "But honestly...I don't think you have anything to be worried about."

"What do you mean?"

"The man looks at you like you are his world, Calla. You need to give him a chance to prove your fears wrong."

"Easy to say," I say, tucking my head onto her shoulder. "You got one of the good ones."

"Are you forgetting how much we had to work through to get to this point? Hell, you could have stuck a neon sign over my head, and I wouldn't have admitted my feelings." She reached out, lacing my hand with hers. "Sometimes, the only way to get past your fear is to push through. You taught me that."

As I weighed her words, a brisk knock came from the other side of the porch before Cole came closer. "Hate to interrupt, but do you mind if I steal my fiancée for a little bit?"

"Ugh," I teased. "If you have to. But I demand joint custody."

"You always know I loved you first." Alex pulled me in for a tight hug. "But I think there's someone else you should talk to tonight."

Cole arched his brow but didn't comment. He just took Alex's hand, pulling her in for a light kiss when she pressed up against his chest. He nodded at me. "Do me a favor, Calla. Get Theo out of his cabin more tomorrow? The guy already called it a night. God knows he's probably buried himself in emails."

"Not likely," I laughed. "I took his laptop charger."

"Cold, Winters," Cole chuckled.

As they walked back inside, I considered joining them. It'd be nice to spend some more time with everyone. I'd missed the town more than I thought I would, and it felt amazing to be surrounded by so much love and comfort. But with Devyn hiding out in her cabin all day and Theo leaving without saying goodnight, I couldn't bring myself to go back in.

I walked back to my cabin, trying not to let my thoughts run away from me. It was tempting to go to Theo and tell him all about my insecurities, to tell him that I was falling for him and that I hoped like hell he'd be there to catch me.

Peeking over my shoulder, I glanced at his assigned cabin, frowning when I saw all the lights were off. Disappointment furrowed deep in my chest, hating that his absence left such a gaping wound in my heart.

But I didn't get a chance to dwell on it for too long, because when I approached my cabin, I found Theo sitting on my front step. I sucked in a sharp breath when his dark eyes met mine, so full of longing and lust that my knees shook.

"Theo?' I called out.

"I believe we have a score to settle."

FROM THE MOMENT the cabin door closed behind us, a heaviness filled the room. A heady mix of lust and need tried to take me out at the knees, my body willing me to throw myself into Theo's arms. I needed him, every part of my body practically singing with it. But I also needed answers, ones that could potentially change the way he looked at me. And while I hated the idea of things shifting between us, I couldn't keep living in this bubble forever.

Theo leaned in to kiss me, but I placed my hand on his chest to stop him. His eyes widened in surprise. "Calla, everything okay?"

"I don't know." I reached down to take his hand. "I've just been thinking, and I..." I sighed and looked up at the ceiling. "How do you feel about me?"

"What?" Theo asked.

"I need to know how you feel about me. You say you choose me, that you're in this, but I need to know what that means. Is it for now? Is it until someone finds out about us? Or is this thing between us real?" I inhaled slowly, hating the shakiness in my throat. "Because I'm falling for you, Theo. And it scares the hell out of me–"

Theo stopped my thoughts with his thumb on my lip. He tilted my head down, forcing me to meet his eyes. "How could you think I'd settle for anything less than all of you, Calla? Being with you is the most real thing in my life." He smiled slowly at me before dropping his forehead to mine. "You're not the only one scared, you know. I'm terrified of how much I care about you, how deeply you've carved yourself into my heart already. Because it only started working again when you showed up, Calla. I'm pretty sure if I lose you, the damn thing will never work again."

"You mean that?" I looked up at him, tears clinging to my lashes.

"Every word, beautiful." Theo gripped the back of my neck, bringing my lips to his. "I will never be perfect. I work too much, take on too much stress, and lord knows I'm not great about keeping my anger in check. Those things may never completely go away, but I promise to try every day. For you, Calla." He pulled back to look me in the eyes. "Ever since you first walked into my office, I've been yours, beautiful. Please tell me you're mine."

"I'm yours," I whispered, crushing my mouth to his. Theo wasted no time, lifting me so my legs could curl around his waist. He pressed me up against the door, his erection growing against my stomach. It was almost comical how much I wanted this man, how much I needed his touch after a few weeks of space. It was like he was the air I needed to breathe, only able to exhale now that I was in his arms.

Theo's lips drifted down my neck, slowly languishing my collarbone and chest with his mouth. As soon as he reached the neck of my dress, I heard a loud rip, the fabric now pooling off me. I smacked him in the shoulder. "I liked that dress."

"I'll buy you a new one," Theo smirked against my skin. "And when it gets in my way, I'll destroy that one too."

"Seems like an endless cycle."

"Yes, it does," he chuckled. "In fact, when we're alone, you probably shouldn't wear anything at all—at least nothing you're fond of."

I chuckled as he moved us to the bed, laying me out in front of him. As I pulled off the remnants of my dress, Theo palmed himself through his trousers, staring at me like I was his prey. He sighed, taking a step forward to massage my thighs. "I have to admit, beautiful, I'm losing control here. I want to take you nice and slow, but I don't know if I can hold back tonight."

"Don't," I whispered, sitting up with my elbows to meet his eyes. "Fuck me, Theo. Mark me, own me. Show me I'm yours."

TWENTY-EIGHT

Theo

"Show me I'm yours."

The words had barely left Calla's lips, and I was on her, needing to make her feel as desperate as me. Fuck this distance nonsense. I wanted her in my bed every night, to wake her up with my tongue between her legs every morning. Her taste was quickly becoming an addiction I never wanted to break.

With her dress torn in half at my feet, all that remained on her lithe body was a set of matching maroon lace bra and panties. I toyed with the lace around the crest of her breast, brushing my finger over her peaked nipple. "Did you wear these just for me, Calla?"

"Yes," she breathed, arching her back to deepen my touch.

"Not yet, beautiful." I dragged my finger in light circles across her skin. "I promised that I'd show you you're mine, and I will. But right now, I need you writhing and desperate for me."

"What?" Calla squeaked, shifting to try and sit up.

My hand splayed against her stomach and stopped her, anchoring her in place. The other grabbed her wrists, placing them above her head. "Keep them there," I demanded, leaning down to nip her lower lip. "If anything is too much, tell me to stop. Everything ends the moment you say so."

"I understand, *sir*," Calla added with a smirk.

Fuck, that word would be my undoing. My lips found hers immediately, but there was nothing delicate about this kiss. It was primal, all need and pure adoration at this woman's trust in me. But before I could lose my entire mind, I lifted back, removing my belt and bringing it back to Calla's wrists. I twisted it around her delicate skin, checking that it wasn't cutting off circulation before wrapping the other end around the footboard of the bed. "Too tight?"

Calla shook her head, pure lust clouding her own eyes. "No, it's good."

She must have thought I was about to resume my touch, but instead, I tugged off my tie, running it through my fingers as I stared down at the girl at my mercy. "Now, beautiful, do you remember the first time I had you like this?" She stared at me, confusion furrowing her brow. I chuckled, continuing as I moved back over her, "You told me to beg for a taste. And I did. I would beg a thousand times if it meant you'd come on my tongue. But tonight, the only one begging will be you."

She pulled her lip between her teeth, and for a moment, I was afraid I'd gone too far, that she wouldn't be able to handle my darker urges. But instead of nerves, all I saw reflected at me was excitement in those honey-hued irises.

"This is going over your eyes now, beautiful. But remember, any time you want to stop, it comes off immediately."

She nodded as I slipped it over her head, tightening it only enough so she couldn't peek at me. As soon as her eyes were covered, I leaned back, taking her in like a masterpiece. Fuck the paintings that hung on my walls. This was a sight I'd pay any amount of money to see every day. Calla was my salvation, my heart, and for tonight, every inch of her would be mine. But as much as I wanted to take her right now, patience was going to play off in the long run when she was screaming my name and clenching around my cock.

Shedding the rest of my clothing, I climbed back over her, letting my lips explore her chest and breasts. Between kisses, I nipped at her flesh then blew on the same patch to soothe it. By the time I finally brought my mouth around her peak, she was practically squirming underneath me, desperately trying to add more friction between us.

"Is there something you need, beautiful?"

"God, please touch me, Theo," Calla said, her voice tight and strained. "I'm losing my mind waiting."

"I don't know...." I teased, drifting my lips down her stomach, bypassing where she wanted me. Instead, I focused on her thighs, loving the way they were trembling in anticipation. "I think I've heard better begging."

"Theo, please, I need you to touch me," Calla cried. "Fuck me, lick me, I don't care, as long as you do something, please. Please, Theo."

"That's better, baby," I crooned as I parted her pussy, licking along her seam. Calla's back bucked off the bed, bringing her even closer to me. I chuckled against her sensitive skin. "You really are such a needy little thing, beautiful. You're making a mess all over my sheets."

"Theo..." she cried out as my tongue flicked her clit right as my finger entered her.

"Relax, baby, and I'll take care of you. Just remember to breathe."

Without another word, I dove back in, letting my tongue explore every part of her, mapping out all the moves that made her ignite. It didn't take long for her to start clenching around my finger, but I wasn't finished with her, not yet. Another finger joined the first as I sucked her clit, savoring her essence. Only a few more strokes of my tongue, and Calla came while screaming my name loud enough to wake the whole campground. It only made my dick harder. I kept working her through her release, not wanting to waste a single drop.

Once her breathing evened out, I lifted myself, kissing her lips to let her taste the same sweetness as me. She chuckled as I leaned back. "God, what did I do to deserve you?"

I reached down, needing to see her eyes. Her soft, satiated smile shot right to my heart, and I knew right then I was in love with this girl. It wasn't the kind of love I felt before, a natural progression, slowly building until you realized you were in it. No, falling for Calla was more like being struck by lightning, igniting every fiber of your being and knowing your life would never be the same. I'd never recover from this woman, nor would I want to.

"Please, Theo. Please fuck me." Calla shifted to reach her lips to mine. "I need to feel you inside me."

"Greedy girl." I smirked, reaching up to release her wrists. I pulled them to my lips, kissing the reddened skin. "But you need to earn this cock, baby. Get on your knees and suck me. Take all of me. Show me how desperate you are to come again."

Calla didn't even hesitate, twisting until she was kneeling in front of me. With me sitting back on my haunches, she placed her hand around my length, twisting it a couple of times before her mouth descended. *Fuck.* Her tongue swirled around my tip, and I almost blew right there. But when she took me deeper, letting me hit the back of her throat, all the thoughts left my mind. All I could think of was the goddess in front of me, sucking my dick like it was all the nourishment she'd ever need. And when she took my hand, placing it on top of her head? I said a silent prayer to whoever sent her my way, unsure what I'd done to earn this beautiful girl.

As she continued her movements, it was getting harder and harder to maintain control. After a few more bobs of her head, I pulled her off me. "Need to come inside of you, baby. Another night, I'll paint the back of your throat, but tonight, I want to feel you pulsing around me when I come."

"Fuck yes." But when I twisted to grab a condom, she stopped me. "I'm on the pill, and I was tested when I moved to the city."

"What are you saying?"

"I want you bare," Calla said. "Nothing between us, Theo. If you've been tested–"

"I was," I answered her. "Three months ago. I haven't been with anyone since. All good on my end." I lifted my hand, brushing my thumb along her cheek. "Are you sure?"

She nodded. "More than anything. I want you, Theo. Every piece of you."

That was all the reassurance I needed. I lifted her into my lap, lowering her onto my dick, inch by inch. I slowly stretched her, raking my nails down her back as she struggled to take all of me.

When I was buried to the hilt, our eyes met, pure need darting between us. I originally planned to fuck her hard, but with the way she was staring at me? It was almost impossible. I wanted her in my arms, wanting to hold her close as she fell apart. I'd always heard about people making love, and honestly, I thought it was a myth that there could be anything between two people other than carnal desire. But tonight? I felt it with Calla. While we both needed this release, it was about so much more between us.

When she started to fall apart, Calla placed her hand on top of my heart, as if she knew the thing only beat for her. "Come with me," she whispered, her lips meeting mine. "Come with me."

As if I had any other choice. When it came to Calla, I'd blindly follow her wherever she led, especially when she was gliding along my cock like she was made for it. As soon as her walls started to constrict around me, I felt my spine start to tingle, and I was crashing alongside her.

When we finally came down from our highs, we collapsed against the pillows, grinning at each other. Calla reached up, tracing the lines of my face with her forefinger. "Thank you," she whispered.

"For what, beautiful?" I asked, turning so I could hold her even closer.

"Being you," she said. "Even when you're being rough, I feel safe with you." she nuzzled against my chest. "And for caring about me, all of me. You make me feel like I'm enough."

I tilted her chin to make her meet my eyes. "You are more than enough, Calla. And I'll spend forever trying to get you to see that too."

THE NEXT MORNING, I woke up feeling like everything was right in the world. With my girl in my arms and the quiet country around me, I'd slept better than I had in years. Every moment I spent in this town, the more I saw its appeal. I'd never be able to live here full-time, but I could get used to weekends like this.

Kissing Calla's cheek, I climbed out of bed, my stomach grumbling and in desperate need of coffee. I opened the door, sparing one last look at Calla before I walked out into the summer heat. Hopefully, she'd sleep a bit longer, and if not, I hoped returning with fresh coffee would make her forgive me for leaving her in bed alone.

I walked into the main building of the resort, letting my nose lead me toward food. I was surprised when I stepped inside and found Adam at one of the tables, sipping from a mug and staring out the window. I cleared my throat as I came closer, waiting to see if he even acknowledged me.

Our last conversation had been tense, and he'd been ignoring my calls and texts since then. I hated this rift between us, hated that he was floundering and I was unable to help.

Adam looked up and nodded his head, motioning for me to join him.

I sighed as I dropped into the seat next to him. "Didn't know if you'd want to talk to me. Thought you might still be pissed."

"Nah," Adam answered, not looking at me, instead keeping his gaze trained on the view. "If I was, watching you try to play corn hole last night would have killed the last of it. How in the hell are you so bad at it?"

"City kid, remember?" I chuckled.

"Forgot," he sighed. "Look, Theo, I know you mean well, but right now, I just need to take a step back. I've got a lot going on in my head, and being on set..." Adam sighed. "That's the last thing I need. I know this fucks with your job—"

"I don't give a shit about that." I shook my head. "I just want to make sure you're good, Adam. You haven't seemed like yourself in months. I'm not going to push unless you really need it, but you need to know I'm here for you. Not as your agent, but as your friend."

Adam nodded, keeping his eyes trained low. "Thanks, Theo." He sighed, toying with the cup in his hand. "It's just—"

"*Thank fuck*," a voice came from the other side of the dining room. We both looked up to see Grayson Anders rushing toward us. "Theo, I've been calling your phone all goddamn night! I need to talk to you."

I glanced back at Adam. "Can it wait?"

Adam waved me off. "Go help Gray out. There's not much you can do for me anyway." He nodded at me. "But if I need to talk, I know where to find you."

"Make sure you do," I said sternly. "If you keep going radio silent on me, I'm going to show up at your house and drag you out into the world."

Adam chuckled. "You can try."

As I walked away from Adam, I looked at Gray, trying to figure out what I was walking into. The man looked like shit. His long, dark blond hair was wild, and his eyes were blood-shot red. If I didn't know any better, I would have sworn the man was coming back from a bender. He pulled me into a side room, one set up like a small sitting room with a library against the wall.

I took a seat in one of the chairs while Gray paced the room, muttering to himself. I leaned forward. "Anders, I'm here to help, but you're going to have to tell me what's going on."

He paused, crossing his arms as he looked at me. "I need you to get me out of my contract."

"You want to retire?" That made me stand up. The man was in the prime of his career, likely to have his pick of teams when his contract expired next year. "What the hell is going on, Gray?"

He stared me down, as if weighing how much he wanted to let me in. Well, tough shit. If I was about to risk my neck to get him off his team, then he'd better start trusting me. After a long moment, he ran his hand through his hair. "Fine. But if I tell you, this needs to stay between us and us only."

"Deal."

"I mean it, Theo. You can't tell anyone, not even Calla." His steel gray eyes stared back at me with more determination than I'd ever seen. "*Especially* Calla."

I almost said no, not wanting to keep any secrets from her. Hiding something from her already was a bad plan, and everything in me wanted to say no.

But looking at the desperate man in front of me, I knew that wasn't an option. When he signed his contract with my agency, it became my job to help him, even if it put me in a tight spot.

I nodded. "No one will know. Tell me what's going on."

TWENTY-NINE

Scowling through my windshield, I stared at the building in front of me, waiting for some sort of sign. The clock ticked on my dashboard, boxes sat in the backseat, and yet I was stuck, unable to move out of the driver's seat.

The Isadora looked the same as it always did—pristine and welcoming, an idyllic setting for visitors to our small town. But what once was my home now felt foreign to me, as if a black cloud was shrouding it.

I probably shouldn't have come here. No, I *definitely* shouldn't have come. But so many of my belongings were still inside, probably packed in dusty boxes and hidden in the corner of the storage room. I'd put off grabbing them for so long, knowing that it was the final string tying me to my old home.

But it was time to let go.

I took my first steps in the Isadora's ballroom and broke my arm on the back lawn at thirteen. This was the place where I nursed my first heartache and where I mourned the loss of my grandparents. My dad's ashes were sprinkled on the private beach, the place he'd met my mother for the first time.

My life was built inside the Isadora's walls.

But it didn't mean I'd always belong here.

Trying to distract myself, I checked my phone for the thirtieth time, wondering what had Theo so occupied. When I woke up alone, I figured he'd just gone to find breakfast. Then he texted, saying that he had to deal with a work situation. I expected him to want me to help him through the problem, but he not only didn't ask me, he pointedly told me that he wanted to handle it alone. And maybe it was juvenile of me, but being shut out stung.

My original plan was to borrow Alex's jeep, quickly grab what I needed for the hotel, and get back before anyone saw me. But when I pulled into the parking spot that used to be mine, I stared at the white colonial building, unable to go inside. I had no doubt my mother would be furious if she found me sitting here, especially after our run-in on Friday. That was almost enough to make me climb out of the car.

But as soon as my hand touched the handle, I froze, unable to take that next step. Maybe it was because the last time I'd been inside, a security guard was ushering me out, only a handful of my belongings stuffed into whatever boxes Alex and I could find.

Out of all the things my mother could have done, that was something I never would have expected. I could handle being cut off from the family funds. I could even deal with the distance between us. But the coldness in her eyes when she cast me out of my home? When she locked me out of the place I'd loved the most? That was something I'd never forget.

Someone knocked on my window, and I almost jumped out of my skin, my hand flying to my chest. My friend, Javi smiled on the other side, pointing for me to roll the window down. "Geez," I chuckled. "Hasn't anyone ever told you it's rude to sneak up on someone?"

"About as rude as creeping in the parking lot of your former home," he answered, leaning to kiss me on the cheek. "Or is there another reason you're sitting out here?"

"Guilty." My cheeks flushed with color. "I was going to grab the last of my stuff, but then I got here, and I couldn't get out of the car."

Javi turned to follow my eye-line. As the newly appointed manager of the Isadora, Javi knew better than most how wicked my mother could be. But he was one of the few she liked working with, and I knew since Alex left, she'd been relying on him more and more. She couldn't afford to have him leave, not when all the guests raved about him. I squeezed his hand. "I didn't get enough time to talk to you yesterday. How's Drew?"

"Good." Javi beamed at the mention of his husband. "Busy with work, as usual, but he's been trying to cut back and spend more time at home with me." He smiled conspiratorially at me. "We decided that we're going to start fostering."

I opened the car door, pulling him in for a tight hug. "That's amazing! What made you decide to go that route?"

He shrugged. "We spent a lot of time looking into options, but nothing felt right. It was Drew's idea, actually. He'd talked to one of his friends who's a county caseworker. There's a real need for families, especially with older kids. We went to an information session, and now we're waiting to get our first home visit."

"And you're feeling good about this?"

"Yeah." Javi smiled widely. "I know there's going to be times when it's hard or it hurts like hell, but I want to give these kids some stability, give them a safe place to land, for as long as we have them. I think it'll be good for all of us."

I placed my hand on his arm. "This is going to be *great*, I know it. These kids are going to be lucky to have you guys in their lives." I reached up to hug him again. "If there's anything you need, do not hesitate to call. I want to help in any way I can."

"You could come back to work," Javi chuckled. "Did you hear that Marina quit?"

My jaw dropped open. Marina had been the events coordinator at the Isadora for *years*. Sure, she'd started cutting corners in the last couple of years, and most of her decor options were from the eighties, but she was still a staple on the staff. She'd let me shadow her for years, even allowing me to make suggestions and design different elements for some of our biggest weddings. Even though I knew she did it to make her life easier, it was the first time I got to stretch my wings and try something just because I enjoyed it.

I shook my head. "I had no idea. Who's taking over for her?"

"Good question," Javier grumbled. "Your mother has been interviewing, but in a shock to no one, things haven't been going very well. We're all holding out hope that she's going to come to her senses and hire you back. Everyone knows you were the true talent in that department."

I shook my head. "I have a job, Javi. And even if she asked, I don't think I'd ever want to work for my mother—not after what happened."

He sighed and glanced down at his phone. "I've got to head back in." He leaned in to kiss my cheek. "But think about what I said. Marina leaving left a huge void around here, and we both know you've got the talent to make this opportunity something incredible."

Reluctantly, I nodded my head. "Fine, I'll think about it."

"That's all I ask." Javi waved over his shoulder as he walked toward the employee entrance.

I'd just started pondering his words when my phone dinged in my pocket. I pulled it out, smiling when I saw Theo's name on the screen.

THEO

Change of plans. I have to head back to the city tonight. Can I convince you to come with me? If not, I can set up a car service for you.

CALLA

Not necessary. I'll go with you. I just need to let Alex and Cole know we're heading out early. When do we need to hit the road?

THEO

ASAP.

My stomach sank when I saw that word, and I wondered if this had anything to do with what had kept him all morning. I pulled the car into reverse, sparing one last look at the Isadora in my rearview mirror, leaving it in the past where it belonged.

"ARE you sure I can't convince you to come over?" Theo asked, his lips leaving a trail along my neck.

I shook my head, gently pushing him away. If he kept teasing me like that, I'd mount him right here in front of my building. "Not tonight. I need to shower and get ready for the week. And as much as I'd love to be in your bed, I should also check in on my sister. She left so quickly that I didn't even get a chance to talk about what happened with her case."

"Fine," Theo jokingly groaned. "But promise me you'll come over tomorrow night."

"Who knew you were so needy?" I chuckled as I pressed a light kiss to his lips. "But yes, I'd love to come over."

"Good. Now get your ass inside, beautiful, before I kidnap you for the night."

I rolled my eyes but couldn't help the smile that spread over my face. Even after the long drive, I was still floating, loving every extra moment I got to spend with Theo. I could tell that something was on his mind, but I decided not to pry. He'd tell me what was going on whenever he was ready.

My mind stayed in the clouds as I got into the elevator, humming as it climbed the floors. Hopefully, Devyn would be home, especially given the way she bolted from the party on Saturday. She claimed it was a work emergency, but it seemed like a convenient excuse. From the moment Gray and his parents showed up for the party, she was on edge, sticking close to the exits. She left only an hour later.

I chewed on my lower lip, hating that I'd put Devyn in that position. I should have known the Anderses would make an appearance, given how close they'd grown to Alex over the past few years, but I hadn't expected Gray to be there, not with the season in full swing. It was clear that Devyn didn't expect him either, not with the way her face paled when their eyes connected.

An apology started to form in my mind as I pushed my key into the lock, shoving the door open with my hip. "Honey, I'm ho—"

But the word died on my tongue as I looked into our kitchen where my sister was kissing a shirtless man. It took my brain a moment to catch up and realize who she was holding.

"Jack?"

THIRTY

Calla

Nope. This was not happening. The scene in front of me was like a messed-up nightmare. I must have fallen asleep on the way home, tucked into Theo's passenger seat while he hummed along to an eighties rock song. I was not standing in my apartment, watching my sister make out with Jack, my co-worker. I refused to believe this was my reality.

"Wake up, wake up," I whispered, but when I peeked one of my eyes open again, the view was the same. How the hell had this even happened? As far as I knew, when they met at the gala last month, Devyn and Jack barely interacted. She hadn't mentioned that they connected, much less that they were hooking up behind my back.

With my foot, I slammed the door closed, the sound reverberating through the whole apartment. They jumped apart, Jack hiding behind the kitchen island as Devyn's eyes widened dramatically.

"Calla!" she squeaked out, wiping the back of her hand across her mouth. "I didn't think you were going to be home until tomorrow."

"Clearly," I scoffed. "Theo had a work emergency, so we

decided to come back early." I shook my head, rubbing my hands over my face. "Jack, I already saw you, so you might as well come out now."

He sheepishly stood up, rubbing the back of his neck. "Hey, Calla. How was your weekend?"

"Don't hey Calla, me." I pointed my finger between the two of them. "How long has this been going on?"

"It's not," Devyn said at the same time, as Jack answered, "Almost a month."

Devyn glared at him, her hazel eyes narrowed in annoyance. She sighed, rolling her eyes as she turned back to me. "Technically, we hooked up after the gala, but it was supposed to be a one-time thing. And after this weekend, I just..." She shook her head. "I called Jack, and we talked for a while. But this is just a hook-up. We are not dating."

"Yet," Jack called out from behind her.

"Never," Devyn snapped back. "In fact, you should leave, Jack. There's no reason for you to hang around, especially now that Calla's home."

He chuckled and kissed her on the cheek. "I already warned you, Dev. I'm not giving up that easily."

"Keep dreaming."

"You called me, angel." He winked as he walked back toward her bedroom, emerging a couple of minutes later fully dressed. He waved at both of us as he walked out the door but blew Devyn a kiss as it shut. Her cheeks turned a furious shade of red, and she did everything she could to avoid my stare.

"Seriously?" I said when I was sure Jack was gone. "Out of all the guys in the city, that's the one you decide to sleep with?"

Devyn shook her head, walking back into the kitchen without answering my question. I followed her, "I mean, I'm not trying to be judgmental, but I'm shocked, Devyn. I didn't even think you talked to him, much less–"

"Fucked him?"

I placed my hands over my ears. "Things I do not need to know about!" I lowered them, staring back at my sister. "And this is..."

"Nothing." She shrugged. "It was an itch that needed to be scratched. We're not dating; I've made that clear to him. And trust me, this arrangement suits him just fine."

"So it's going to be an ongoing thing?"

Devyn paused, tapping her fingers on the counter. "I don't know. Maybe. It works for both of us, so why not enjoy it a little longer?" She let out a long breath. "I don't know why any of this matters to you."

I rolled my eyes, moving to the fridge to grab a bottle of water, even though it was tempting to grab the vodka instead. "Because it's something major happening in your life? And that there's someone who might be around our apartment?" I closed the door and leaned against the fridge. "Besides, these are things sisters usually tell each other, Devyn."

"Like you told me you were sleeping with Theo?"

The water almost slipped from my hand. My mouth hung open, unsure what to say. Not telling Devyn was one thing, but downright lying when she asked me about Theo? I couldn't bring myself to do that. "How... Why do you think that?"

"Because Theo told Jack," Devyn crossed her arms. "And then he asked me because he assumed I'd know. Because that's the kind of thing *sisters* share, right?"

"That's different," I muttered, but even as the words left my mouth, I knew they were a lie.

"You could have told me, Calla," Devyn said. "I would have kept your secret, even if I thought it was a bad idea."

"And that's why I didn't tell you," I answered. "I didn't want to hear what a bad idea this was. All my life, Mom's been in my head, questioning every one of my choices. I wanted to do something just for me because it was what I wanted. He makes me so happy, Devyn." I looked back at her. "I didn't want to hear the negative. I didn't want to talk about the potential fallout. I just wanted to hold onto this happiness a little bit longer."

Devyn reached forward, encompassing me in a tight hug. It'd been a long time since my sister held me like this. I'd forgotten how good it felt, like she was taking all my cracking edges and holding them together for me.

"That's why I didn't want to say anything about Jack. I know that you think there's something off about him, but he's fun, Calla. And for the first time, I don't want to second-guess everything. I'm not imagining a future with him. I don't want anything serious. I just want to enjoy my life a little." She chuckled into my shoulder. "And I didn't want you to judge me."

"I'd never judge you." Devyn pulled back, giving me a knowing stare. "Okay, maybe a little, but only because I don't trust Jack. I don't know what it is about him, but there's something there that bothers me. But," I took a deep breath, "I want to know what's happening in your life, Dev. I want to be there for you."

"I want that too."

After several silent moments, Devyn pulled back, brushing the tears away from my eyes. "I can't lie to you and say I think everything will be okay, but if Theo makes you happy, hold onto that for as long as you can. And no matter what happens next, know that I am always in your corner, Calla. I'm not Mom. Yeah, maybe I have some concerns, but as long as you're happy, that's what matters most. You love with your whole heart, and you deserve someone who will love you the same way."

"So do you. And if that's Jack..." I swallowed, trying to ignore all the red flags popping up in my mind. "I don't want to stand in your way either."

"Not all of us get that great love story," Devyn answered sadly, squeezing me once before stepping out of my embrace. "And some of us don't deserve one."

But before I could ask what she meant, she left the room, shutting the door on the rest of our conversation.

Calla

Now that we were no longer hiding our relationship from Devyn, I spent every night at Theo's apartment. We'd developed an odd new routine. During the day, we kept as much distance from each other as possible and then collided together the moment we got behind closed doors. And at first- keeping this secret was exhilarating, like we were living this secret life together. But as the days dragged on, it was starting to wear on me.

I hated that I couldn't hold Theo's hand in public, that I had to weigh every one of my words before I spoke. All I wanted was to dive into this man and not have to worry about the potential fallout.

But that thought would have to wait. With the partners arriving in a few short days, Theo's mind was fixated on making everything perfect. From sun up to sunset, he met with agents, reviewing rosters and ensuring that every contract was top-notch. When he wasn't in meetings, we were working on the week-long itinerary, ensuring that the partners got to experience the best parts of New York. He was burning himself out, and I wasn't far behind. As I shifted in my chair, studying his exhausted expression through the glass wall, a plan started to form in my mind. With a thorough Google search and a shopping list in hand, I walked up to Theo's door and knocked lightly. He smiled when he realized I was the one standing there, but it didn't do much to hide his stress.

It was so hard to stay rooted in my spot, to not go to him and soothe some of his worries. I wanted to hold him, kiss away the stress lining his eyes. A few more hours, and we'd be back in our bubble. As long as he agreed to my plan. Then we could leave the stress at the door for one night. "Do you mind if I head out a little early?"

Theo's brow furrowed. "Everything okay?"

"Yes," I answered quickly. I shifted on my feet, trying to remain in the doorway. "But I think we both could use a night away from this place, so I'm working on a little something for you."

"I can't." Theo shook his head. "You know I want to, Calla-"

"Please, Theo."

Perhaps it was a dirty tactic to use that word with him, knowing there were very few things he'd refuse me if I asked. But I swallowed the guilt because it was for his own good. If he kept going this way, by the time the partners got here, he'd be falling apart. And that wouldn't help anyone.

Theo sighed, running a hand over his face. "Okay, but only because you're the one asking."

I ducked my head to hide my grin. "It'll be worth your while."

I STOOD IN MY KITCHEN, studying everything I'd gathered. Various vegetables and other ingredients lined my counter, prepped and ready to go. I'd already rinsed off all my new cookware after realizing that Devyn only had one pot in her cabinets. I'd even found a cute apron while I was shopping. The only thing missing was Theo. Looking down at my phone, I checked the time. *Fifteen minutes late.* Shaking my head, I opened my text messages, hoping I missed one from him explaining what happened.

ME

Where are you?

But before I could press send, a knock came from the door. When I pulled it open, Theo stood on the other side, holding a brilliant bouquet of varying colors. "I'm sorry," he said. "I got distracted, but I promise, that's it for the night. I'm all yours."

I playfully rolled my eyes. "You're lucky I know how much you're leaving at the office to be here. It means a lot, Theo."

"Anything for you, beautiful."

He ducked his head, giving me a soft kiss before looking around my kitchen. "What is all of this?"

He passed me the flowers and I started rooting through cabinets to try to find a vase. Luckily, there were a couple of dusty ones tucked into the back corner. "I thought we could try that recipe again." I said as I placed the flowers in water. "Moghrabieh, right? I know it's not your mother's recipe, but I found a few online and thought we could tweak them as we go."

Theo turned, staring at my face like he'd never seen me before. For a moment, I worried that I'd crossed a line, inserting myself into a memory that had nothing to do with me. But before I could start to really stress, Theo pulled me into his arms, holding me tight against his chest as he brushed his lips against my forehead. "Thank you."

"Don't thank me yet," I chuckled. "Hopefully, it turns out okay."

Theo nodded, consciously avoiding my stare as he walked

into the kitchen. He looked over the ingredients, sniffing the spices and smiling to himself. There was a glisten in his eyes, one I had never seen before. Even though he rarely spoke about his mother, it was easy to see how much he cared about her and her impact on his life to this day.

I placed the recipe in front of him, and we reviewed it, Theo crossing off things that he knew his mother would never do. Once we started, we seamlessly worked together, Theo prepping the chicken while I finished peeling the onions. As he worked, a calm serenity washed over his expression, one I hadn't seen in a while. Deciding to press my luck, I voiced the question that had been weighing on me. "Can you tell me more about her? About your mom?"

Theo nodded. "She was the strongest woman I ever met. My mother, Rana, came here with little more than a backpack. She created this whole life for us and never asked for anything in return. All she wanted was for me to be happy, to have the American dream."

"She sounds amazing," I said. "And your dad?"

Theo shook his head. "She never spoke about him. Even when I asked, she refused to say much. When she left Lebanon, he stayed. I don't know if it was because he wanted to stay, or if she never gave him a choice, but either way, he's never been a part of my life."

"I'm sorry, Theo."

He shrugged, "I've tried to tell myself it's fine- that it's impossible to miss something you've never had. But I would have liked to know him, even just to understand why she left."

"I know the feeling. My dad died when I was five. I don't remember much about him, just the stories that everyone tells." I glanced up at him. "And sometimes, that hurts worse than not knowing at all, that everyone else has these memories of him, and my mind is basically blank."

Theo stared at me for a long moment. It was full of understanding, empathy for my own loss. It made my heart sing out to him even more, grateful to share these pieces of our past, when we were hopefully building our future together. I shook my head, pushing away the thought. "So, your mom taught you this recipe?"

"Taught is a strong word," Theo chuckled. "When she fled Lebanon, it was in the middle of a civil war. She never talked about what she saw, but it wasn't good. When she came to America, it was her fresh start, and she left a lot of her culture behind. She always said, *we're Americans. That's what matters the most.* She never taught me a lot about her home, but when I was sick or having a bad day, I'd watch her make this stew, and she'd sing songs from her childhood. It was a little piece of comfort for her, even if she didn't necessarily see it that way."

After we finished browning the chicken, we left the broth to simmer before moving to the barstools. Theo clasped his hand around mine, holding tightly. "Thank you for this, Calla. I didn't even know how much I needed it until I got here."

I lifted our joined hands, pressing a kiss to the back of his. "I'm here for you, Theo, even if it means getting you out of your own way."

He leaned forward, brushing an errant hair behind my ear. "I mean it, Calla. And not just for tonight, but for making my life better than I ever dreamed, just by being you."

I ducked my head, not used to earning such high praise. It felt foreign, strange to hear, even after all the times Theo had complimented me. He reached out, lifting my chin so I could meet his eyes. "Don't hide from me, beautiful. I promised I'd never take you for granted, and I meant it."

"I'm not used to this," I answered honestly, vulnerability leaking into my words. "I've wasted so much time floundering because I refused to look beyond what was comfortable." I stared up at him, studying the darkened swirls of his eyes. "But I can't help but be thankful I did, because it led me here."

Theo pulled me in, kissing me as if my lips belonged to him. In truth, they did. He possessed every part of me: my body, my heart, every fiber of me. All I wanted was to fully dive into him, to let go of that last tendril of doubt.

But until our relationship was out in the open, I didn't know if I could.

THIRTY-TWO

The partners' visit arrived faster than I anticipated. On the morning of their arrival, I stood in the lobby, Eloise waiting by my side. We'd spent the last two days ensuring that everything was ready. There was no room for error, not when the man I loved was the one on the line.

The thought snapped a tether inside of me. *Loved.* I loved Theo. It was nothing like what I felt in the past, what I'd assumed love was supposed to feel like. Instead, it was all-consuming, overwhelming, and yet the most natural thing I'd ever experienced.

My heart pounded in my chest when the elevator bell dinged, and the doors opened to reveal a group of well-dressed men and women. I tried to push away my nerves, knowing that Theo was waiting on the other side of the office doors. He wanted to greet them personally and then have us welcome them as they came inside. As he pushed the doors open, our eyes met, and I could feel his nerves. I smiled, trying to pass some of my faith onto him.

Theo paused in front of me. "Allen Wallace, this is Calla

Winters, my assistant. She's the one who keeps the office running smoothly."

I tucked my head, hiding my blush from his praise. I reached out and shook the man's hand, trying to portray as much confidence as possible. "It's nice to meet you, Mr. Wallace. I hope you enjoy your trip."

His smile was warm and genuine, not at all what I was expecting from the CEO of the agency. "Same to you, Miss Winters. We've been looking forward to this trip."

After passing out folders filled with various facts and figures, Theo led the team into the main conference room to review the agenda for the next few days. As I watched them settle into their chairs, I finally exhaled, hating that he was in there alone.

While I stared at my boss, I caught Jack coming over out of the corner of my eye. It was tempting to avoid him, especially after the last time our paths crossed. I'd like to never see that sight again, but for Devyn, I'd try to play nice. It had been years since she even attempted to date, so if Jack was the person who got her to open up, I wouldn't stand in their way.

"What's the verdict?" Jack asked, leaning on his elbows on Eloise's desk. "Are we all heading back to LA?"

"They've been here ten minutes," I answered flatly. "Have some faith in Theo."

"Oh, I have plenty of faith in our fearless leader, but we both know his head hasn't been in the game as much lately." He smirked at me. "Know anything about that, Calla?"

My eyes narrowed at him, not wanting to dignify his comment with a response. Eloise leaned forward. "What do you mean? Are our jobs in jeopardy?" She wrung her hands together. "I just signed a year-long lease. I can't afford to get fired!"

"No one is losing their job," I snapped, staring daggers at

Jack, but he didn't even notice. He was too busy staring into the meeting, as if he wished he was in the room as well. "Theo's got this. As long as we have his back, this visit will be a breeze."

That snapped Jack out of his daze. He smiled at me. "Actually, Calla. I need to have a word with you. Can you come to my office?"

"Of course." I smiled tightly.

I followed Jack to his office, a corner section on the opposite wall from Theo's. And that wasn't the only way they were opposites. While Theo was neat, almost on the side of compulsive, Jack was a mess. Files and folders were tossed on almost every surface, as if a tornado had ripped through his space. I stood in the doorway, not daring to come any closer.

"Come on," Jack chuckled. "I won't bite."

"Good, because I'm pretty sure I need a tetanus shot from just being in here. I don't want to get a rabies one as well."

"Funny," Jack huffed. He leaned against his desk, motioning for me to take a seat in the chair across from him. After I shoved a few folders to the side, I took a seat, staring up at him. He tapped his hands on the surface, smiling cheekily at me. "Look, I've been trying to play it cool, but my patience is up. Tell me you're coming to work for me."

"What?" I snapped, leaning away from him. "I'm not—"

"Shit." He ran his hand over his face. "Theo didn't tell you?"

My mind raced, trying not to let my mind get the best of me. There was no way Theo would transfer me, especially not without speaking to me first. And even if he did think it was a good idea, there was no way in hell I'd choose to work for Jack of all people. Besides, I mainly liked this job because of how well Theo and I worked together. Without that, would I really want to stay?

Jack sighed, leaning back to watch my reaction. "I'm sorry, Calla. I thought you guys had already the shift. He mentioned that he wanted to wait until the partners left to make any changes, but I thought he'd talk to you about it beforehand. But look, no matter how this plays out, know that I'd love to work with you. I've seen how well you run things around here, and I know we'd be a great team."

His words should have meant a lot, but I couldn't really let them sink in. Not when I was on edge, not sure if Theo meaningly hid something from me or simply forgot. Either way, it was a crappy feeling. I smiled at Jack tightly. "I'll let you know."

Without another word, I slipped out of his office, breezing past the conference room. I refused to look through the walls, afraid that if Theo met my gaze, I'd fall apart. Instead, I grabbed my laptop and the spare set of keys from Theo's desk and walked toward the isolated back office. At least in there, I could fall apart without everyone staring at me.

I'D BARELY GOTTEN an hour in the silence before Theo came busting into the abandoned office, a look of concern covering his features. He stared at me, lingering long enough on my eyes to know I'd been crying. He shut the door with a little more grace, moving to my side before I could get a world out. Theo reached down, brushing his thumb along the trail of tears left behind on my cheeks. "What happened?"

I scoffed, pulling out of his grasp. Turning back to my computer, I focused on the screen instead of his features. "Jack pulled me into his office for a little chat. Asked if I was willing to come work for him once you were done with me."

Theo stepped back, covering his mouth with his hand. I glanced up at him, unable to hide the hurt in my eyes. "So you were planning on getting rid of me?"

"What?" he snapped. "Of course not, Calla. It wasn't like that."

"So explain it to me." I slid back in my chair, pushing so I could stand to meet his gaze. There was a lot of conflict brewing in his stormy expression, yet I couldn't latch onto a single emotion. Not that I really cared. I was too angry, too hurt, to worry about his feelings over mine. "Because it sure as hell sounds like you were."

Theo cursed under his breath, then turned back toward me, "Jack and I were talking a while ago, trying to figure out how we could keep seeing each other and both keep our jobs. He threw out the suggestion, and I didn't shut him down."

I wasn't going to think about the fact that he'd told Jack about us. There were more pressing things to worry about. "Why? Why would you even entertain that idea?"

"Because it made sense!" Theo snapped. "This was not some devious plan to get you out of my life, Calla. It was to give you a more permanent place in it! There's no way we can keep going this way. It fucking kills me to see you here and not be able to hold you, to kiss you whenever I want. You know how hard it was to watch you come down here upset and know that I had to bide my time to go to you? I wanted to fucking leave in the middle of a goddamn meeting with the men who hold my fate in their hands." He turned to look at me. "We've always known there was going to be a moment, one when we'd have to choose. I choose you, Calla. I will every fucking time. Because I'd rather have you at my side as my partner than as my assistant."

"Oh," I said, all my anger deflating at his words.

"Yeah, *oh*. But I was a coward. Every time I tried to bring it up, I imagined being here without you, and it hurt. I love working with you, Calla. I love the life you've brought into my office. So I kept things going the way they were, holding onto this moment for a little bit longer." He stepped forward, placing his hand on the back of my neck, using his thumb to tilt my chin up to meet his gaze. "I am sorry for that. But know this: I never would have made the final call before talking with you. You'll always have a place here, one of your choosing, for as long as you want it."

I chewed on my lower lip, debating his words. As much as I loved working in this office, it was also a placeholder for my real goals. I'd invested so much in Theo because I believed in him, because we were a great team. Did I want to see if I could find that dynamic with someone else?

No.

"I don't want that." I placed my hand on top of his. "I think we both know that the reason this job works for me is because of us. Otherwise, it's given me a convenient excuse to delay finding out what I really want to do." I paused, looking up to search his gaze. "And it's probably time for me to figure that out."

Theo sighed, pulling me into his embrace. His hands clenched my back, and an immediate sense of rightness washed over me. This was meant to happen. We both knew it, and as much as it would sting to not see him every day, there were better things ahead of us.

"Everything you're saying makes complete sense. I can't lie and say I haven't had the same thoughts myself." Theo pulled back, brushing my hair away from my face. "But when I think of walking into that office and not seeing your face, I don't want to go back either."

I laughed, placing my hands on his chest. "You've worked too hard to walk away now, Theo, not when you're so close to becoming a partner." I lifted up to my toes, kissing him softly. "And yes, it'll be hard not to be there for you, but I'll give you most of my nights, and then we can share our days like a normal couple."

"I do like the sound of you being here when I get home every night." He tightened his hold on me. He nodded. "Fine. As much as I hate it, I'll see if I can help you find something else. But I need one favor."

"Of course."

"Wait until after the partners leave. It'll be enough stress with them looking over my every move. I don't want to have to worry about having to train a new assistant."

"You got it, Sunshine." I smirked up at him. "I have a condition of my own."

"Anything."

"After I leave, you need to take me on a real date. I mean dinner, drinks, the works."

Theo chuckled, lifting me into his arms. "Beautiful, do you know how long I've been waiting to show you off? I'm counting down the minutes until I can tell everyone you're mine."

THIRTY-THREE

Theo

"This is a huge mistake."

Calla glared at her reflection in the mirror, staring at her half-made-up face. The mascara wand was still in her hand as she stormed back into her bedroom, rooting through her closet for the tenth time this evening.

I laid back on her bed, watching as she ripped dress after dress off the hangers. I'd tried to intervene earlier, and all it earned me was a scowl. I quickly learned that my role tonight was a supporting one, only muttering compliments when she asked me what I thought of her new outfit. That was easy, because she always looked gorgeous to me.

Calla sighed, placing her hands on her hips. I slipped off her bed, twisting her so that she'd face me instead of the offending mirror. She sighed as she relaxed against my chest. "I know I'm being ridiculous, but this feels like one of those scenes in a horror movie when the whole audience is screaming, '*don't go in there*', and the dumb character does it anyway." She pointed to herself. "Dumb idiot screaming 'who's there?' in the pitch-black basement." She groaned as she dropped her forehead to my chest. "Why did I think this was a good idea?"

In truth, I had no idea. When Calla told me earlier in the week that she'd decided to attend dinner with her family, I immediately wanted to tell her no—to keep her away from their hurtful words and judgments a little longer. But the more she talked about it, the more it made sense. It wasn't for her mother or stepfather; it was for her—a final chance to see if she wanted them in our lives moving forward.

As much as I hated it, I respected her choice. I was just pissed I couldn't go with her.

Today marked day three of the partners' visit, and everything had been going smoothly so far. Everyone, even the founding partners, seemed impressed by how much we'd accomplished in such a short amount of time. There was even chatter that they'd be naming a new partner before they left in two days. The general assumption was that it was going to me, but I refused to believe anything until it was definite.

Unfortunately, tonight, I was expected to play host at a dinner and a play, which so happened to collide with Calla's family gathering.

I sighed, holding her tight and inhaling her sweet scent. "I hate that you're doing this alone."

"I won't be." She smiled up at me, but it lacked its usual sparkle. "Devyn will be there. Laurel made some excuse, probably not wanting to be in the room when my mother and I come face to face again." She kissed my chest and then returned to the closet to grab a black dress. "Probably for the best. She's basically an extension of my mother. At least without her there, Diane won't have any backup. Lord knows David doesn't care enough to get involved."

"And you're sure you don't need me there?" I asked, trying to soothe the nagging feeling in my chest. Over the years, I'd missed hundreds of things due to a work event. Guilt and shame were familiar companions, but I'd push through every time.

Tonight, though, I couldn't help but feel like I was making the wrong choice.

Calla came out of the bedroom clad in a dress that was so unlike her, I almost had to do a double take. It was stuffy, buttoned up to the neckline. No color, no embellishments, nothing that usually suited her. She stepped in front of me, placing her hands on my shoulders. "I'm sure, Theo. Yes, I would love to have you there with me, but tonight is important for you. Honestly, I'm tempted to blow off my mom and join you instead." She kissed me softly. "I promise, if anything happens, you'll be my first call."

"I better be." I placed my hands on the back of her thighs. "Text me anytime you need me. Even if it's that the food sucks, I want to know about it."

"No," Calla chuckled. "You need to focus on the partners. That's what's important tonight."

I gripped her a little tighter. "Beautiful, you need to get it through your head that you are the most important thing in my life. Tonight, tomorrow, it doesn't matter. If you needed me, I'd gladly tell them all to fuck off."

She stared at me, her eyes bouncing back and forth between mine. If she was looking for a lie, she'd never find one. I meant every word. It'd taken me a long time and one pain in the ass assistant to get here, but I was finally living again, and she was the only person I wanted to spend my life with.

I loved her. The words hit me like a lead balloon, desperately wanting to escape my mouth. I wanted to scream it out, to make her understand how deep my feelings for her ran. But with our limited time tonight, I held them back. She deserved a grand admission, something she could look back on years from now and know that she would always be loved that fiercely, not some rushed declaration before we both had to deal with different obligations. So I settled for the next best thing. "I'm yours, Calla. Nothing is going to change that."

She smiled so brightly that the rest of the city looked dim in comparison. "I don't think I'll ever get tired of hearing you say that."

"Get used to it, beautiful." I chuckled and brought her knuckles to my mouth. "Because you're going to be hearing it for a long time."

"I'm yours just as much as you're mine, Theo." She reached up to kiss me softly. Holding this woman in my arms, I knew then that she loved me just as much as I loved her. There were no doubts, no fears that we weren't in the same place. Even without saying the words, I knew I held her heart, and I'd guard it more fiercely than anything else in this world.

Now, I just had to make it through an excruciating dinner before I could officially tell her.

MY LEG BOUNCED against the tiled floor, trying to keep my focus on the conversation around me. But after sitting at this table for hours, my give-a-shit meter was running low. I'd barely heard from Calla all night, unsure if that was a good or bad sign. She had less than thirty minutes to text me back, or I'd hunt her down and make sure she was still in one piece.

Needing a break from the non-stop chatter, I excused myself to the bar, finding Jack already waiting there with a drink in hand. He smiled as I approached, passing me a second scotch I didn't see when I arrived. Taking a long sip, I sighed. "Thanks for that."

"No problem." Jack nodded to his side. He turned around from the bar, plastering on a false smile as he looked out to the crowd. "Down that fast, because Allen's coming over, and from the look of it, he's heading right for us."

Fuck. I inhaled the rest of my scotch in one sip, turning to give Allen the same phony smile as Jack. As the CEO and founding partner, he was one who decided the fate of our office. Based on past meetings, he was a challenging read, not someone open to a lot of change. I'd known he would be the hardest to impress, so I couldn't let my demeanor slip just yet.

"So, Theo," Allen said as he slipped onto a bar stool at my side, "how are you liking New York so far?"

"It's fine."

"Tell me how you really feel, son," he chuckled. "Regardless, things seem to be going well for you here."

I paused, placing my phone on the bar to stare at the man. Yes, he held my future in the palm of his hands, but I was getting tired of these little games. My work should speak for itself. Why the hell did I need to kiss their asses when I'd brought more revenue to our agency than most of them combined? "Allen, why don't you ask me your real question so we can get down to what tonight is really about?"

"Theo..." Jack warned from my side.

Allen laughed, unfazed by my comment. "You know, I was originally against this expansion. Thought it was a gigantic waste of time. But now, being here, I can admit I was wrong." He nodded to the rest of the partners back at the table. "We've been talking about continuing to grow, possibly looking into international options. If we decide to go that route, we want you on the ground, replicating what you've done here. Of course, it would come with a title change and salary increase, maybe even a named partnership, but we'd discuss that when the time was right." He stared at me. "Is that something you'd be open to?"

"Holy shit," Jack whispered under his breath. "What the fuck are you waiting for, Theo? Say yes."

But I couldn't. The word refused to leave my mouth. The job might be the opportunity of a lifetime, but the idea of leaving New York made my stomach twist into a gigantic knot. This was supposed to be my chance with Calla, a chance to start our lives together. Hell, her resignation letter was sitting on my desk, just waiting until the partners left to make it official.

She could always come with you, the voice in my head called out, but I quickly pushed that thought away. She'd been clear; she didn't want to have to start over again, not when she was just getting settled in New York. How could I ask her to follow me to another city, possibly another country? And what if this kept happening? What kind of man would I be if I asked her to pack up and move every few months? She wanted the fairytale, the home with the picket fence and the partner by her side, not a man who was always flying off somewhere, too preoccupied with work to make her happy.

I started to say no, but that word also died on my tongue. As much as I wanted to refuse, to turn it down in favor of a life with Calla, there was a small part in the back of my mind that wondered if I was acting too impulsively. Was I ready to throw away a decade of hard work with one simple word? Even if I decided to take the job, it didn't mean I couldn't make things work with Calla. She was my person, my constant in this world. There was no other option but for it to work between us. But this was the selfish route, the one that put my career over her needs. The man I was before would jump at this opportunity, would have said yes before even consulting her. However, I'd promised to change, and the least I could do was give her a choice, to seek out her input on this potentially life-altering decision.

"I–" I swallowed the lump in my throat. "I need to think about it."

I didn't miss the look between Allen and Jack, both as

shocked at my answer as I was. However, I didn't care about that too much, not when my phone suddenly rang out, Calla's name on the display. "Excuse me," I muttered as I walked away from the table. Pressing the screen, I brought my phone to my ear, "Hey, beautiful, you okay?"

"Eh," she grumbled. "About as good as I can be. Luckily, a couple of David's co-workers are here, so they're acting as a buffer. But I wanted to call and check in."

"Your mother isn't being too hard on you?"

"Nope." A loud bark of laughter came through the other side of the line. Calla sighed. "I have to get going. If I'm late to dinner, my mother will have a fit."

"Yeah, I should get back to it too."

"You're right," Calla said but didn't hang up the phone. She sighed into the receiver. "Only a few more days, right?"

"Only a few more days," I repeated, hating the weight that fell on my chest at her statement. Only a few hours ago, I was floating, on the top of the world, elated that I got to call this woman mine. But now, all my fears had suddenly grown teeth, making me nervous that a lifetime with Calla wasn't as promised as I thought.

THIRTY-FOUR

"Thank you for finally joining us," David scoffed as I took a seat at the table. Just my luck that everyone had already found their place when I stepped back into the room. Maneuvering around the table, I found the inscribed card with my name, the elegant script almost mocking me. After all, who needed assigned seating for a family dinner?

Diane Winters, that's who.

As soon as the appetizers were served, I zoned out, already bored by the same mundane conversation I'd heard a million times before. David's coworkers would blow smoke up his ass while my mom pretended to be the picture-perfect wife without a single hair out of place.

The chatter died down as David's guests, whose names I hadn't bothered to remember, turned toward Devyn and me. "Calla..." the shorter one sneered, talking more to my breasts than me. "What is it that you do? Do you work with your father?"

"No," I answered coolly. "I don't work with my *stepfather*. I'm an assistant at a talent management agency."

"Ah." The man turned back toward David with a pity-filled

smile. "One of those bleeding, artsy hearts, huh? I have one of those myself." He patted my hand. "When the money dries up, we all know where you'll turn, child."

"Exactly," David scoffed. "It's all rebellion until they learn the value of a dollar."

I opened my mouth to say something, but Devyn kicked me in the shin, shaking her head subtly. My jaw hung open in shock. She'd never been good at ignoring out their nonsense—at least when she was a kid. Now, it seemed like she'd drunk the Kool-Aid and become one of the prodigal daughters, the ones whose names meant something—unlike me, the black sheep of the Winters clan.

"It's just temporary, Richard," my mother interjected. "Calla wanted some independence, so we encouraged her to branch out and expand her horizons." She lifted a brow at me, at least as much as she could with the amount of filler pumped under the surface. It was a look I knew well, one that promised hell if I embarrassed her. "We're planning on her returning to the fold once she's had a taste of how the other half lives."

"I'm not so sure about that." I tried to keep my voice calm. "Even if I don't end up staying there long term, I'm not planning on working for David."

My mother's eyes narrowed in my direction. "We'll be discussing that later, Calla." She smiled back at her guests. "I apologize for my daughter. She's still at that willful age where all children believe they need to find their passion. But she knows our family values well. She'll make a great addition to David's staff someday."

Family values? I almost choked on my sip of wine. If I'd learned anything from this family, it would be that appearance matters more than anything, and your value is defined by the money in your bank account. None of those values were ones I wanted to emulate. As the conversation started to resume around me, I couldn't bite back my words anymore. After years of being shoved into a box, only expected to smile and wave as the cameras passed me by, I was done.

My mother cast me out of her life months ago, so what else was there to lose?

"Actually, Richard..." I downed the rest of my wine glass. "That's not true. In fact, I'd rather chew off my own toes than spend a single day working for David. And since I don't hate myself that much, I think I'll stick with my current job—the one I got *without* any intervention from the two of you."

"Calla," my mother hissed. She looked at her guests. "I apologize for our daughter's outbursts. She hasn't been herself lately." She tilted her head, as if in a secret code that only the upper class knew. There'd probably be whispers later that I had a problem, something vague enough to give an excuse for my behavior without making my family look bad.

I scoffed, accepting that there was no hope of us reconciling. I'd come here with good intentions, hoping that after months apart, my mother and I would be able to turn a new leaf. But instead, all I'd gotten were snide comments and insinuations that my absence was due to more nefarious reasons than reality.

And I was done.

"You know what, Mom? That's fine. Tell your lies, twist your truths. I don't care. If you want to spend your life looking down on others, I can't stop you. But I'll be damned if I have to spend another minute listening to it."

Staring out at the shocked faces, I stood from the table, feeling a new level of thrill for finally standing up for myself after years of snide comments and remarks. Without another word, I stepped out of the dining room, heading straight for the foyer. I paused, looking around the apartment that housed me for so many years. While I'd always appreciate my family giving me the very best money could provide, that didn't make it a loving home, and I was tired of settling for something less than that.

Not when Theo had shown me what it meant to be loved unconditionally.

Before I could find my purse, my mother stormed into my space. "Calla Marie, what the hell was that in there? That man could have helped you secure a good future, a career, and you practically threw it all in his face." She crossed her arms and shook her head. "What has gotten into you? You are not the girl I raised."

"I take that as a compliment."

She narrowed her eyes, "You will not speak to me this way. Not in my own home."

"Precisely why I'm leaving," I scoffed before turning to face her fully. "Don't you ever get tired of this, Mom?"

"What do you mean?"

"This act. Constantly pretending you have it all together. Don't you just want to scream that everything is not perfect?" I sighed, watching as her eyes widened in shock. "All of my life, you've tried to make me into someone I'm never going to be. I'm done, Mom. I love you, and I appreciate everything you've done for me, but until you can accept who I am, flaws and all, I don't want to see you."

"Calla..." Her voice cracked, and she dropped her gaze down to her hands. "I know these last few months have been difficult."

"That's the thing, Mom," I said. "They haven't. I thought when you kicked me out, my entire world was falling apart, that I'd be forced to come running back to you. But I figured it out, and I've made a life for myself that I love. Without you in it." I grabbed my purse from the entry bench, looking at her one last time as I pressed the button for the elevator. "I want you to be happy, Mom, but I want to be happy too. And it seems we can't have it both ways." The doors opened, and I stepped inside. "So I need to choose me."

***

I FOUND myself in front of Theo's apartment, barely even thinking twice when I told the cab driver the address. Not for a moment did I think about going home. Maybe it was too soon, but this already felt more like my home as opposed to my room in Devyn's apartment.

After all the shit that today had brought, I needed grounding, the kind that only Theo could provide. A night in his arms would soothe away all the bumps and bruises of the past few hours, making me feel whole again.

As if he knew I was approaching, Theo came rushing out of the building at the exact moment I tried to push the doors open, almost colliding with me. As I took a step back, his strong arms grabbed me, keeping me from landing on the nasty sidewalk.

"Shit, baby," Theo said, holding me out to check me over. "Did I get you?"

"Nope." I offered him a shaky smile. "Are you heading somewhere? I can head back to my apartment if you–"

"No." Theo shook his head. "I was coming to get you. Devyn texted that something had gone down, but I was in the shower, so I didn't get it until now." He stared down at me. "Are you okay? What did your mom do?"

"Nothing she hasn't done a thousand times before," I sighed. "But this time, I didn't put up with it. I'll probably die of embarrassment about my actions tomorrow, but tonight, it felt so fucking good to say what I've wanted to for years."

"I bet it did." Theo smiled down at me. "I'm proud of you, Calla."

"It was because of you," I admitted quickly, feeling the color rush to my cheeks. You gave me the strength to say no, to not accept anything less than I deserve." I placed my hands around his neck, pulling him down closer to me. "You are a good man, Theo, and finding you is the best thing that has ever happened to me."

Theo sighed, but his smile felt off, like it was painful to hear those words come from my mouth. Alarm bells rang out in my head, already on edge because of earlier. I placed my hand on his cheek. "What's wrong?"

"Nothing," Theo said. "It's been a long afternoon with the partners, and my energy is spent. But I'm happy you're here."

His words didn't ring true, but I couldn't bring myself to question him, not when I was already feeling so raw. Selfishly, I needed him to hold me up right now, and I didn't want to think about anything that could come between us.

But as he led me up to his apartment, I couldn't shake the feeling that something was about to do precisely that.

THIRTY-FIVE

Theo

As Calla stepped into the shower to wash the remnants of the day away, I sat in my bedroom, holding my head in my hands. Ever since Allen brought up the promotion, my mind had been spinning, trying to figure out how to get everything I wanted. But no matter what, I'd have to choose.

For the first hour, it felt like an insurmountable decision to choose between the woman I loved and the career I'd fought so hard for. Even though she wasn't here to witness it, I felt like I was betraying my mother's dreams, throwing all her sacrifices back at her. She'd wanted me to succeed, and this promotion was the next step. However, as much as I craved for it to be a straightforward choice, it never would be. Not when it meant potentially losing Calla.

I planned on talking to her about it, but when I saw her face after the dinner, all I wanted was to hold her, to tell her everything would be alright, even though I didn't know if that was true. And maybe I'd regret it one day, but at that moment, I knew I would choose her over anything else. Work would come and go, spitting me out at the first possible inconvenience. Calla, however, had already proven that she was at my side. The least I could do was return the favor as she worked through these issues with her family.

Besides, I liked living in New York, liked the team I was leading. Maybe it wasn't going to place my name on the letterhead, but it was a job I'd be happy to keep for a long time.

As Calla emerged from the shower, wrapped in a white terry cloth towel, the decision cemented in my mind. This was the life I wanted. She walked over to me, standing between my legs. She ran her hand through my hair, smiling softly down at me. "What's going through that mind of yours?"

I peered up at her and, once again, the words were on the tip of my tongue. I wanted to tell her I loved her, to promise her that my heart would always be hers, but yet again, the timing failed me. This night was not the night for bold declarations, not when her mind was already so frazzled with thoughts of her mother and the fallout of her actions. Instead, I'd show her my love with quiet declarations, show her how much she meant to me without words.

My fingers teased the knot of her towel, letting it fall to her feet. Seeing her body bare in front of me made my cock harden in my pants, but there would be time for that later. Placing my hands on her hips, I pushed her back slightly, enough to get past her and to my dresser. I grabbed one of my shirts and pulled it over her head, loving how it barely grazed the tops of her thighs. She furrowed her brow, clearly unsure what was happening. I held my hand out. "Come with me."

"That's what I thought we were doing," Calla muttered to herself before placing her palm in mine.

I chuckled, leading her across the hall into my barely-used office. I'd planned this surprise earlier, thinking it would be a great segue into telling her how I felt. But now, it would stand alone, hopefully enough for her to read the meaning into it.

Looking into the space, I was flooded with memories of

lonely nights, hunched over my computer screen, a time before a certain redhead had crashed into my life and made me re-examine all my priorities. Now, this office was barely used, almost like a relic of my past life. I thought coming in here would have been a sharp reminder of what I once wanted, but all it did was reinforce the choices I'd made. I looked at Calla over my shoulder. The choices that had led me to her.

She walked over to the bookcases, touching the now empty shelves. "What is this?"

"You were running out of room for your books at Devyn's." I leaned back against the wall, watching her. "I thought you could bring some here."

She turned, a confused expression furrowing her brows. "You're giving me space in your office?"

"Calla..." I stepped toward her. "You might feel like you don't have a place within your family, but you'll always have a place here, with me. Even if it's just your books for now, I like there being pieces of you in my home."

"Are you sure about this?" She chewed on her lower lip. "My books are going to make this office all cluttered and chaotic, break up the black-on-black motif you have going on."

"You've done it before, beautiful, and my life got better for it."

She pressed onto her toes, kissing me with enough force for me to stumble a little. Calla chuckled as she pulled back. "This is the best surprise I've gotten in a long time."

"Give it time, beautiful. I plan on spoiling you for a lot longer."

THE NEXT MORNING, I kissed Calla goodbye before the sun came up, heading straight into the office. As I walked inside, I passed by my office, instead going toward the conference room where Allen was already waiting. I'd texted him late last night, knowing that he was as attached to his phone as I used to be. Without much information, I told him we needed to talk first thing in the morning.

"Have a seat, Theo."

I did as he requested, taking the spot opposite him. Yet again, his expression gave nothing away. I didn't know what he expected from this meeting, but I hoped I would still be in his favor when it was done.

He leaned back in his chair, steepling his fingers over his stomach. "You called this meeting, so let's get into it. Why did you need to speak with me?"

"I appreciate the opportunity you presented me. As much as I would like to lead a new office, I'm afraid I can't. I've got a good thing going here in New York and would like to continue to manage this office. You've seen what we can do in a few short months, so let me show you how successful we can be in the long term."

Allen stared at me, probably in disbelief over my words. In truth, I was too. Six months ago, when Calla first walked into my life, I never would have thought I'd be here. But now that I was, I had no regrets, no reason to fear the future. Even if I never achieved every one of my goals, I'd be content with my lot in life as long as I had Calla at my side. That mattered more than my job title.

"Listen, Theo," Allen sighed. "Some new information has come to light, and I'm afraid that won't be an option."

My heart stalled in my chest.

"Excuse me?"

"As of next month, you will no longer be in charge of the New York office."

There were no words to describe the deafening sound in my

ears, the way my chest felt like it had caved in at his words. Out of all the possibilities, that was the last thing I thought he would say.

I shook my head, my hands shaking in my lap. "I don't understand. Just last night, you were saying how well this office is running. You wanted me to run another office because this one's been such a goddamn success." I slammed my hands on the table, lifting myself up to stand. "Why the fuck do you think that's happened? *Me.* I've killed myself to make this office work, and now you're saying I'm fired?"

"No," Allen said calmly. "That is not what I'm saying at all. We see your talent, Theo. We know what an excellent leader you are, which is why we're offering you a choice. Either lead the new expansion, or you can return to your old position in the LA office."

What the fuck?

"Just not here," I scoffed. "Why, Allen?"

He looked up at me, and for the first time, I saw a flicker of emotion. Regret? Annoyance? I wasn't sure, but either way, he didn't like what he was about to say.

"How long have you been sleeping with your assistant?"

THIRTY-SIX

Theo

I'd never been as nervous as I was in this moment. I'd sat across the table from movie stars, legendary singers, and hall of famers from almost every sport. None of them were as terrifying as staring into the eyes of the woman I loved, knowing that what I had to say could change our relationship forever.

As soon as my conversation with Allen ended, I returned home, hating that I was being put in this position. Not once did I think our talk would go that way. I'd wracked my brain the entire trip home, trying to figure out how he'd found out about Calla and me. An anonymous source had come forward with their suspicions. That was all he told me. And while there was no direct evidence to link us together, I wasn't going to lie about our relationship either. To tell Allen it was untrue would have probably been the smart move, but once I opened my mouth, I couldn't deny how much I cared about Calla. To say anything less than the truth would have cheapened our relationship, cheapened the bond between us.

Even if it cost me everything.

"Theo?" Calla called out as she stepped out of the kitchen

and came closer to me. "What's going on? You're freaking me out a little bit."

I rubbed my hand through my hair then dropped it down to grip the back of the couch. I needed something to hold me up, something to give me strength when I had none to spare.

"Last night, at dinner, Allen said that the agency is potentially opening up another satellite office." I inhaled slowly, forcing the words past my lips. "And if it passes, they want me to head the new location."

The moment it escaped my lips, Calla's whole demeanor shifted, like she was actively closing the walls around her heart. I couldn't blame her; nothing about this situation would have been ideal for either of us. And she didn't even know the worst part yet.

I inhaled slowly, continuing without meeting her worried gaze. "I told him no. At least, I *tried* to tell him no."

"Tried to? What does that mean?"

"It means he knows about us." I lifted my eyes to meet hers. Her gaze had widened, her whiskey-colored eyes already filling with tears. I hated it, hated that I was the cause. "He gave me two choices: either lead the next office or return to LA and go back to my previous position. But either way, if I want to stay in New York, I'm going to have to find a new job."

Calla let out a little gasp, her hand flying to her mouth. As she started to pace, she shook her head. "What evidence do they have? Maybe we can fight this, find some excuse for why–"

"I told Allen the truth."

She turned, staring at me in shock. "Why would you do that?"

I stepped forward, taking her chin in my hand, crushing her lips to mine. "Because I don't give a fuck what it costs me. I'm never going to deny how I feel for you. Never."

"Theo..." Calla's tears spilled down her cheeks, soaking into the fabric of my suit. As soon as they started falling, she pushed away from me, turning to take a seat on the couch. She curled her legs under her, staring out the window, as if the city held all the answers. I hated that expression, wishing I could say anything to take it away. But I had no solutions, no answers that would soothe the ache in her chest, not when the one inside of mine was tearing me apart.

"What happens now?" Calla whispered.

"I told Allen I needed to think about it," I answered, sitting in the armchair across from her. Never before had we sat like this in my living room, and it hurt even more having the space between us. "I don't know what to do, Calla."

"And if you say no to both options?" She asked, still refusing to meet my eyes.

"Then I'm out of a job." I pushed air through my lips. "But I'd be able to stay here. I don't know if I'll find something at the same level, but at least we'd be together."

She glanced up at me, her warm eyes bigger than I'd ever seen before. But gone was the usual light that shined within her, and I hated myself for being the one to dim it. "Is that what you want?" she asked quietly, staring at anything else but me. "To stay here and start over?"

I swallowed. "Of course it is."

"Theo..." Calla sighed as she stood up to face the window. She inhaled slowly then turned back toward me. "I think we both know that's not true."

I was on my feet before my brain could even process it, moving to be as close to her as possible. My hand found the back of her neck, pulling her forehead to mine. "I want *you*, Calla. No matter what else happens, *you* are the only thing I'm sure about."

"Right now," Calla whispered. "But this thing between us is so new, and I don't want you to make a decision based on me."

"What are you saying?"

She looked up, studying my eyes. Hers sparkled with unshed tears, making her irises even more vibrant. I wanted to stay like this, in this moment, the one before I knew everything would change between us. "If I wasn't a factor, would you take the promotion? Would you want to lead the new team?"

I took a step back, hating that she voiced that question. It was one I didn't want to answer, didn't want to admit the words that had been playing out in my head. Because absolutely, I would take this job if she wasn't here right now. I would have said yes without an ounce of hesitation. But none of that mattered, not while Calla was in my life.

"That's not important," I finally muttered. "It doesn't matter what I would do in that situation."

"It matters to me," Calla whispered, her voice cracking. She shifted closer to me, placing her hands on my chest. "Theo, you know how I feel about you. Part of the reason I fell for you was your drive and ambition. I know what your career means to you, how hard you've worked for this chance. From the moment we met, you've been dreaming of an opportunity like this."

"But that was before—"

She placed her hands over my lips. "I refuse to get in the way of your goals, Theo. I care about you too much to ever hold you back." She lowered her hand, placing it back over my heart. "So tell me, if I wasn't in the picture: would you take the job?"

I sighed, closing my eyes as tightly as possible. "Yes."

"Then you should take it." Calla smiled up at me, but it didn't meet her eyes. "For what it's worth, I think they're lucky to have you, Theo. You're going to be incredible."

"Come with me." I took her hands in mine. "As my assistant, girlfriend, I don't care what your title is, as long as you're there with me."

Calla shook her head. "I can't. I want to, but then I'd just be building my life around yours. As much as I want to go with you, I can't do that to myself, not when I'm just starting to feel free again. I need to carve my own path."

I swallowed, hating the weight on my chest. It felt like I was being dragged into the depths of the ocean, and I had no one to blame but myself. Each breath was a struggle, and my eyes stung with the threat of tears. I cleared my throat, unable to meet her gaze. "Where does that leave us?"

"I don't know," Calla admitted. "I want to be with you, Theo. More than anything. You're the person I want to build a future with." She paused, her voice cracking with emotion. "But maybe that future isn't supposed to start right now. Maybe after we both figure out what we want, we can find a way to meet in the middle."

"No."

I broke her hold on me, storming over to the other side of the apartment. "We're not giving up. Not yet, not like this. Not when we were so damn close to having everything."

Calla shook her head. "Please, Theo, don't make this harder than it has to be."

"Fuck that," I spit, wanting to rip my heart out of my chest and lay it at her feet. Maybe then, she'd realize how much this conversation was killing me. It was so tempting to tell her that I loved her, that I knew she loved me too, but it felt like cheating, pulling out a trump card when I was about to lose. I wanted to say those words because I wanted to give them, not as a desperate ploy to keep us together. I walked up to her, cupping the back of her neck so she had to meet my eyes. "Don't do this, Calla. Don't give up on me."

"I'm not." Tears filled her eyes. "I'll never do that. But right now, you need to take this opportunity. Try to see if this is what you want. If it's not, I'll be here, waiting for you. If it is, then I'll be happy for you, knowing that you finally achieved your goal."

She pressed a kiss to my chest. "Neither of us can live with regrets, Theo. And if you don't take this leap right now, we're going to spend the rest of our lives wondering what if. I don't want that for either of us."

My lungs wanted to give out as she said those words. I shook my head, my hands holding her against me. Maybe, if I held on tight enough, I'd never let her go. "I hate this."

"I do too." Calla wiped away a few stray tears. "But I'm still so incredibly proud of you, Theo. I hope you know that."

"Thank you." I leaned down to kiss her forehead. "And know that no matter where I am in the world, you call, I'm there."

"You can't promise that."

I seized her chin, forcing her to look at me, to see the seriousness in my eyes. I might have failed this girl in many ways, but this promise would be one I'd keep. This was not goodbye; I refused to let that be the case. And if she called, I would be there, no matter what.

"I promise you, Calla Winters, that if you need me, I will be there for you, no matter what is happening in my life. Because I'm yours, and that's never going to change. Not tonight, not ever. Maybe I don't get to have you right now, but there is no way I am walking away from you forever." I lifted her chin. "Do you understand me?"

Calla nodded then pressed her forehead against mine. As we stood there, both of us breaking down at the thought of being apart, something solidified in my chest. This might have been goodbye for now, but no matter what happened next, Calla was the other half of my heart.

Neither time nor distance would never change that.

THIRTY-SEVEN

Calla

The bouncing cursor on my screen taunted me, relishing in the lack of words coming from my brain. It felt like my hands had been perched on my desk for hours, staring at the open document on my computer.

My resignation letter.

Today was supposed to be our defining moment, the moment we got to tell the world we were together. To stop hiding, stop living in fear that someone would find out and we'd be forced to choose between our careers and each other.

Turns out, fate is a cruel bitch after all.

At least before, I would have had Theo. My job was a price I was willing to pay to have the man I loved in my life. But now, I was left with nothing—no job, no boyfriend, and no more will to keep a smile on my face. It was worse than when I arrived in New York all those months ago because, at least then, my heart had been in one piece.

After our tears finally dried last night, Theo and I agreed on a relatively clean break. It would be hard enough to say goodbye to him as it was; I couldn't imagine how it would have felt if we'd kept going as we were, knowing there was a hanging clock over our heads.

He was under the impression I'd still be here with him for two more weeks, but I knew I couldn't do it. I couldn't watch as he accepted the promotion, no matter how much I wanted him to take it. I can't bear to watch his office get boxed up; all our memories gone as well. It was better this way.

I steeled my resolve and started typing, adjusting the dates on the page. There was no way Theo would fight me on this. At least, I didn't think he would. He wanted the best for me, and right now, that was being as far away from this place as possible. After pressing print, I grabbed the letter and darted down the hall, hoping to have this whole process done before Theo got out of his meeting with the partners.

We'd barely crossed paths this morning, but I could feel him everywhere—the little trinkets he'd left on my desk, his sloppy handwriting all over the files. Even his cologne hung in the air, the notes of leather and pine taunting me with each breath.

As I reached Jack's office, I knocked on his door, waiting until he called out before heading inside. His brows rose in surprise when I came in, and he shut the door behind me. "Calla?" he asked, standing to greet me. "Not that this isn't a pleasant surprise, but what are you doing here?"

"I need to give this to you." I pushed the letter in his direction. "It's my resignation. I gave it to Theo two weeks ago, but I don't know if he ever filed it with everything going on. Today is my last day."

He unfolded it, reading the words so slowly that it felt like my skin was ripping apart. I needed to leave, to get out of this building as quickly as possible. Every minute I stood here, I was closer to losing control, to completely falling apart. And if I saw Theo... I refused even to entertain that thought.

"Why?" Jack asked. "Because he's leaving? Calla, but you have a job here. I'll make sure of it."

"I can't," I whispered, crossing my arms around my stomach. "It would be too hard, being here without him." A single tear fell down my cheek, and I hastily pushed it away. "We're done. And even standing here...it hurts, Jack."

He cursed under his breath, running his hand over his face. "Look, I know this isn't my place to say this, but it's probably for the best."

"You're right. It's not your place," I scoffed, turning toward the door. But before I could, Jack shifted in front of me, blocking the exit. "Let me go," I sneered, not wanting to hear another word from his mouth.

"Two minutes," Jack said. "And then I promise, I'll never bring up Theo again. Just let me explain. Let me tell you why you're better off without him."

I DIDN'T EVEN MAKE it into the cab before I started to break down. The entire drive home, I sobbed in the backseat, hating that I had been so naive. The driver just stared at me in the rearview mirror, concern and irritation lining his eyes, but I didn't care what he thought about me.

Once I stepped inside my apartment, the tears only got more forceful, to the point that it was hard to breathe. I pressed against the door, letting it guide me down to the floor. I bunched up my knees, burying my face in my hands. I didn't even realize anyone else was there until Devyn curled up to my side, pulling me into her lap. The tears continued as her fingers twisted through my hair, comforting me in the way she did when we were small.

When my breathing evened out, she finally spoke. "What happened?"

"I quit," I whispered, my throat hoarse from crying. "I went to give Jack my resignation letter, and then he told me that Theo played me, that this was his usual routine. He'd have these secret relationships and then find a convenient excuse to end them." I brushed my hands along my face, not even wanting to know what I looked like right now. "And as much as I don't want to believe it's true, what if it is? What if he was lying to me that whole time, and this new job is a convenient excuse to end things?"

She hummed, waiting a few minutes before answering. "Did you talk to Theo about it?"

"I can't, Dev. It hurts to much to even breathe. If I talk to him, I don't know if I'll survive it," I whispered, pulling out of her lap. "I don't believe it's true, but I also don't know why Jack would lie to me about it."

"I don't know either," Devyn said. "But I agree: nothing he's saying makes sense. Maybe Theo has done stuff like that before. We all have pasts, and it can be hard to share the darker pieces. But I saw that man with you, Calla, and I have zero doubt that he loves you. He would have given up the world if you asked him to." She tucked my hair behind my ear. "He only gave you up *because* you asked him to. He was willing to walk away from his dream job to make you happy. People only do that for someone they love."

"I don't know," I muttered, rubbing my hands over my tired eyes. "I almost would rather there be some devious plan in place. It would be so much easier to hate him than love him and not be able to be with him."

"You don't know how true that is." Devyn held my hand to her chest. "But for Theo and you, that's not the case. You know what you shared, no matter what anyone else says. Hold onto that. Let it keep you going." She kissed the top of my head. "And hope this isn't the end of your story."

THIRTY-EIGHT

Theo

Staring out at the city surrounding me, I waited for some emotion to hit me. With only hours left until I boarded a plane to London, this was the last time I'd stand in this office, the last time I would call New York City my home. However, it was hard to feel any sort of loss when I was barely surviving.

When the partners called me in to announce my promotion, I was sick to my stomach. It only got worse when I exited the conference and was met with the sight of Calla's deserted desk. It was as if the last remnants of my heart had been reduced to ashes. She'd left without saying goodbye, not a minute to spare for one last moment together. It would have been a solace to believe she didn't care, but I knew the truth. She was as shattered as I was, both of us bearing the wounds of a relationship that had left us battered and bruised.

That had been almost a month ago. A month without her laugh, thirty days without her color igniting my world, and it was already clear that I would never move on from Calla Winters.

There were so many times I walked into Allen's temporary

office, ready to hand in a resignation letter of my own. But Calla's words played out in my mind, reminding me that this was what I had worked for. If I turned down the job, not only would I be disappointing my mother, but Calla's sacrifice would have been for nothing. I owed it to both of them to give this a shot, to see if I was meant to take this path.

As I kept studying the city's skyline, trying to commit each detail to memory, a soft knock came on my door. "Come in," I called out, not bothering to turn around.

"Wow," a familiar voice called out. "This is a far cry from the mailroom."

My brow furrowed, shocked when I turned around to see Natalie darkening my door. It had been years since we stood in the same room, and all our communication was going through our lawyers. She'd left me countless messages over the past few months, but I never bothered to respond, leaving that part of my life behind.

"Nat," I sighed, running my hand over my face. "What are you doing here?"

"I had some business in New York, so I figured I'd come to check in on you." She stepped closer to me, gripping the handle of her bag. "You haven't returned any of my calls."

"I know, I just—"

"I get it," Natalie cut me off. "Everything between us has been so tense; I can't say I wouldn't have ignored your calls either. But I need to speak with you, and this seemed like the next best option."

"Is this about my alimony payments?"

"Nothing like that," she chuckled. "But I got an offer on the house, and we agreed that if I sold, you would get half the profits. I need your signature before I can agree to their terms."

"Shit." I rubbed my hand over my forehead. "Do you have it with you?"

She nodded, opening her purse to pull out a stack of documents. I placed them on top of one of my boxes, reading through all the details. Natalie paced the room as I read, looking through all the boxes. "Are you moving?"

"Yeah, to London."

"London," she sighed. "Same old Theo. Always on the go."

I ignored the barb, not having the heart to battle it out with Natalie anymore. In truth, the animosity between us was born out of hurt feelings and poor communication, and there was no reason to continue that toxic pattern. Before Calla, I would have called my ex-wife the one who got away, but now I knew that wasn't true. We were a lesson, one we should have learned without trying to crush each other. But now that I knew what love was supposed to feel like, I realized I never gave Natalie my all, never loved her the way she deserved.

I exhaled slowly. "I want to apologize."

Natalie wasn't expecting that, because she flinched like she'd been struck. She shook her head. "I'm sorry, what?"

"I'm sorry, Nat," I repeated. "I've been holding onto this resentment ever since we got divorced, and I'm finally realizing it was more about me than it ever was about you. Because of how I treated you while we were married." I ran my hand over my hair and leaned forward on my desk. "I promised you that I would make you a priority, and it never happened. Instead, I buried myself in work, especially when our relationship started to get rocky."

Natalie shifted in her heels and cleared her throat. "Wow, Theo. Thank you for that. I honestly didn't know how much I needed to hear that until now." She offered me a half-hearted smile. "For what it's worth, I'm sorry too. I let resentment get the better of me, and it became toxic."

"We were never meant to work, no matter what we tried. I

want you to be happy, Nat." I glanced down at her finger, which now held a giant diamond ring. "It seems like you are?"

She nodded, tucking her chin to hide her blush. "I am. Blake. He's a great guy."

"Blake? What is this guy, some money manager from the eighties?" I joked.

Natalie smirked back at me. "Actually, no. He's a real estate agent. He's the one selling the house. When he did the first walk-through, he asked me out to dinner." She looked down at her ring and smiled. "We're getting married next month." She winked at me. "You'll be off the hook for any alimony checks."

"Thank fuck for that," I chuckled. "If I ever meet this guy, I'm shaking his hand."

"What about you?" Natalie asked. "Any women in your life?"

I cleared my throat. "There was."

She arched a manicured brow at me. "What did you do?"

"It doesn't matter." Natalie placed her hands on her hips, able to see through my lies. After years together, she knew my tells, having heard enough of my excuses to read the lies. With her staring at me, I finally snapped, unleashing the words I'd been holding back. "She was my assistant."

"I knew it." Natalie smirked. "That girl was too protective of you just to be an employee."

"Yeah, well, we were trying to keep it under wraps because it was against the rules. But someone reported us, and the partners told me I'd have to transfer offices. They offered me a promotion to sweeten the deal. I wanted to say no, but Calla wouldn't let me. She thought if I didn't take the job, I'd start to resent her, that it was the wrong way to begin our lives together."

"And that's not how you feel?"

"I don't know," I answered honestly. "I see her logic, and I know why she feels that way, but every fiber of me is screaming that this is the wrong choice." As the words fell from my tongue, the stronger they felt. "Ever since Calla left, I've just been going through the motions, not really living without her. I can live without this place, without this job. God knows I've worked my way up from nothing before. But none of it matters if she's not there to celebrate with me." I smirked to myself. "I'm such a fucking idiot."

Natalie smiled at me. "Then why are you sitting in here talking to me? Go get her. And make sure you rehearse that speech a few times. Really get in there and grovel."

"Shit," I hissed. "I've got to go. I have to tell Jack—"

"Wait, Jack? As in Jack Fischer? The one from your old office?" She grimaced as she leaned back against the wall. "I didn't know you were still working with him."

"Why do you say it like that?"

"I don't know," she sighed. "Jack always gave me a bad feeling. He would say all the right things to your face, but there was always a hint of animosity there. Jealousy, maybe?" She shrugged. "I never liked that you two were so close, but it wasn't my place to say."

"And you were kind of hoping he'd screw me over?"

She smiled boldly at me. "Maybe a little."

I shook my head. "Jack would never—"

But the rest of the words wouldn't come. Looking back, he was the only person I told about Calla, the only one who knew the truth about us. I thought we'd been caught by accident, but what if that wasn't the case? I never suspected that Jack would betray me, not when he was pushing me to take the risk the entire time.

Calla tried to warn me, to tell me that something about him

made her uncomfortable, but I let our past speak for itself, not stopping to wonder about Jack's motives and his shady antics.

"That motherfucker."

Natalie headed toward the door. "I know that face, and I'm getting out of here before you confront Jack. But Theo? Do me a favor? Tell Calla you love her, because every day that you wait is another day she's starting to move on. And that's not what you want, is it?"

"Fuck that," I growled. "We're not done."

"Good." Natalie arched a brow. "So go, Theo. I'm only forgiving you if you promise to make it work this time. Learn from our mistakes."

MY MIND WAS COMPLETELY blank as I walked down the hall, leaving a trail of smoldering ashes in my wake. On most days, one or two people would try to stop me to chat, but today, no one even looked in my direction. That was good. I had one task on my mind, and God help the person who got in my way.

When I got to Jack's office, I headed straight for the door, ignoring his assistant as she asked if he was expecting me. Her voice was like a low whine, unable to break past the buzzing in my head. The beast within me needed vengeance, and it wouldn't stop until I got what I was owed.

As I stepped into Jack's office, he stiffened the moment we made eye contact. He held up his hands. "Look, I don't know what you heard..."

It didn't matter. Not when my fist had already connected with his nose, feeling the satisfying crunch beneath my knuckles. "Fuck!" Jack screamed out, pulling a cloth to his nose. "What the hell was that for?"

I got an inch away from his face, pointing my finger so close to his eye that one wrong move, and it would make contact. "I trusted you, asshole. I told you about Calla because you were my friend, and then you turned around and sold us out? For what? So you could have the corner office?" I shook my head, my breathing heavy. "If you wanted the job so fucking badly, take it. I'm just glad I'm finally seeing your true colors after all these years."

Jack laughed, the sound low and full of condemnation. "Who I am? That's rich coming from you, buddy." He grabbed a tissue and slid it under his nose, pulling it back to see blood still draining from it. He hissed as he placed it back, staring at me with the promise of vengeance in his eyes. "Do you even remember how you heard about the New York job?" I searched my memory, unable to recall what had happened. "It was from me," Jack continued. "It was *supposed* to be mine. But then you went and got yourself a few big-name clients, and suddenly, my name didn't mean shit. You *took* it from me, Theo, and you never even thought twice about it. I tried to be the bigger person, tried to get over it. But then you started acting like you were better than me, and I said fuck it. You took my promotion from me, I was going to take *everything* from you. Your job, your girl, anything if it meant knocking you off your game." He laughed again. "And honestly, you should be thanking me for getting you away from Calla. That girl was poison, killing all your drive. If she'd stuck around any longer, you would have been left with nothing. For what?"

My hands clenched at my sides, and I was so fucking tempted to hit him again. Tempted to go to Allen and tell him everything. But none of it mattered, not while Calla was out there, thinking that I could live without her. As I looked over at Jack crumbled in his chair, I shook my head. "I feel so fucking sorry for you, Jack. You have no idea what it means to love someone like that, to have someone see you at your worst and still decide that you're worthy." Jack shook his head as I turned away from him. "Keep the job. I don't give a shit. I hope it's everything you hoped it would be."

"And where the fuck do you think you're going?" Jack called out.

"I'm going to get my girl back."

THIRTY-NINE

"Okay, I think this is the last of it."

I dropped the box in the hallway, looking over the sparsely decorated apartment. Move number three this year was finally finished. Javi looked up at me from his spot on the couch. "That's what I heard ten boxes ago. You need to do yourself a favor and purge some of this shit. There is no way you need all these books.:"

"Bite your tongue," I snapped back. "These are my collectibles. One day, when I'm old and gray, I'll pass them down to my children."

Drew, Javi's husband, chuckled as he walked in the doorway. "I doubt your children are going to want your smut collection, but what do I know? My dad tried to give me his collection of novelty spoons."

"Which you made me put up in the kitchen," Javi answered, standing to kiss his husband on the cheek. They both looked around the place, the one they'd shared for years before buying a cute little cottage downtown.

Originally, I planned on staying in New York, but after I quit, everything about the city reminded me of Theo. Walking down each block was like poking at a healing wound, asking for it to open back up. It was impossible to move on while surrounded by the place where we fell in love. In the end, it was an easy choice to move back to Saint Stephen's Lake, especially when Javi and Drew offered to let me sublet their old place for a fraction of the actual value.

Between my savings from working for Theo and Marta offering me some shifts at the Lost Tavern, covering my rent wouldn't be hard. And with my new free time, I was determined to commit to a career path finally. Once I sat down and cleared out everyone else's expectations, it was an easy choice. Besides working for Theo, the time I'd been the happiest was when I was helping plan events at the Isadora. Seeing couples' dream weddings come together was my ideal career; I loved that I was getting to create people's happily ever afters, the moment that they would look back on for the rest of their lives.

As soon as I rolled into town, I contacted Marina, the former event coordinator at the Isadora, asking for her advice. She chuckled, asking what had taken me so long. After leaving my mother's employ, she'd decided to open a private shop, working more in Saratoga and the capital area. She forwarded me all her local connections, offering to serve as a mentor while I got myself set up.

Luckily, Marina had logged all my hours working for her, so that would count as hands-on experience. Now, all I needed to do was pass my online classes, and by this time next year, I'd be able to take on clients.

But as much as everything was looking up for me professionally, my personal life was a completely different story.

Living without Theo was like living underground. Nothing seemed to break through the layer of gloom and darkness surrounding me. Every day, I woke up expecting it to hurt a little less, for it to finally be the moment my heart started to mend itself. Instead, all I felt was more grief, hating that I was taking this next step alone.

After speaking with Devyn, I decided to forget the conversation I had with Jack. Even if it was true, I wasn't going to taint my memories with those sour thoughts. I knew the truth of our relationship, and I would hold onto it, hoping that, one day, our paths would cross again. Besides, she promised to deal with Jack herself, and I knew better than to get in the way of Devyn's wrath.

But just because I chose to ignore Jack's words, it didn't mean I didn't have my doubts in the late hours of the night. I was barely sleeping, and when I did, my dreams were all of him. Of how I thought our lives were going to turn out, or even just doing mundane tasks together. The especially tortuous ones were when I relived moments between us, mostly when we were wrapped in each other's arms all night. Those were the ones that made it hard to wake up.

Over the last couple of weeks, I'd replayed our last conversation a million times in my head, wondering if I made the right choice. Would it have been so bad if I had decided to follow him around the world? Sure, I wouldn't be here, dreaming of owning my own business, but I'd be happy...right?

I shook my head, refusing to go down this path again. I'd made my choice, and ninety percent of the time, I accepted that fact. But it was in those quiet moments, when something significant happened in my life or when I crawled into my bed at night, that I could weep from missing him. It was an excruciating loneliness that only time could heal, and I was starting to doubt even that would work.

As Javi and Drew left, I looked over my new place, admiring the space. While Devyn's apartment never felt like home, this one already felt more like me. Most of the walls were painted a cheery yellow, while the furthest one was exposed brick, still showing signs of the old factory that used to take up most of main street. That was my favorite part. When you looked out the window, you were right in the middle of town, able to see almost all the businesses. It felt right, being here, even if it was hard to come back alone. And while I had hesitated about coming back, as soon as I settled into the apartment, I knew I'd made the right choice.

I was home.

"ORDER UP!" the line cook called from the kitchen window. I dashed across the dining room of the Lost Tavern, praying my feet would hold out a little longer. It was only my second shift, and I was already exhausted. I knew from experience that the weekends were always packed here, but I wasn't expecting the same level of rush on a Tuesday night.

With summer starting, most of the other restaurants in town were swimming with tourists, and it remained that way until the fall. The Lost Tavern was a staple in these busy months for locals, our place to get away from the ever-present crowds. That meant that, tonight, I'd been on my feet since the moment I arrived, turning over tables as fast as possible to accommodate everyone.

After dropping off the order, I glanced up at the clock. Only a few more minutes, and I could go home and crash. So much for finishing my book tonight—just when the freaking enemies were about to become lovers. That big revelation would have to wait until tomorrow, because I was barely hanging on. I would barely have time to strip off my uniform before crashing into bed.

I dropped off my last check to Marta at the register, propping my head on my hand as I waited for change. She chuckled. "It's a lot to get used to."

"I'm good." I waved off her concern. "Just need to invest in a better pair of sneakers." I pointed to my flats. "These are pinching my toes something awful."

"Good call." She placed the bills in front of me. "Oh, and before I forget, you're probably going to be seeing Gray around here more often. He's going to be moving home for a little bit."

"Really?" I asked, my face rearing back in surprise. "But it's mid-season…and I thought he had a couple more years on his contract." At least, that's what I'd seen when Theo was looking over it. The memory blew through my chest, leaving a wrecking ball-sized hole where my lungs used to be. That day in the diner was one of the first times Theo let me in, let me see the man hiding underneath his cocky exterior. It was when I started to fall in love with him.

Marta shook her head, pulling me out of her daze. "Decided to retire early. There's some personal stuff going on, so he decided to come home for a bit." She smiled brightly. "As much as I loved watching my boy live his dream, I sure did miss him. It'll be good to have him here."

"I think so too. I'm going to drop this off and head out unless you need anything else."

"Nope." Marta leaned in to give me a tight squeeze. "Get your butt home and get some rest, kiddo. We'll see you next week."

I darted out of the restaurant quickly, heading home as fast as possible. My pores would hate me tomorrow, but I was even willing to forgo a shower to get to bed quicker. Maybe tonight was the night I'd get a full eight hours. I couldn't even remember the last time that happened. By the time I got the door to my apartment open, I was downright giddy.

I dropped my purse on the counter, counting out the tips I'd gotten. Not too bad for a weeknight. I placed half in my savings jar while sliding the other in an envelope to take to the bank. When my courses were done, I'd need some capital to start my business, so hopefully whatever I made from the restaurant would cover my expenses. The one negative of waitressing was that the money could be inconsistent, so I wanted to make sure I wasn't dipping into my savings too much.

After washing my face and brushing my teeth, I walked into my bedroom, prepared to drop right onto the mattress. But before I could, a knock sounded on the door.

My brow furrowed, glancing at my phone to see if I had any missed calls or texts. Nothing. I walked to the door, opening it slightly to poke my head out. When I saw who was standing on the other side, I pulled it open all the way, my mouth gaping.

"Mom?"

FORTY

"Mom?" I asked as I stared out my doorway, unsure if I trusted the sight in front of me. I had no idea that my mother even knew I was in town, much less where I lived. She looked so out of place standing in my apartment, and the way she clutched her purse to her arm made it clear she was as uncomfortable as I was.

She cleared her throat, adjusting her jacket. "Can I come inside?"

Still in shock, I nodded, stepping aside to let her in. I instantly cringed when she looked around the apartment, mentally preparing for a critique. Was that why she'd come here? To drag me back, kicking and screaming?

I crossed my arms around my middle. "What are you doing here?"

"I heard that you were back in town, and I wanted to make sure you were all right." She turned, a rare vulnerability flashing over her features. "This place is cute."

"Mom," I groaned, rubbing a hand over my eyes. "What is this? Even when we were speaking, you'd never stop by late at night, so please, tell me why you're here."

"I miss you." She said it so simply, like it should have been my logical conclusion, but the thought never even crossed my mind. I dropped down to the couch, hoping that she would take the hint and join me. After running a hand over the surface, she sat down at my side. While I fully sank into the material, my mother sat on the edge, as if afraid my couch would swallow her up. I would have laughed, but it was hard to focus on anything except the way she was staring holes into the side of my head.

"Why now?" I asked, turning to face her. "We haven't spoken in months, and in case you forgot, the last time we saw each other was a disaster. So if you came here to rehash all that stuff, please, just go. I'm too tired to deal with anything else from you right now."

"I know," she sighed, rubbing her temples with her fingers. "The last time I saw you, I was...hurt. I'd convinced myself I was doing what was best for you. But after that dinner, seeing how much you had grown without me? How much of your life I'd missed? I realized that all I'd done was push you away." She reached over, taking my hand in hers. "I don't care what you decide to do in life, Calla, just as long as you're happy and I get to be a part of it. I can't excuse any of my past behavior, but I am trying, and I am going to do better for you and your sisters. I've started seeing a therapist and she's helping me work through my need for control. And I know I have a long way to go, but I thought you should know that your words hit their mark. I want more out of my life, and it starts with a better relationship with you girls, especially you, Calla."

My eyes clouded with tears as I gently took my hand from hers. "Mom, I want nothing more than to say okay and make things better, but it's not that simple. You talk about repairing our relationship, but you don't realize that you've been breaking it down for *years*. Every time I'm around you, I'm bracing myself, waiting for the passive-aggressive comments, for you to try to manipulate me into following your lead." I inhaled slowly. "I can't do that anymore, Mom. I won't. As much as I want you in my life, you need to change for yourself, because you *want* to be a better person. It can't be about me, because I'm not ready to have you in my life, at least not right now." A lone tear dropped from my eye, and I rushed to wipe it away before she saw.

But instead of admonishing me for showing my emotions, my mom lifted her thumb, brushing it away. I finally looked up and saw tears forming in her eyes as well. It broke down that final wall in my heart, and there was one question at the center.

"Why wasn't I enough?" My voice cracked. "Why couldn't you just love me as I am?"

"You've always been enough," my mother answered. "It's me. I'm the one who let you down." She inhaled slowly. "What do you remember about your father?"

"Not much," I admitted. "Little bits and pieces like a photo album. And his laugh."

"He had the best laugh." She smiled fondly at her hand. Looking down, I saw her old wedding ring from my father on her right hand, and she was toying with it when she spoke. "Your father was the love of my life. We met when I was sixteen, and I knew I'd never love anyone else as much as him." She exhaled, staring out at the window. "When he died, he took a part of me with him. It was easier to keep everyone at a distance, to be cold, than to risk any sort of pain like that again. It changed me for the worse."

"It changed all of us!" I stood, needing to work off some of the excess energy now coursing through my veins. "I was five years old, Mom. Five! I'd just lost my dad, and then my mom went from my hero to being the villain. We were all hurting. We were all broken! But instead of healing together, you pushed everyone away, turning into a fucked-up version of a Stepford wife."

"I know," she admitted quietly. "I failed you when you needed me the most. Without realizing it, I pushed all my children away, especially you." She looked up at me. "You have always been so much like your father. You have the same fire inside you. And I'll admit, sometimes, it hurts to be around you, because it just makes me miss him more." She let the tears fall down her cheeks. "Losing the love of my life almost killed me, Calla. I wouldn't wish that pain on my worst enemy." She stood up and moved in front of me, cupping my damp cheek with her palm. "But it doesn't excuse what I've done. I will never be able to atone for all my mistakes, but if you are willing to give me a chance, I would like to try to move forward."

The devastated, broken little girl inside me wanted to say yes, to cling to the mother she lost along the way, but there was too much damage to forgive that easily, not when words were all she was offering.

"I'm sorry, Mom. I'm not ready for that."

She nodded, "I understand." She ran her hand over my hair once, then pressed a kiss to my forehead. "If that ever changes, you know where to find me. You are always welcome at the Isadora. It's just as much yours as it is mine." She pulled back to look in my eyes. "I love you, Calla, exactly as you are. I'm sorry it took me so long to tell you that."

As my mother turned toward the day, I tried to stay strong. I tried to hold onto all the anger I'd suppressed, but by standing my ground, that tension loosened, leaving less resentment behind than before.

When the handle turned in her hand, I called out for her. "I'm not ready yet, Mom." She shifted, turning to face me with a hopeful gleam in her eyes. "But if you keep showing up and putting in the work, maybe I can be, one day."

She nodded. "That's all I ask."

———

I STARED at my phone on the coffee table as I paced in my living room, debating what I should do next. As much as I wanted to talk to someone about my mother's visit, the only person I wanted to tell was Theo. Unfortunately, over the last month, we'd completely cut off all contact, foolishly thinking it would lessen the blow of our separation.

For me, that was the furthest thing from the truth.

Every day, I hoped it would be the day I stopped missing him, the day I stopped feeling like I was missing a piece of me, but it never happened, and I was starting to doubt it ever would.

Refusing to question it anymore, I followed my instincts, grabbing my phone and scrolling until I found his number. His contact had been changed to *DON'T EVEN THINK ABOUT IT*, but I dialed anyway, needing to hear his voice, even if it was just his voicemail.

"Calla?" his breathless voice answered after a single ring.

That was all it took for me to break, for everything I'd been holding back to rush to the surface. I placed my hand over my mouth, trying to hide the sound of my tears. It wasn't enough, though, because Theo spoke a few seconds later. "Fuck, Calla. Please don't cry. It breaks my heart to hear you upset."

"I can't help it," I sniffled. "I miss you so much, it hurts, Theo. I'm so happy for you, and I'm incredibly proud of you, but I think we made a mistake. I made a mistake."

"Calla..." he cooed, his voice breaking. "I miss you too, more than you even know. I've been falling apart without you."

"You have?"

Maybe I should have hated that he was hurting, but hearing the pain in his voice soothed those broken pieces inside me. For the first time since I left his office, I felt like I wasn't alone. Just talking to him again pumped air into my lungs, and I was finally able to breathe fully.

"How can you even question that, beautiful?" Theo chuckled. "Do you have any idea how awful it has been here without you? I can't even walk into my apartment without getting mad that you're not in it. Hell, I've been reading the books you left behind every night because it feels like you're sitting here with me."

"Yeah, I know the feeling," I exhaled shakily. "So, this whole clean break thing—can we both agree that it was a terrible idea?"

"One thousand fucking percent."

I smiled through my burst of tears. I wanted to hold him, see him, spend the entire evening reacquainting myself with his body. It had been too long since he had been inside of me, and I craved his touch more than my next breath. But, in the back of my mind, I still wanted to support him. I needed him to know I would be there to support his dreams, even if it was hard. "I know you're going to be busy for the next few months, but I want to visit you, to see you in action in your new office. Maybe make sure your new assistant doesn't get any ideas."

"You don't have to worry about that, beautiful. You're the only woman I see." He exhaled slowly. "But yes, I'd love that. We can talk more tomorrow and figure out all the details."

"That sounds perfect." I laid in bed, propping the phone on my pillow so I could talk to him more. "Guess who came to see me tonight?"

"Do I even want to know?"

"Not like that," I chuckled. "My mom came over."

Theo paused, probably unsure what to say. "How did it go?"

"About as well as could be expected."

As I dove into the story of my mother's visit, I couldn't help but feel content for the first time since we last spoke. His calm, quiet voice soothed me, and I drifted off in the middle of our conversation, finally able to sleep peacefully through the night.

FORTY-ONE

Calla

The next morning, my eyes reluctantly opened, glaring at the bright light that shone through my bedroom window. My legs and feet ached, but I felt incredibly well rested. I glanced at the clock, seeing that it was after nine—probably the latest I'd slept in for months.

After my mother's visit, I spent almost an hour on the phone with Theo, catching up on everything that had happened over the last month. Honestly, even after talking it through, I was surprised that my mother had come here. She never admitted when she made a mistake, never talked about our father. It was like seeing the woman behind the mask and not knowing if I could believe the sight. Only time would tell if she meant what she said.

But I had to admit, realizing how much she loved my father did soften me a little to her situation. My heart had broken just because Theo moved away. I couldn't imagine what I'd do if something happened to him. Would I be the same person after that? *Probably not.* And while it didn't excuse any of her actions, grief made people act in unusual ways. All I could hope was that she found a way to work past it and make amends with the people in her life.

As I stretched in bed, my phone started to ring on the end table. I pulled it closer, seeing Alex's name. I frowned as I slid the bar to answer the call. "Everything okay?"

"No," she sighed. "One of our cabins' pipes leaked, and it's completely flooded. Cole's starting to work on it now, but it's kind of an all-hands-on-deck situation. Can you come help?" she asked. "Pretty please? I would love you forever."

"Of course I will," I chuckled. "Give me a little bit to look more human, and then I'll be on my way."

The drive to Fox Creek was a quick one, and even though my body was rioting at the thought of manual labor, I was more than happy to help my friends. When I was living with them last year, I'd gotten a first-hand look at all of their ideas for improving the campgrounds. It was amazing to see it all finally coming together, even if Alex was cursing the plumbing right now.

When I pulled up to the main lodge, I looked around, noticing that no other cars were waiting in the lot, not even Cole's work truck. I shook my head. Maybe he'd run out to get supplies. Considering that the closest Home Depot was thirty miles away, he'd be gone for a while.

I knocked on the office door when I heard Alex on the other side. She came out, closing the door behind her. "Ugh, thank you for coming out so fast." She pulled me into a hug. "This has been the longest fucking morning of my life."

"I'm sure it'll be fine," I chuckled, holding her closer for a moment. "At least it's just one cabin, right?"

"Yeah..." She sighed. "But selfishly, I've always loved number nine. That's the one that overlooks the lake just right, so you get that great sunrise in the morning."

I stalled, remembering that sight all too well. That was the cabin Theo and I shared when we came up for the soft opening. It felt like a lifetime ago when I bared my soul for him and he promised to catch me every time. It was the first time I realized I was falling in love with him.

I shook my head, pulling myself out of the memory. "Hey, where's Cole? I didn't see his truck outside."

Alex's face blushed, and then she chuckled a little too loudly: "It isn't. That's weird. Maybe he ran out to grab a few tools from his boss or something."

"Are you okay?" I asked, placing my hand on her forehead. "You're turning all shades of red."

"I'm fine," Alex snapped, glancing down at her phone. She sighed, pulling me toward the back porch. "But how are you? You know, after everything with Theo?"

"We actually talked last night." I sighed, smiling to myself. "And we both agreed that trying to stay apart wasn't working. With any luck, we'll get to see each other soon, but it still hurts, you know? Like I'm missing a major piece of myself because he's not here with me." I groaned, dropping my head into my hands. "The long-distance thing is going to be hard, but hopefully, it'll be worth it in the end."

"Well, I'm pretty sure you have nothing to worry about on that front," Alex said as we approached the cabin. As I looked at the stoop where I found Theo that night months ago, a tear threatened to spill from my eye, but I pushed it down, refusing to break down again.

"Shit," Alex hissed, patting her pockets dramatically. "I forgot a couple of things in the office. You head in; I'll be right back."

I scrunched my face, "Why are you being so weird today?"

She rolled her eyes. "Just...ignore me. Get your ass in that cabin before I drag you in there."

"Would love to see you try," I muttered under my breath as I stepped up the stairs and Alex ran off toward the main house. At least there weren't any signs of damage out here. I would have hated for them to have to knock down any of their cabins, but to see this one go would have broken me, not to mention Alex and Cole. While I had some incredible memories tied to this place, it was their baby.

I pushed open the door, trying to mentally prepare myself for the damage. To my surprise, once I stepped inside, not only was there not any damage, but candles and vases of wildflowers covered almost every single surface. I glanced around, trying to let my brain catch up with the sight in front of me. Looking over at the bed, I spotted an envelope set on the mattress, the light blue color calling to me. I grabbed it, smiling when I recognized the terrible handwriting.

To a lifetime of more nights together.

I held the card to my chest, wishing I was holding Theo close instead. Shutting my eyes, I replayed all of the memories we'd made together, from his smile down to the subtle scent of his cologne. I was just about lost to the past when a pair of arms looped around my middle, pulling me into a hard chest.

But before I could make sense of what was happening, a low chuckle came from behind me. "Did you really think I'd be willing to wait to see you again?"

I squeezed my eyes even tighter, hoping I was truly awake. Because I knew that voice, knew it better than my own. It had spelled its way into my heart, and even after weeks apart, it hadn't lessened its hold. I slowly turned, forcing my eyes open. When I did, I was met with the same dark-colored gaze that haunted my dreams, the ones I reached for but could never quite grab.

"Theo?" I asked, pressing my hands to his chest. "What are you doing here?"

"I'm here for you, beautiful."

My eyes darted between his, unsure how to process what was happening right now. "But you're supposed to be in London. The job—"

"Doesn't matter to me."

I shook my head, hating that I was about to repeat the most devastating conversation of my life. But before a single word could escape my lips, Theo placed a finger on them. "Last time I saw you, you made a fairly good argument for me taking the job. It's taken me a little longer, but I have a counterargument." He put his hand down. "I love you, Calla. I have been in love with you since the moment you rearranged my office without asking. You make every one of my days better by just existing." I opened my mouth to respond, but Theo gave me a look to silence me. "You thought that job was my dream, and for a while, so did I. But it's not. You are. I'm not going to regret walking away from it, but walking away from you? That would have destroyed me. I don't want to waste another minute without you."

I rolled my lips together, trying to hold back the tears filling my eyes. "Can I go now?"

"Shit, yes," he chuckled. "Sorry, I practiced that speech about fifty times and wanted to make sure I got it right."

"It was a good one." I placed my hands on his chest. "And I love you too, Theo, so much that being away from you physically hurts. If you're happy with your choice, then I'm happy too. All I ever wanted was for you to achieve your dreams, even if they took you away from me."

"That's never going to happen." Theo slid his hands to my hips, holding me tightly. "If this last month was a taste of life without you, I never want to experience it again."

"Me neither," I chuckled, running my hands along his chest. "I can't believe you're here."

"I was always coming home to you, Calla. It just took me a bit longer than it should have." He leaned down, capturing my lips in a fiery kiss. I sighed into it, finally knowing that this was where we were meant to be, that I'd been right to hold onto my faith in Theo, my faith in us.

"I love you," Theo whispered as he pressed his forehead to mine.

"I love you too." I reached down to link my fingers with his. "So what's next, Sunshine?"

"Now, beautiful, I finally get to take you on a real date."

FORTY-TWO

Theo

"I think I'm going to throw up."

True to her word, Calla's face paled as she looked up at the Isadora Resort, unable to hide her nerves. All morning, she'd been fretting over her choice to come here. She shook her head and glanced up at me. "This was a mistake. I think it'd be better to tell them in a letter. Oh! A postcard! Who doesn't love getting those? It really is a lost art if you think about it."

I chuckled, pulling her into my arms. "If that's what you want, we can do it that way, but I think it's better to get it over with."

She groaned, placing her forehead against my chest. "I hate when you make sense." She sighed and stood up straighter, linking my hand with hers.

In the weeks since we got back together, we were rarely apart, already having enough separation for a lifetime. After I stayed true to my word and took Calla on an official date, we sat down and talked about our future together. As much as she loved the city, Calla didn't want to move again, especially not after getting her books in just the right order. We compromised on a split-time arrangement. If I had to go into the city for work, she'd join me, but otherwise, our home base would be Saint Stephen's Lake.

After taking a couple of weeks to plan my next move, I decided I wanted to set up my own shop. I took out what I didn't like about the agency, designing something smaller and focusing more on individual clients. And the best part? I was able to do most of my work remotely, only having to fly out to LA or New York for client meetings or other important events. With my client roster at a reasonable number, I was able to keep a good balance between work and my home life. While I'd never be the guy who logged off exactly at five, it was easier to walk away when I knew Calla was waiting for me.

It was a beautiful balance, having her at my side but watching her carve out her own career. I loved being the one to cheer her on along the way, already knowing how successful she'd be one day. She was passing her courses with flying colors and already had requests from people in town to plan their weddings. She'd only accepted one, though—Alex and Cole. They were getting married in the fall, right in the middle of their campgrounds. It would be small, but Calla was already burying our apartment in samples and center-piece options. It was chaos compared to what my apartment looked like when I was single, but I wouldn't have it any other way.

I followed as Calla pulled me inside the hotel, stopping to look around the place. I'd never taken the time to appreciate the building before, too buried in my job to take a minute to look at the world surrounding me. But now, I noticed everything, all the pieces that helped form the wonderful woman at my side. This place was a part of her, so I didn't want to miss a thing.

She kept tugging me until we hit the restaurant at the side of the lobby. My breath loosened as I looked around the room, the white walls covered with wide windows that showcased the lake outside. Calla's hand gripped mine harder when she spotted her family sitting in the corner.

I held her hand a little tighter. "You say the word, and we go home."

She nodded, lifting her gaze to meet my eyes. She pressed a kiss to my cheek before walking over, hugging her mother and sisters before taking a seat. I followed her lead, holding out my hand to her mother. "Diane."

"Theo." She smiled at me. "Good to see you again."

While this woman would never be my favorite person, even I had to admit she was trying to do better for her daughters. She finally served her asshole husband with divorce papers. She moved into the hotel full-time, devoted to bringing her family's vision back to life. The overall morale at the hotel seemed to be getting better, but there was still a long way to go before she could fully be cleansed of her sins.

But Calla was willing to take slow steps toward repairing their relationship, and I'd support her if that was what she wanted. However, I'd also be at her side, making sure her mother didn't step out of line. Never again would Calla have to question her worth, not while I was around.

I nodded to her eldest sister, Laurel. She was the one who was the most removed. Part of me wondered if it hurt her, watching the bond between Devyn and Calla, but she never reached out to Calla and never stood up for her before, so I wasn't going to push for a relationship.

Devyn wrapped me in a tight hug. "How's it going with the new gig?"

"It's going," I chuckled. "Never thought I'd want to be a one-man operation, but it works for me. How about you? Any headway on that joint project we spoke about?"

A sly smile filled her face. Calla was right- Devyn could be terrifying when she wanted. "It's getting there."

I chuckled, changing the subject before we incriminated ourselves further. "And work? Any news on the partnership?"

She scoffed. "They gave it to some asshole with less time than me. Pretty sure it's never going to happen, but I also can't bring myself to leave."

"If you ever decide you want to change gears, I could use you on my team."

"And stick around here more than necessary?" She shook her head. "No, thanks. I'm good where I am for now." She tilted her head to the side. "But if that changes, I'll keep you in mind."

With greetings out of the way, we all took our seats, perusing the brunch options. Calla found my thigh under the table and squeezed it. She wasn't wasting any time. As the waiter took our drink orders, she inhaled slowly. "We have something to tell you."

All three sets of eyes turned to her, Devyn speaking first. "Shit, are you pregnant?"

"Absolutely not!" Calla chuckled. "That's going to be way, way down the line, after we've got our businesses running smoothly for a while."

"I don't know if I'd say way down the line, beautiful," I teased in her ear.

"Don't even think about it." She shook her head and turned back to her family. She sighed, reaching into her purse, and pulled out two silver rings, handing me mine before slipping hers back on, then intertwining our fingers once again. My finger instantly found the slender band on hers as I sighed with relief. It had only been off for a few minutes, and that was already too long for me. Now that I had gotten it on her, it was not coming off again.

Calla held our hands up. "Theo and I... We got married."

As her family stared at her with wide-eyed expressions, we just smiled at each other, reliving the night we'd made things official. It wasn't something we planned, but just like every other choice we'd made, it felt right. When we were in the city last week, I'd spontaneously popped the question at breakfast, wanting to make Calla my wife as soon as possible. We went down to the city clerk's office an hour later and got our marriage license, only to return the next day to the same office to exchange our vows. It was simple, spontaneous, and perfectly us.

And the best part? I got to call Calla my wife. Nothing had ever seemed so right as the first time those words slipped from my lips.

As if the spell broke at the same time, all three Winters women started to ask rapid-fire questions. I was about to snap when my wife held up her hand, silencing all of them. "Before you start, you should know that we're planning on doing a ceremony next spring with everyone in attendance. I wanted to wait until my courses are done before I try to plan anything." She turned and stared up at me with adoration in her eyes. "But we didn't want to wait that long to make things official." She turned back to her family. "This is what we wanted to do, and if you have anything to say that is less than supportive, we don't want to hear it."

Her mother got up, and for a moment, I thought she was going to walk out of the room. But she kneeled in front of Calla, placing her hands on her daughter's cheeks. "I'm so happy for you." She smiled at me. "Both of you. All I ever wanted was for you to find what makes you happy, Calla, and you've done that and more. I'm so proud of you."

Tears filled my wife's eyes as she lunged forward, wrapping her arms around her mother's neck in a tight hug. By the time they parted, almost everyone at the table had misty eyes, but Calla waved them away. "Now it's someone else's turn. I've been on edge all day, waiting to tell you guys the news."

Devyn took over, discussing the latest ridiculous client that was making her life hell. But I didn't listen, too distracted by the beautiful woman at my side. I placed my arm around her shoulders, pulling her into my side.

For so long, life felt like a game I was doomed to lose, too wrapped up in my career to see the light on the other side. But with this woman, *my wife*, in my arms, it was all worth it. This life might be a far cry from what I'd planned, but it was better than I could have ever dreamed.

Calla

EPILOGUE

THREE MONTHS LATER

The night sparkled with bright stars, illuminating the Fox Creek campground in an ethereal glow. Lines of fairy lights and garden blooms surround the filled dance floor, burlap-lined tables circling around its edges. It was the ideal backdrop to what had ended up being a perfectly imperfect day. Between the last-minute guests who showed up and a mix-up with their cake, for a moment this morning, it felt like Alex and Cole's wedding day was cursed.

Thank goodness Theo was by my side, helping me work out all the kinks. As much as I wanted my first planned wedding to go off without any issue, my mentor, Marina, assured me it was never going to happen.

Luckily, all those issues faded away as soon as Alex put on her dress and walked down the aisle. Her groom cried before she even reached him. Cole's hand shook as he held hers, only having eyes for his new wife. At the end of the day, that was all that mattered—that they got to say their vows and declare their love for each other in front of their friends and families.

After the ceremony ended and the food had been served, the dance floor was packed with friends and family from near and far. While Alex and Cole originally tried to keep the wedding small, almost the entire town of Saint Stephen's Lake wanted to celebrate with them. Alex and Cole didn't care, and they were all too happy to welcome every last person who showed up.

I watched from the sidelines as they swayed in each other's arms, just as they had for most of the night. It was clear how much love passed between Alex and Cole. For a long time, I thought that would never happen to me, that I was too lost to see my way through the fog.

A set of arms wrapped around my waist, pulling me into a broad chest. Theo's lips tickled the shell of my ear. "What's the look for, beautiful?"

"Just thinking about how lucky we are." I turned in his arms, kissing him lightly. "I never thought I'd find someone like you."

"Same here," he chuckled, holding me close. He nodded as Adam joined us, letting me turn to face his friend. Theo held out his hand, clasping Adam on the shoulder. "How's it going?"

Adam nodded, letting out a long breath. "It's good. You were right; being up here full time has been good for my head."

As much as Theo was dying for Adam to take a role, he still refused to commit to one, claiming that he needed more time. I thought there was more to it than that, but it wasn't my place to pry. We just made sure that Adam knew our door was always open if he needed to talk.

Since he wasn't sure how long he'd been staying, Alex and Cole offered to let Adam use one of the cabins for as long as he needed. So far, he'd been up here for almost a month, and it seemed to be working wonders. He wasn't looking as tired, no longer checking over his shoulder every few minutes. It was nice to see him smile again.

I nudged him in the side. "I met your neighbor earlier."

He arched his brow. "Who?"

I nodded across the field to a brunette tucked between Marta and Curt. They'd taken the girl under their wing since she showed up, nervous at joining such a tight-knit group. "Victoria." I turned to Theo. "She's Cole's sister. Apparently she's been up here for a week, and I'm just meeting her now." Now facing Adam, I asked, "How long is she staying?"

"Not sure," he answered, but his eyes were still stuck on Victoria. "They gave her an open invitation to stay as long as she likes."

Theo snorted, "They do know those are supposed to be for paying guests, right?"

I knocked my elbow into Theo's stomach. "There are ten other cabins, Sunshine. And besides, it's what we do for family around here."

But Adam didn't respond, too busy watching Victoria. When she smiled back at him, he ducked his head and cleared his throat. "You okay over there?" I chuckled.

"Shit...yeah." He ran his hand over his face. "She just, uh, looks a lot more grown-up now."

"When was the last time you saw her?"

He shrugged. "Before I left for LA almost ten years ago. Tori... She had to be thirteen, maybe fourteen?"

I chuckled, placing my hand on his arm. "That tends to happen after a decade. Go over and say hi. She's been quiet all night because she doesn't know most of these people."

He nodded, taking another long pull of his drink before walking in Victoria's direction. Theo chuckled in my ear. "You sure that was a good idea? From the look in Adam's eyes, this might not end well."

"What do you mean?"

"He's not looking at her like she's Cole's little sister, beautiful."

I shrugged. "They'll figure it out. Besides," I reached for his hands then pulled him toward the dance floor, "I want to dance with my husband."

"Anything for you." Theo smiled, pulling me into his arms. As we swayed to a slow song, his lips met my forehead, his arms holding me close. "Does this make you regret our wedding?"

"What?" I pulled back to search his eyes. "Why would you ask that?"

He glanced around the field, "This is so much more than ours. I don't want you to have any regrets, Calla. Even if we're doing the real thing in the spring—"

I silenced him with a kiss. "Our wedding was perfect. All I want is to be your wife, Theo. Everything else is extra."

He smiled brightly back at me. "That's how I feel too. Every time I get to call you my wife, it feels better than the last."

"To think," I chuckled, holding myself tighter in his arms, "all of this started because you took a chance on an assistant with no experience."

"Best decision I ever made."

ACKNOWLEDGMENTS

Ahhh, I can't believe I am writing another one of these. This book has been such a labor of love. When I first started planning out this story, Calla had a completely different journey (and love interest). But Theo kept screaming in my ear, and as soon as I put them on the page together, I fell in love.

As with any book, it takes a village to get to this point. To my family, I could not do this without you. From being my biggest supporters to listening to me scream, cry, and moan when my characters wouldn't cooperate, thank you for helping me achieve my dreams. I know none of this would be possible without you.

To my fantastic team of readers. Emily- my forever alpha reader, what would I do without you? From your tough love to your unwavering support, you have had my back at every turn. Thank you for supporting my writing, not with just this book, but for the past few years. I know that none of this would have been possible without you in my corner.

To my beta readers—Heather, Meghan, Brandi, Katie, Katherine, and Nikki—you guys are AMAZING! Thank you so much for reading through the unedited version of this story and helping me shape it into this final product. I am beyond grateful for your time, your kind words, and your feedback.

Lemmy at Luna Literary Management—Girl, I have zero words for how much I've loved working with you. I told you my goals, and you literally blew them out of the park. You are so talented and supportive that every person who works with you is better for it. The book community is so lucky to have you.

To Alexa, my editor, thank you for all of your time and support. I literally do not know how you have time to achieve everything you do, but I am in awe of you. I am so grateful that we found each other in this vast book community.

To Anna- what would I do without your fantastic artwork??? From designing the cover that made me cry to the incredible scenes you've brought to life, your talent knows no bounds. I am so thankful that you were willing to work with me on this series.

To Books & Moods- what can I say about the discreet covers you've created??? I am the worst at describing my ideas, but you manage to take my fragmented notes and make something out of this world. I am so grateful for your talented designs.

And last, but never least- thank you to my readers. Every time I hear from someone on social media, I get embarrassingly emotional. The fact that you not only take the time to read my stories, but to love my characters as much as I do? That is a feeling I will never recover from. From the bottom of my heart- thank you. I will never be able to thank you enough.

Now, onto Adam's story...

ALSO BY K.C. BROOKS

Saint Stephens Lake Series:

(Un)Expected

Cole & Alex's Story

(Un)Planned

Calla & Theo's Story

(Un)Spoken

Coming Fall 2024

ABOUT THE AUTHOR

K.C. Brooks is an avid romance reader who has always dreamed about turning her ideas into a book of her own. She lives for sunny days, iced cold coffees, and stories that make your heart ache for more. When not living in the fantasy worlds of her books, she resides in upstate New York with her husband, two children, and two fur babies.